A Bird in the Hand

Through the half-open door, I perceived a complete stranger seated at Holmes's desk. This bewhiskered rascal was reading a letter with great interest. The man had a sharp, wizened face that peered from behind thick glasses. His back was bowed with age, but that did not incline me toward an abandonment of caution. I well-remembered the evil menace of the ancient Colonel Sebastian Moran, the second most dangerous man in London.

On tiptoes, I retraced my steps to secure my army-issue handgun. In Holmes's absence this white-haired interloper was not going to make free of our habitat if I could help it. Back at the sitting-room door, I eased my Webley to full cock and was about to confront the bounder when a familiar voice called to me.

"Dear chap, don't come through the door spewing bullets like some desperado of the American West!"

As I staggered back in amazement, the figure at the desk arose. With the sweep of a sinewy arm, the white wig was removed. The bowed back straightened, and before me was the familiar figure of Sherlock Holmes!

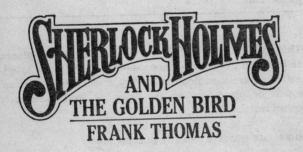

SHERLOCK HOLMES

AND
THE GOLDEN BIRD
FRANK THOMAS

PINNACLE BOOKS   NEW YORK

SHERLOCK HOLMES AND THE GOLDEN BIRD

Copyright © 1979 by Frank Thomas

An original Pinnacle Books edition.

First printing/September 1979
Third printing/April 1985

ISBN: 0-523-42510-4
Can. ISBN: 0-523-43467-7

Printed in the United States of America

PINNACLE BOOKS, INC.
1430 Broadway
New York, New York 10018

Contents

Preface   vii

A Note to the Reader   ix

Chapter
1	The Problem	1
2	Into Action	11
3	The Battle at the Nonpareil Club	19
4	The Solving of a Message	31
5	To Berlin	41
6	Our Singular Client	51
7	The Hatchet Men	63
8	In Constantinople	75
9	Back to Baker Street	87
10	St. Aubrey	97
11	The Famous Chair Fighter of the Andaman Islands	105
12	The Meeting with that Frightening Man	121
13	Our Quarters Under Seige	135
14	The Removal of the Bird	147
15	Holmes Plans Our Defense	161
16	The Attack	173
17	More Light in Dark Places	181
18	The Taking and the Rescue	191
19	The Revelations of the Royal Jeweler	203
20	The Deadman's Code	217
21	The Resolution	227

Preface

In bringing previously unpublished cases of the world's greatest detective to the attention of readers, one is faced with the persistent questions: "How did you come by these adventures, and why have they not been published before this?"

There is no mystery here. The unpublished stories are frequently referred to in the four novels and fifty-six short stories that Doctor Watson made available during his lifetime. Nor is there doubt as to where the voluminous case books, carefully compiled by the most diligent chronicler of all times, were placed, for Watson told us on a number of occasions. They were filed in that famous dispatch box in the vaults of Cox's Bank at Charing Cross. The reasons the good doctor denied the eager reading public of the world access to these adventures was also plainly stated. A number of Holmes's exploits dealt with sensitive government matters best allowed to remain in limbo for the time. Others cast light on social scandals of the late Victorian era and Watson, always the soul of propriety, felt they should not become public knowledge while those involved were still alive. In addition, there were certain cases which Watson rather cryptically described as being of such a nature that the world was not prepared for their revelation. I have often wondered if the months Holmes spent in research into coal-tar derivatives in a laboratory at Montpellier, in the south of France, is classified in this last category.

The adventures were certainly recorded and preserved and the only singular matter is how this editor came by them. I have been vague on this point in previous writings, but the whole matter will be in the open before long because of legal questions regarding ownership. There is, in Anglo-Saxon law, the Treasures of the Realm act of which I have been made alarmingly aware.

It was during the height of the wartime blitz that Cox's Bank was devastated by bombs. Since I was in London at this time, my only thought on that fateful night was to seek refuge from the explosions that seared the darkness with a nightmare of flame, falling masonry, dust, debris, death. By pure happenstance the aged dispatch box and I were thrown together and happily we emerged from the kaleidoscope of horror relatively undamaged. One thing is certain, had I not been in the ruins of the bank, the dispatch box with its historical and irreplaceable contents would have been lost forever, reduced to cinders by the German firebombs.

Such is the statement I shall make when the matter comes to court.

But this unpleasant legal confrontation lies in the future, which must unfold according to the blueprint of destiny. Let us now part the veils of time and walk back into the past. Back to the wondrous world of Baker Street.

The game is afoot, or more appropriately, the bird is on the wing.

—Frank Thomas
Los Angeles, 1979

A Note to the Reader

For the purpose of this work, it was necessary to authenticate, in depth, certain elusive historical facts regarding ancient treasure.

The dedicated research of Elsie Probasco of Reno, Nevada proved indispensable in this regard.

As was the case with previous publications dealing with Mr. Sherlock Holmes, the author was able to lean on the encyclopedic knowledge of the greatest Holmesian of our times, John Bennett Shaw of Santa Fe, New Mexico.

We shall mention last what came first. Walda, in whose presence the Golden Bird first took wing. Without her, this book would have been completed six months earlier.

SHERLOCK HOLMES
AND THE GOLDEN BIRD

1

The Problem

It was a night in late autumn and the wind, which had brought an Arctic cold to the streets of London, had died down. But on its heels came a thick fog that blanketed the metropolis. Neighboring buildings loomed momentarily like blurred objects and then disappeared under swirls of moist eiderdown. There was a chilling wetness everywhere and I had built the hearth fire high, in hopes that the leaping flames would defy the inclemency without.

Sherlock Holmes had been idle for several days, spending the time arranging his voluminous files. He seemed in excellent spirits, unusual when there was no test for his highly trained talents. During a tasty dinner prepared by the solicitous Mrs. Hudson, he had regaled me with tales of that tiny and little-known country of Montenegro with which he seemed so familiar. While removing the dishes, our kindly housekeeper gave Holmes a letter that had just arrived by special messenger. As his thin, dexterous fingers extracted the single page and his eyes flashed over it, the relaxed, somewhat languid mood of the world's only consulting detective disappeared. His manner sharpened with interest and he gave the message a long second look before passing it to me.

"An unexpected communication, Watson. From Lindquist, you know."

As I took the letter from his hand, I regarded my

intimate friend with a blank stare, prompting him to continue.

"Possibly, you do not know of him. Rather brilliant chap. Was of considerable service in connection with that matter of Mrs. Farintoch's opal tiara."

The message I read had more than a touch of urgency.

My dear Holmes:

Am hopeful that this finds you in your chambers and that you will be there come nine o'clock when I shall arrive. Time is of the essence and there is no one but you to turn to. In desperation, I am . . . Nils Lindquist.

My eyes elevated to Holmes. "The chap seems in need of your unique services."

"A visitor at a late hour on a night like this would have desperation as a spur. However, Lindquist was always a cool one, not given to flights of fancy." Holmes was rubbing his hands together with a satisfied air. "Which leads me to think his visit will unveil a matter of interest."

The signs were obvious. Holmes was, again, thirsting for action—hungry for puzzles and mysteries in which to subtly insert the probe of his specialized knowledge and experience.

"You mention his association with a previous case," I began, then let my voice dwindle away, knowing he would pick up the conversational lead.

"While Lindquist's fame is limited to a small circle, he's a top-notch gem expert with an extensive knowledge of *objets d'art*." Holmes indicated the stationery in my hand. "Do you deduce anything else from his message?"

Holding the paper up to the light, I tried to emulate my friend, mimicking the manner with which he had viewed countless messages in times gone by.

"I note the paper is Neeley-Pierpont bond. I'd say it fetches a good price."

"My dear Watson, you fill me with delight! Obviously, our years together have not been wasted."

Holmes usually had only sparing praise for my powers of observation and I was much heartened by his tone of commendation. Therefore, I desperately searched for further clues.

"The chap writes in a precise manner, conserving space since his lines are rather close. Might I hazard the guess that, in his role of art expert, he makes his reports in longhand rather than using a machine?"

"Better and better! Pray continue."

"Alas, I cannot. There seems little else to note."

Holmes assumed an air of resigned patience, which did not fool me one whit. I well knew that he delighted in producing his little surprises and gloried in his ability to do so.

"I must, ol' fellow, let you read a pamphlet I published some years back: 'Handwriting as a Guide Towards Vocation and Attitude.' It does have some points of interest. Now regard Lindquist's message. The letters slant forward and the writing curves down at the end of each line. The mark of tragedy, Watson. Also regard the first sentence in which he used the word *that* twice, as well as *this* and *there*. In each case, the first letter *t* has an elongated bar at the top. This is further proven by the first word of the second sentence *time*, where the capital *T* is crossed with an even longer stroke."

"A characteristic of his hand."

"Agreed. But the cross bar dwindles out. While I am not familiar with Lindquist's penmanship, I contend that in former times this characteristic would have been firmer, more definite. In several instances, there is a waver that denotes weakness. I fear he is a sick man, which may explain the urgency in the note."

"Despite our long association, Holmes, you continue to amaze me. A short message like this and you deduce

3

that the writer is low in spirits and failing in health. Astonishing!"

"Not really," remarked the great detective, with unusual modesty. "It is just knowing what to look for."

Holmes broke off our conversation and busied himself with a case book. I noted it was the *F* file and assumed that he was going over the Farintoch Case, possibly looking for a sample of Nils Lindquist's hand. I was not to learn if he found one for the hour of nine was upon us and the sound of a distant church bell blended with a ring at the outer door of 221B Baker Street. Shortly thereafter, footsteps were heard on the seventeen steps leading up to our chambers. Alerted by Holmes's deductions, I noted that they were not steady, but indicated that our visitor paused twice, as though to gain strength, before continuing his ascent.

When Billy, the page boy, ushered the man through our door, I was not surprised to note that he was very thin. Fair hair had receded in front but still made a brave showing on his head. It was the unusually high color around his cheekbones and the feverish glitter of his eyes that captured my medically trained eye. "By Jove!" I thought. "Holmes called the shots again. This chap does appear to have had it."

Holmes's introduction of Nils Lindquist was brief and as I busied myself with the tantalus and gasogene, our visitor seated himself gratefully in the low armchair by the fire. His breathing was labored and had a hoarse, rattlelike sound that affected the hackles of hair on the back of my neck. His voice was strong enough, and while his English was certainly of Oxford, there was the rising inflection of the Scandinavian to it.

"Doctor Watson's training and your unerring eye, Holmes, have doubtless revealed an unpleasant fact to you both. Certainly unpleasant to me," he added with a grim smile.

Holmes could be soothing and reassuring when called upon, but he seemed to sense that Lindquist did not seek sympathy nor would he welcome it.

"You have secured expert opinion, I assume?"

"Three leading specialists are in agreement. The verdict is definitely in. Which explains my call."

"How can I help?" questioned Holmes as I gave Lindquist liquid refreshment.

He thanked me with his eyes and drained half the glass in a single draft as if to bolster waning strength. Then he leaned forward in his chair with purpose.

"As time grows short, one does develop a severe case of ethics. You might bear that in mind, gentlemen. There is an obsession to clean the slate. A month ago, I accepted a commission from one Vasil D'Anglas of Berlin. The matter was handled by mail and I received a money order for one thousand pounds to locate or arrange for the return of the Golden Bird."

Since Holmes's face remained impassive, Lindquist cocked an eye. "I see you are not familiar with the object. No reason that you should be. In any case, D'Anglas agreed to the payment of another thousand pounds upon recovery of the object as well as reasonable expenses incurred in tracing it. I sent out feelers in the art world but uncovered little. Actually, I should not have accepted the case. My health made the necessary travel impossible, but I needed the money."

There was a furrow between Holmes's brows. "Your reference to travel I find confusing. Did not this gentleman in Berlin expect the art object to be here in England?"

"D'Anglas was somewhat vague regarding that. He had purchased the Golden Bird from a dealer in Constantinople, Aben Hassim. The bill of sale was mailed to D'Anglas, making him the legal owner. However, the Bird was stolen from Hassim's shop immediately prior to its being sent to Germany. My employer, for reasons he has not revealed, is of a mind that it will show up here in England. Actually, I should have gone to Constantinople, interviewed Hassim, and picked up the trail from there. Instead, I hired Barker, an inquiry agent of

5

Surrey, to try and find a lead in the London under-world."

There was a half-smile on Holmes's face. "My rival," he stated, with a quick glance at me. "You will recall that our paths crossed relative to that matter of Josiah Amberley."

" 'The Retired Colourman,' " I responded automatically.

"Such was the title you used in your recounting of the affair," commented Holmes. His eyes swiveled back to Lindquist. "But what is this Bird which, by the size of your fee, must be valuable?"

"It is that. The Golden Bird stands twenty-three inches high, and is mounted on a pedestal of good size. The detail work is that of a master. The entire figure and base is said to be of twenty-four carat gold."

"My heavens!" I said, without meaning to.

"I am inclined to doubt that," added Lindquist quickly. "The Golden Bird has a unique history. It keeps disappearing."

Holmes was nodding. "I follow your reasoning. If this Bird is much traveled, undoubtedly there must be a percentage of alloy to provide rigidity."

"Eighteen carat sounds more reasonable." Lindquist and Holmes seemed in agreement on this. Frankly, their discussion was over my head.

"What kind of a bird is it?" I asked.

"A roc."

"Well, now," said Holmes with a pleased expression, "this gives us a touch of melodrama. The legendary giant bird of Arabia, so huge that it carried off ele-phants in its claws." Then the shadow of a thought crossed his face. "A strange subject for the artisan. You mentioned disappearances, which I assume were due to the criminally minded."

Lindquist leaned back in the chair as if rallying his limited strength. "See what you make of this sketchy his-tory. The Golden Bird is said to have first appeared in Samarkand, part of the treasure of Tamerlane, the great

Tartar conqueror. From drawings it would appear to be of Greek workmanship, though I cannot be certain of that. It was next heard of in the Russian Court of Peter the Great around 1720. This tsar was a great fancier of gold objects. Around 1790 it is definitely referred to as being in France. The royalist owners are said to have sold it to raise money desperately needed during the French Revolution. Then it fell into the hands of Napoleon, who used it as a pledge to borrow money from Dutch bankers. At the turn of the century, the Bird was in the possession of an art dealer named Weimer, of Amsterdam. Weimer's shop was gutted by fire and the Bird disappeared. Around 1850 it showed up on the Island of Rhodes. Evidently, it had been gathering dust in a small shop there until it was stolen by Harry Hawker."

Holmes, who had been gazing throughfully into the fire as he listened to this strange history, suddenly turned toward the speaker.

"Ah-ha! Hawker, the expert thief, who had been in his youth a disciple of Jonathan Wild, London's master criminal of the last century. His sharp eye would indeed recognize the value of the Bird."

Lindquist resumed his narrative. "He escaped with the statue to Budapest. To whom he sold it is unknown. It finally reappeared in Constantinople in the shop of Aben Hassim. A reputable dealer, Hassim spread the word that the Bird was in his possession and the Turkish government upheld his claim of ownership. At this point, my client entered into negotiations with Hassim."

"Only to have the elusive object disappear again." Holmes's eyes were glistening. Obviously, he was intrigued by the story.

"Now you and Dr. Watson know what I do," said Lindquist.

He was suddenly seized by a violent fit of coughing. I hastened to replenish his glass when the attack subsided.

"But," said Holmes, "surely Barker came up with

7

something. His methods are unorthodox, but he is effective."

"Was," stated Lindquist. "Barker was on his way to my lodgings on Montague Street when he was run down by a four-wheeler. On hearing of the accident—if it was indeed that—I made my way to the hospital. Barker was in a coma and the doctors gave him no chance. However, he regained consciousness at the very last. I could see recognition in his pain-filled eyes. He said but one word: 'Pasha.' Then he died."

Holmes's face was stern. I remembered Barker vaguely. An impassive man who wore gray-tinted glasses and had a large Masonic pin in his tie. Evidently, the death of a fellow professional had an effect on my friend and his words buttressed my observation.

"We can't just have people killing off private investigators. You suspect, I gather, that Barker's death had sinister overtones?"

Lindquist nodded. "The four-wheeler has not been located. The fact that Barker was on his way to meet me, and the importance that he seemed to attach to that final word, makes me suspect foul play."

Holmes nodded. "Pasha! Does it mean anything to you?"

Evidently, it did not. Our visitor seemed to have recovered somewhat from his racking cough. At least, his color had improved.

"What would you have me do?" asked Holmes.

"I give you little to work with." Lindquist removed two envelopes from his pocket, handing one to Holmes. "Here is what remains of my original fee. If you agree, I shall mail this letter in my hand to Vasil D'Anglas in Berlin informing him that I have turned the matter over to you because of ill health."

"I see you have the letter to Germany already stamped," observed Holmes.

Lindquist exhibited a wry smile. "I was in hope you would agree for—shall we say—old times' sake."

Holmes responded with a single nod.

Our visitor had some difficulty rising from his chair. His manner indicated that he wished no assistance. "I am in your debt, thought I doubt my ability to honor the obligation. Let me bid you good night, gentlemen. A case report is with the limited amount of money in that envelope. It is my hope that, if you need me further, I will be available."

Nils Lindquist made his way to the door (and out of our lives, for word reached us the following day that he had died).

Holmes was idly fingering the envelope given him by the art expert, and gazing into space with that faraway look which I knew so well. Finally, he tossed the envelope on the side table and turned to me.

"I dared not refuse the poor man the fee he offered. It would have offended him. To be truthful, I would have undertaken the commission just for the interest it inspires."

I felt this an appropriate moment to introduce one of my small ploys. The strange tale of the Golden Bird had certainly intrigued me and I was desirous of learning what was really going through Holmes's mind. Therefore, I respond with a hackneyed remark.

"It seems but another pursuit after wealth. Somewhat like a search for pirate treasure, don't you think?"

"Financial gain is always a strong stimulant," my friend replied. "But there are other points of interest. Harry Hawker was not without means. At the time Lindquist refers to, when he stole the Bird in Rhodes, he must have been at the end of his notorious career and a much-wanted man. Why did he risk capture for this statue? An object the size that Lindquist described, even of the purest gold, surely could not be that valuable. There was no mention of jeweled eyes or an incrustation of precious gems. The prize does not seem to justify the risk."

"Could it be the workmanship?"

"Lindquist felt the object was of Greek origin. Were it created by the likes of Cellini, the great Italian gold-

9

smith, its worth would be far in excess of the precious metal alone." My intimate friend was thoughtful for a silent moment. "Then there is the possibility of an unknown alloy. 'Tis said the ancients were adept at electrum, which is a natural gold-silver alloy. Possibly, it is the method of metalwork that makes this relic so sought after."

This idea puzzled me. "Surely, an artisan of olden times could not be superior to our experts in Birmingham and Sheffield."

Holmes indulged in a chuckle. "My dear fellow, cement was a lost art during the Middle Ages. Even today, our best men cannot duplicate a means of tempering copper developed by the American Indians. It is a bit far-fetched, but let us not rule out the theory of a lost process."

"I suppose there are any number of possibilities," I said, tentatively.

"None of which we can either ignore or accept. Our starting point is Barker's death. For the nonce, we shall assume that our late acquaintance was the victim of assassination. This leads us to the thought that Barker had learned something—something which someone did not want relayed to Lindquist. But now to bed, for I feel it in my bones that there are busy times ahead."

Shortly thereafter, the lights were extinguished at 221B Baker Street. Sleep came hard, however, for my mind was tantalized by the story of the Golden Bird. When dreams came, they were filled with gigantic rocs and strange alchemists creating weird fantasies in a mysterious laboratory that was very reminiscent of a morgue. As a distant bell tolled an early morning hour, I woke with a start to recall that a morgue was exactly where Barker, the former investigator from Surrey, was at that very moment.

2

Into Action

The following morning, when I noted the time of my awakening, I sprang from bed full of misgivings. The hour was late for one associated with the great detective. Seizing a robe and stepping into my bedroom slippers, I descended to the sitting room eager to learn what Holmes's first move would be, or possibly had already been. But my progress came to an abrupt halt when, through the half-open door I perceived a complete stranger seated at Holmes's desk, who had the effrontery to go over papers on it. At least, this bewhiskered rascal was reading a letter with great interest. He had a sharp, wizened face that peered from behind thick glasses. His back was bowed with age, but that did not incline me toward an abandonment of caution. I well-remembered the evil menace of the ancient Colonel Sebastian Moran, the second most dangerous man in London.

On tiptoes, I retraced my steps to secure my army-issue handgun. In Holmes's absence this white-haired interloper was not going to make free of our habitat if I could help it. Back at the sitting-room door, I eased my Webley to full cock and was about to confront the bounder when a familiar voice called to me.

"Dear chap, don't come through the door spewing bullets like some desperado of the American West!"

As I staggered back in amazement, the figure at the desk arose. With the sweep of a sinewy arm, the white

11

wig was removed. The bowed back straightened, and before me was the familiar figure of Sherlock Holmes.

Carefully lowering the hammer of my Webley, I entered the sitting room, gazing at him reproachfully.

"What need for this charade? You make me feel the fool indeed."

Holmes curbed his mirth, and concern touched his thoughtful eyes. "Watson, you have my abject apologies. However, you constantly perform a great service, for if one of my little disguises can take you in, need I fear detection from other sources?"

Unable to find a response to this, I felt somewhat mollified.

"I suppose those keen ears of yours heard me, though I cannot imagine how."

Holmes was lighting a cigarette with his nonchalant manner.

"When you descend of a morning, your feet unconsciously follow the same path. There is a distinct squeak in the third step which you have heard so often you are probably not conscious of it. I was rather mystified to hear you backtracking, but the click of the hammer on the portable cannon which you cherish was informative."

Thrusting my pistol within the pocket of my robe, I responded testily, "At least, it is an effective piece of ordnance and not a popgun like that hair-trigger 'salon' piece you practice with on occasion."

"*Touché!* But what need have I for a heavy weapon with my trusty Watson on guard?" He indicated a letter on the desk while pouring me a cup of coffee. "It has been a profitable morning, ol' boy. A visit to the morgue revealed that the body of Barker has not yet been identified."

Holmes shook his head. Inefficiency constantly amazed him.

"Baffling, wouldn't you say, since Lindquist visited him at the hospital? On the theory that Lestrade and his cohorts can well use the practice, I did not solve the riddle for them but rather directed my steps to the neighborhood of Lindquist's hotel. Barker was run down close by. Had he come a distance, he would undoubtedly have used a conveyance, since he seemed to be in haste. Here my encyclopedic knowledge of the byways of London came to my aid. I concluded that there were but three rooming houses in the immediate vicinity that Barker might have reasonably chosen. The second one produced a landlady who immediately recognized my description of the dead man. His room proved rewarding."

I gazed at the sleuth with a startled expression.

"Good heavens, Holmes, you don't mean you burgled the place?"

"Of course not. For some reason beyond my comprehension, the landlady assumed that I was of the legal calling and handled Barker's affairs. She was delighted to show me the room he had rented several weeks before."

"Beyond your comprehension, eh?" I regarded him with obvious disbelief, well knowing how Holmes could inspire and nurture a false conception without actually resorting to fabrication or falsehood. He chose to ignore my skeptical tone.

"Imagine my surprise to find a letter addressed to Mr. Sherlock Holmes of 221B Baker Street."

"The devil you say!"

" 'To be delivered should harm befall me.' Such was the notation on the envelope."

I was at a complete loss for words and my expression revealed that fact.

"Not so strange, Watson, that both Nils Lindquist and Barker's thoughts should follow the same path. Both were involved in the matter and both had had previous association with us."

Holmes was consistently generous in his use of the word *us*, but I well knew to whom the art expert and the Surrey investigator had turned as a court of last resort.

Holmes had crossed to the desk with that quick ner-

13

vous stride, which indicated his full powers were channeled to a matter of interest. Gone was the languid theorist and in his place was the finely tuned, nay predatory, sleuth, hot on the scent. He again indicated the letter, which he had evidently been rereading on my arrival.

"Let me give you a brief summation of this. Barker refers to his being employed by Nils Lindquist, the art expert. He draws my attention to a familiar name, should harm come his way. None other than old Baron Dowson."

"Again he crosses our path," I exclaimed. A sudden thought caused me to switch subjects. "Barker must have anticipated that he was in peril."

"At least we can say that he knew that information he had come upon was dangerous knowledge," conceded Holmes. "The letter is couched in vague terms, full of references to previous cases which only you or I would understand. The substance is that he had uncovered a lead to Baron Dowson in connection with a job he had undertaken."

"The Golden Bird matter!" I exclaimed.

"He does not specify it. Barker secured employment at the Nonpareil Club as a means of investigating Baron Dowson."

"Good heavens, Holmes, I did not even know the place had reopened!"

"Some time ago, as an elaborate and completely illegal gambling club that is part of the Baron's apparatus. Obviously Watson, Barker had studied those recountings of our adventures which you occasionally foist on a patient reading public. For instance, he makes reference to a surreptitious investigation undertaken during the Inter-Ocean Trust case.* What does that suggest to you?"

"Slim Gilligan, the cracksman."

"Exactly," said Holmes, with a pleased expression.

---

* The Case of the Three Hats.

"Our attention is not only directed to Dowson and the Nonpareil Club, which now serves as the Baron's headquarters, but we are clued in to the fact that Slim Gilligan might provide a key to what the late Barker found."

My mouth was but half-open when Holmes anticipated me.

"I have already been to Gilligan's Lock and Key Shop and he is not on the premises. The establishment is manned by a friend of his, but I have reason to believe that Slim will get in touch with us in the immediate future."

"Could the cracksman be hiding out in fear of the same fate that befell Barker?"

"The possibility crossed my mind. But Slim will appear, of that I am sure. Meanwhile, I have some, shall we say, staff work to do. We are in need of more information before progressing further in this affair."

I had a few house calls to make and was not loath to leave since I well knew that I could be of no assistance at this point in the case. Holmes encouraged me to continue my medical practice in a somewhat limited manner. When I protested that I was merely a part-time practitioner, he assured me that my calls on the habitués of Mayfair frequently resulted in bits of gossip and information that were of considerable interest to him. As to whether he was completely sincere regarding this I could not say. Possibly he just wanted to make me feel useful or, perhaps, my medical duties provided him with breathing space should he wish to work alone. During my absence on this day, I knew he would be following his usual procedure. The web that my friend had spun over London was sensitive to the slightest tug of as unusual incident. Terminating at 221B Baker Street, this unofficial information machine had ears glued to doors and eyes to keyholes. Hansom drivers, shopkeepers, and commissionaires vied with government ministers, industrial tycoons and eminent attorneys in feeding information into this grist mill, which spewed forth information that Sherlock Holmes's retentive brain devoured. What type of relay system serviced this unusual mechanism I could not imagine, but little happened among the six million of the great city that my friend was not privy to in short order.

It was later than I had anticipated when I returned to our chambers. The day had been clear though cold and the fog of the previous evening had retreated to the Thames. As I looked at the warm lights that beckoned the homeward-bound I thought of Holmes's remark years before about a magical flight over the great city and the fact that if the roofs could be removed one would view a vast tapestry of love, hate, and passion, along with incidents that would make *The Thousand and One Nights* of Scheherazade seem like a child's primer on unusual events. The sleuth was a great believer that man was the most fascinating and unpredictable of all the creations in the universe and, considering our adventures throughout the years, who was I to deny this theory?

When I reentered our chambers, I found my eccentric friend pacing the floor of our sitting room and emitting clouds of acrid smoke from the pipe he fancied when dealing with a baffling problem. His manner was almost abrupt as he indicated a single place set at the table.

"I had Mrs. Hudson prepare a sandwich for you, old friend, and there's stout to wash it down with."

Realizing that Holmes was bent on action, I swiftly removed my great coat and followed his instructions. As I devoured the roast beef sandwich, Holmes selected a walking stick from his collection, speaking all the time to fill me in.

"My investigations of the afternoon have not been singularly productive, so we are forced to abandon the realm of speculation in favor of frontal assault. I must inform you that Lindquist died in his quarters at midday."

I half-choked on a mouthful of stout. "Murdered?"

16

Holmes shook his head negatively. "Considering his condition, it is amazing the man lasted as long as he did. However, as he pointed out, dedication is a spur with long rowels. This case is now a bequest. We must not fail."

"Good show, Holmes! Matter of honor and all that."

"Then there's Barker to be considered. From the message which he left for me, it is obvious that he earned the money Lindquist paid him. There can be no doubt that he uncovered a connection between Baron Dowson and the Golden Bird."

"Else why would he have secured employment at the Nonpareil Club?" I agreed, disposing of the last remnants of my sandwich.

Holmes paused to favor me with a smile.

"Excellent, my dear Watson. I note an improvement in your inferential thinking."

Imbued with this praise, I went one step further. "Since Barker was investigating matters at the Nonpareil, no doubt that is where you plan to launch your own inquiry."

"Exactly," replied Holmes. "This point of embarcation suggests a trump card in our favor." Noting my look of puzzlement, he hastened to explain; "It was in 1888 that our attention was directed to the atrocious conduct of Colonel Upwood and the card scandal at the Nonpareil. Surely you recall that the club was a haven for card sharps and others of larcenous intent. Since it served as a hideout for wanted men, there were entrances and exits not recorded in the original designer's blueprints."

My mind flew back to this notorious case, one of the most unusual in Holmes's career up to that point.

"Of course. The secret entrance from the warehouse behind the club through which Victor Lynch, the forger, attempted to make his escape."

"You are in rare form, ol' fellow. Fortunately, you never chose to make that case history available to the

17

reading public and the matter was not dealt with in detail by the journals of that period. My thought is that we may be privy to information regarding the Nonpareil Club that Baron Dowson, its present owner, is not."

3

The Battle at the Nonpareil Club

And so it was that we departed shortly thereafter from Baker Street, looking for all the world like a couple of swagmen. Holmes had a bull's-eye lantern, an assortment of first-class burglar tools in a valise, and his walking stick that concealed the vicious blade of Toledo steel, which he was capable of handling with such dexterity. The weight of my Smith-Webley was reassuring in my overcoat pocket. My intimate friend had a distaste for firearms and I often contended that he had been born several centuries too late as regards lethal weapons. However, if called upon, he could be extremely accurate with a revolver of small recoil, as evidenced by his occasional indoor target practice with his ridiculous single-shot Continental "salon" piece.

The driver of the hansom we hailed was surprised at the address in Soho that Holmes gave him. And small wonder, since this section seemed hardly appropriate for two staid middle-aged men of respectable appearance. However, he whistled to his horse and soon we were approaching the Thames. Needless to say, Holmes had not directed him to our eventual destination but a convenient intersection some distance away.

As we alighted from the conveyance, the driver was still concerned.

"Would you be wishin' fer me to wyte, gov?" he asked.

"No need, good man," replied the great detective,

pressing a coin into the driver's hand. "My thanks for your concern."

Holmes's jaunty wave of farewell had a confidence which I did not share. The night was dark and the dank smell of the river added to the chill in the air. As the hansom clattered away, Holmes led us into a narrow alley and, taking me by the elbow, guided my steps over cobblestones and around corners without pause. As I have mentioned in other recountings of our adventures, his knowledge of the geography of London was uncanny, especially so in those havens of the lawless.

It took us about ten minutes, traveling a devious route, to arrive at a street that barely qualified for the name. It was a scant two blocks in length and there was not a light on it. Various ramshackle buildings studded it, most of them with an abandoned appearance.

I well knew from stories of Holmes, as well as adventures which I had shared with him, that but a block away the parallel street was garishly lit and much-trafficked, for it was a center of the slumming area of Soho. It was replete with gaming establishments, so-called "private clubs" of ill repute that served as after-hour-drinking spots, and even some "houses" in which the world's oldest profession was practiced. I must in truth admit that certain young gentlemen who fancied being called "gay blades" found it exciting to view life in the raw in such establishments. When some eventually paid the piper via narcotic addiction, staggering gambling debts, or venereal disease, it was too late. Reason or words of caution seldom impressed, for the hot blood of youth promotes an intoxication of personal immunity.

My philosophical wanderings were brought to an end when Holmes came to a cautious halt at the entrance to a shabby building, which bore the barely decipherable sign: AUSTRO-EURASIAN IMPORTS. Flattening himself against the warehouse, he indicated for me to do the same and we remained frozen for better than a minute, while Holmes's keen ears were tuned for revealing sounds and his eyes darted to our right and left, studying intently the buildings facing us. Save for traffic noise that filtered from the adjacent street, the Stygian darkness revealed nothing. Occasionally a faint limpid ray of moonlight winked at us, only to be extinguished by the heavy clouds overhead. Eventually, my friend seemed satisfied, for gesturing to me to preserve silence, he tested the warehouse door alongside which we had been standing. The knob turned subbornly under his hand emitting a squeaking sound which seemed to please him. Holmes had his valise open in a trice and worked on the lock with a narrow curved instrument. There was a faint luminosity from the sky now and I recognized the device as one of those developed by Slim Gilligan, who had figured in other cases, some of which I had recorded. If Holmes gave a grunt of satisfaction, it was barely audible. Extracting the device from the keyhole, he secured a can of thin lubricating oil, which he squirted into the lock and then applied to the hinges of the door as well. He leaned close to my ear.

"Luck favors the bold, Watson. This door has not been opened in a considerable time, strengthening our theory that this entrance to the Nonpareil Club is not known."

With another searching glance up and down the street, Holmes inserted his burglar tool and soon there was a click followed by a squeak. Holmes replaced his equipment in his satchel and then opened the door with no more than a faint protest from its newly oiled hinges. We were inside.

Cobwebs brushed against my face, further proof that this modern-day monk's hole was untrafficked. I could hear my own breathing and the soft sound of Holmes's valise being opened. Then there was a circle of light from the bull's-eye lamp. The illumination revealed a small room, obviously office space for the main warehouse, which was on our left. A flight of wooden stairs at the rear of the room led upward. Holmes swept his light over the stairs, imprinting their distance and the height and number of the treads upon his photographic brain. Then the light flicked out again and my friend's face was close to mine.

"The stairs lead up two flights, ol' fellow. They terminate in a room about the size of a large closet that is immediately adjacent to the private card room of the old club. Through certain sources today, I learned that the area now serves as Dowson's private office. But in the old days, this was where unwary dupes were lured into high-stakes games and Colonel Upwood observed their cards through a peephole. If said peephole is still operative, we may owe Upwood a vote of thanks. Though I have reason to believe that the partition between Dowson's office and what we might term the 'viewing room' is reasonably soundproof, let us remain cautious. In ascending the stairs, stay as close to the bannister as possible since this lessens the possibility of a creak. Sound has a strange way of traveling in old buildings. Also, on each step, place your feet in the middle of the tread and apply your weight slowly."

I nodded my understanding and Holmes led me to the stairs in perfect darkness, placing my hand on the bannister after ascending the first couple of steps himself. I do not care to recall our stealthy ascent of the two flights. Holmes mounted them like a shadow but I was not as successful and every sound boomed like the tympani section of the London Philharmonic to me. My thighs and the calves of my legs ached from the slow transfer of weight, and when we reached the top I was sure that another flight would have been too much for me. But the excitement of our situation soon banished physical ills from my mind.

If Holmes's information was correct, we were but slightly removed from the nerve center of one of the most dangerous criminal gangs in London. Dowson had created a sinister organization that almost rivaled that of Moriarty and the fact that he had eluded Holmes for so long was a tribute to his evil genius.

There was no glimmer of light anywhere in the area

22

at the top of the stairs, a fact that I found comforting and which evidently prompted Holmes to incur a necessary risk. He trained the bull's-eye in the direction from which we had come and opened the shutter a sliver. In the reflected light we could make out the confines of the small space in which we stood, but our attention was glued to the wall separating us from the interior of the Nonpareil Club. About five and a half feet from the floor was a circular piece of wood, not unlike a small plate in size. There was a handle screwed to its surface. A small exhalation of satisfaction escaped Holmes as he doused the light again.

"That must be the peephole, Watson. When I open it, I'll be looking through one eye of a man's portrait if the furnishings within have not been altered. Once we become peeping Toms any light, or sound, would be fatal. I want you to move with me to the opposite wall. Press your ear against it, then I'll chance the peephole. You shall be the ears, and I the eyes, in this effort."

Never in our years together had the comfort and security of our chambers at 221B Baker Street seemed so appealing, but despite this thought my chest swelled with pride at the realization that Holmes placed such confidence in me at this crucial moment in a most perilous investigation. Any member of the Dowson gang would have bartered whatever soul they had left to see the end of Sherlock Holmes, and to secure him in that private fortress where his body could be disposed of so easily would have seemed like manna from heaven to that band of unscrupulous ruffians. Creeping to my station, it occurred to me that they would be happy to settle my fate as well, since I was a dangerous witness.

Pressing my ear carefully against the wall, I tried to quiet the pounding of my heart and listened eagerly, but to no avail. Suddenly, there was a scent in my nostrils which alarmed me, until I realized that Holmes had his trusty can of oil lubricating the mechanism of the concealed aperture, a precaution that would never have occurred to me. Then there was faint light in our hiding place and I knew Holmes had opened the peephole.

The light remained for what seemed an interminable time but could have been but a brief ten seconds. Then it disappeared. Holmes's hand located my shoulder and he startled me by speaking, though softly.

"Judging from the width of the wall, sound is not a peril unless the peephole is open. Nothing is happening at the moment, but I judge we are in luck. You can see for yourself."

Guided by his hand, my head was positioned and then the aperture was reopened. At first, it was like looking through gauze but as my eyes adjusted to the light, I made out a small section of the room beyond. The line of sight was narrow but I could see a desk. Seated facing me was none other than Count Negretto Sylvius, Baron Dowson's right-hand man. He seemed in an attitude of waiting, so I judged him to be the only one in the room. I shifted my head but could not see a door or any area beyond that immediately surrounding the desk. It was like looking through a long tunnel. Sylvius's features were distinguishable but blurred. Obviously, the eye of the picture that secreted the peephole was covered with a filmy material that provided concealment. An excellent piece of workmanship I thought, and then recalled that this very deception which we were making such good use of had separated wealthy and titled Englishmen from a quarter of a million pounds, before the nefarious scheme had been uncovered by the world's only consulting detective.

Count Sylvius was idly smoking a cigarette and seemed without a care in the world. As he blew smoke, for a brief moment my heart plummeted. He was looking right at me. It seemed that he had to see me staring at him, but there was no flicker of alarm or even interest and he tapped his cigarette casually against a jade ashtray. The ashtray appeared to be a piece of value, understandable since Dowson was known to have luxurious tastes, but that is not what gripped my eyes. On the desk, within arm's reach of Count Sylvius, was the Bird. It had to be the Golden Bird, for it glistened in the light of the room, a graceful figure of whitish yellow color, an artistic reproduction of the legendary roc. It seemed poised for flight, its claws, greatly out of proportion to its overall size, grasping the pedestal that supported it.

My head jerked back from the peephole and the light disappeared as Holmes replaced its cover. We retreated to the rear wall of the cubicle for a council of war.

"Watson, that is obviously the Golden Bird and it is equally obvious that we have experienced an amazing stroke of luck. The very fact that Baron Dowson is not present indicates that the consummation of a deal is about to take place. If our good fortune holds, we may discover the principals in this most *outré* affair. Now patience is our byword for a climax is imminent."

As I puzzled over Holmes's analysis, we returned to our observation post. Holmes again opened the peephole and I positioned myself by his shoulder to share as much of his view as possible. Count Sylvius was seated as he had been and I envied his calm, self-satisfied air. The next fifteen minutes constituted the longest and most infuriating period I can recall spending, and it was with heartfelt thanks that I heard the sound of a door opening and the murmur of voices. Holmes, after a moment, drew slightly to one side and I could see the hunched figure of Baron Dowson, seated at the desk opposite Sylvius with his back to us. Obviously, there was a third presence for both Sylvius and Dowson were regarding another who was not in our line of sight. Sylvius rose from his chair, taking the Golden Bird from the desk and passing out of view. I surrendered my position to Holmes keeping as close to the opening as possible and listening intently. The voices in the adjoining room were muted but the words were understandable.

"If you will inspect the merchandise, you will find it to be the object in question."

The voice, with a faint quaver of age, could only be that of the infamous Baron Dowson. The criminal conspirator had his fingers steepled in front of his face as he regarded the third presence in the room, still unseen from our vantage point.

"I can thay, without a thadow of doubt that thith ith the Golden Bird."

For a moment, the danger of our situation and the importance of the information we were surreptitiously gleaning was dissipated by an involuntary desire to laugh. The unknown and unseen consort of Dowson and Sylvius had a pronounced lisp, which seemed so out of keeping with the melodrama being enacted before our eyes. I steeled myself to stifle the imp of humor.

Dowson's aged head was nodding. The confirmation of the authenticity of the *objet d'art* being of no surprise.

"Then all that remains is to conclude the arrangements," he said, suggestively.

Sylvius reappeared with an attaché case, which he placed on the desk. At a gesture of the Baron, he released the catches and opened it. My eyes widened instinctively for the case was filled with large-denomination currency bills.

"You will thee that it ith all there, gentlemen. Allow me to uthe the case to tranthport the Golden Bird."

The unseen owner of the voice was of indeterminate age. Sylvius tipped the attaché case, spilling the currency on Dowson's desk. He disappeared from view toward the unknown as Dowson's trained fingers riffled through the packs of currency with the expertise of a banker.

Holmes's figure at my side drew back and, suddenly, the peephole was closed.

"Quick, Watson, we must get out of here. The Golden Bird is on the move again but this time we shall follow it."

His intention was obvious. If we could regain the street and make our way to the entrance of the Nonpa-

26

reil Club the attaché case would identify the unknown who had just paid such a large sum of money for the statue we were pursuing. With a hand on my friend's shoulders, I followed his sure progress down the stairs, suddenly coming to an abrupt stop since Holmes did. I could feel his sinewy muscles tense and then below us heard the sounds that had alerted him.

"We're trapped!" I thought. "Our exit is cut off!"

Suddenly, behind us, within the Nonpareil Club, a shot rang out and it was followed by a volley. There were screams and the silence we had been so intent on preserving was shattered on all sides.

"Back to the peephole, ol' chap," said Holmes. "See what has transpired. I'll hold the stairs."

In the sudden silence that so often follows an outbreak of violence, I heard the soft slither of steel and realized that my friend had drawn his sword blade. There was a pungent odor in the air and the sound of soft footfalls below.

Back at the peephole, I swung its cover to one side. Sylvius was not in evidence. Baron Dowson was extracting a long-barreled revolver from his desk drawer as another man, bearded and with a scarred face, was pushing the desk toward where I judged the door to the room to be. It was the stranger who was speaking hurriedly.

"It all came of a sudden, Baron. The gaming room was swarming with Chinks. The customers made a bolt for the doors naturally enough."

Dowson, gun in hand, lent his frail strength to his assistant. Evidently, they intended to barricade the room.

"How goes it below?" Dowson asked, venomously.

"Our boys are forted up in the kitchen, serving pantry and the bar room. If them heathen Chinee make their way up here, it will cost them."

The conversation was underscored by sporadic gunfire. As I replaced the cover and turned toward Holmes, there was a scream of pain and a body fell down the stairs we had ascended. Now I understood the pungent odor that had registered on my senses—the scent of spices carried by the Chinese dock workers so numerous in this area. Evidently, the Nonpareil Club had been invaded by a small army of Orientals. My Webley was now in my hand as I located Holmes at the head of the stairs. Below were the soft guttural sounds of a foreign tongue and the unmistakable presence of many bodies. It occurred to me that if a light were shown up the stairs, we would be in a very revealed position, an idea which occurred to Holmes as well. He drew me back from the head of the stairs, listening for the sound of movement that would indicate an upward rush at our position.

But the next sound that intruded itself over the chaos in the Nonpareil Club came from above. There was a sliding noise and a brief glimpse of the night sky overhead.

"Good heavens, Holmes, they're on the roof!"

But it was a voice born within the sound of the bow-bells that graced our ears, to my intense relief.

"Mr. 'Olmes, be ya down there? 'Tis Slim."

"Right you are, Gilligan," replied Holmes in his coolest manner.

"Best get up 'ere, sir. Things is a moite warm all 'round the block."

Holmes, warned by some instinct, suddenly hurled his sword blade like a lance toward the head of the stairs. There was another howl of pain and a crash of a falling body. Like an uncoiling spring, the great detective sprang upward toward the outstretched arm of Slim Gilligan, which was extended through the trap door in the roof. Grasping the wrist of the safecracker, Holmes reached the side of the opening with both of his powerful hands and drew his body, with Gilligan's help, halfway through the hatch.

"Watson, grab my legs. We'll get you out of there."

Loosening two shots from my revolver, I reached my left hand overhead and made contact with one of Holmes's ankles. As I was drawn clear of the floor, I sprayed the stair landing with the remainder of my cartridges, dropped my trusty weapon, and flailing wildly with my right hand made contact with Gilligan's hand. As Holmes drew his body clear of the opening I somehow managed to hold onto his ankle and, with Gilligan pulling on my other arm, my portly form was dragged through the hole and onto the roof. Gilligan promptly replaced the trap door as Holmes and I, more than a little breathless, regained our feet.

Sounds of battle continued beneath us and, in the distance, could be heard approaching police vehicles. The street below was full of running people. We wasted no time discussing the situation or the fortuitous appearance of Slim Gilligan, but followed the master cracksman as he led us over the roof of the warehouse. It was a short leap to the roof of the adjacent building. We quickly crossed it and found that Gilligan, who had obviously arrived on the scene in this manner, had stretched a plank across the space to the next roof in the block. Gilligan and Holmes went across this slender pathway to safety in a sure-footed manner but, in trying to emulate a tight-wire performer, it crossed my mind that I was much more suited to the life of a country doctor and, in all honesty, should retire to bucolic and peaceful surroundings rather than try to dog the footsteps of the world's greatest detective.

On the third roof, Gilligan kicked the plank, which had served us so well, free of the side of the buildings, to forestall any pursuit although there was none in evidence.

Behind us the sounds of conflict were dwindling and I assumed the forces of law and order had arrived on the scene, but Holmes seemed to wish to avoid the Metropolitan Police. So the three of us regained the cobblestones of the street in short order and dodged through a series of alleys until it was safe to call a halt to our pell-mell rush and hail a hansom.

The driver of the conveyance had heard the uproar

and questioned us regarding it. Holmes satisfied his curiosity with the guess that there had been a raid on a gambling establishment, which was certainly the truth, though as we well knew it had not been a police raid.

4

The Solving of a Message

When the hansom delivered the three of us to 221B Baker Street, I couldn't help thinking that the domicile of Mrs. Hudson had never looked more appealing.

Billy, the page boy, had the door open before we could ring the bell.

"I give your message to Mr. Gilligan," he stated to Holmes with a shy smile.

"And how fortunate for Doctor Watson and myself that you did," replied Holmes.

I echoed this thought most emphatically, though silently.

In the sitting room, with glasses in our hands, we tried to make some sense from the pattern of madness that had been the road map of the past few hours. Holmes seemed in no hurry as he thoughtfully extracted shag from the famous Persian slipper and fueled his pipe. Nothing could shake the habitual calmness of Slim Gilligan, but then nerves of steel were what had made him the leading cracksman of his day, until he had abandoned the paths of the lawless because of his association with Sherlock Holmes. One felt that Gilligan had seen so much in his colorful career that no surprises remained.

Of course, questions bombarded my poor befuddled brain, but fortunately I managed to preserve my silence as the quickest means of learning what had been going on.

Puffing furiously on his pipe, Holmes finally broke the silence.

"Your *deus-ex-machina* appearance was most fortunate for Doctor Watson and myself, Gilligan. Our thanks."

The former safecracker gestured aimlessly with one of his abnormally long and thin arms, as though rescues from rooftops were a daily occurrence.

"I knew you was on the lookout for me, Mr. 'Olmes. When Billy told me you was investigatin' the Nonpareil Club, I figgered there moight be a little excitement so ol' Slim sneaked up on the locale—sorta. I was a little leery, you see, because of that Barker fella."

"He contacted you?" asked Holmes.

"By post. Kinda caught me off guard 'cause I didn't really know the cove."

"He's dead," stated Holmes flatly.

A nod was Gilligan's response. He passed a sealed envelope to Holmes.

"Some light is coming to dark places," said the sleuth. "Barker sent you a letter for delivery here. He also left a communiqué for me in his lodging. Let me hazard a guess that when I consider this letter in connection with the one already received, the true message that Barker intended will be revealed."

Gilligan's brow was furrowed. "But why would 'e given a message to me iffen I never even knew 'im?"

"Strangely enough, Watson here is the answer to that. Barker was one of his devoted readers. The letter he left me was full of references to those cases that Watson has recorded for the reading public. Obviously, the late investigator from Surrey knew of our close association, Gilligan."

He showed good sense there, I thought, for Slim Gilligan was one of the staunchest of Holmes's allies. The safecracker's head was now nodding in understanding.

"I will study this communiqué later," continued Holmes. "For now other vistas beckon. Have you ever heard of an object called the Golden Bird?"

The name meant nothing to Gilligan and he indicated as much.

"It is an ancient art object, a statue of solid gold."

Gilligan's lips pursed in a silent whistle. "Iffen something like that was 'round, I should 'ave 'eard of it."

"It is but recently in England," said Holmes. "That is not just a rumor, for Watson and I saw the object tonight. Let us try another tack, Slim. Has there been any unusual robbery or incident lately that comes to your mind?"

"Well, sir, always there's somebody tryin' to take somefing from some other bloke. But wiv most of the stuff wot's 'appened, I could make a fair guess as to 'oo is involved."

"As could I," said Holmes. "So let us consider a minor incident, something with an unusual twist but seemingly unimportant."

Gilligan's eyes narrowed in thought. "There was that Chinaman off the *Asian Star*."

"Chinaman?" I said, instinctively. "We were knee-deep in Orientals tonight."

Holmes's questioning eyes remained glued to Gilligan.

"This 'ere Chinee got 'isself knifed. Nothin' unusual about that. Them 'eathens gamble for fair and they got Tongs and feuds wot we don't know nuffin' abaht. The reason the story comes to moind is that there was a fuss abaht 'is belongin's after 'e got 'isself killed. Seems 'e 'ad this 'ere idol. 'E was a common seaman on the *Asian Star* and 'is fo'c'sle mates remember it right enough. But the bloomin' thing disappeared. Couple o' slant eyes turned up claimin' the seaman was a relative and the idol belonged to their family. Well, one Chinee looks pretty much like another. Maybe these blokes was 'is relatives 'n' maybe they wa'n't."

"Was it by chance an image of Buddha?" questioned Holmes, his eyes alight with excitement.

"That's the nyme, Mr. 'Olmes. You 'eard abaht it, eh?"

"No," admitted the sleuth, "but it is common for those of the Buddhist faith to carry an image of their god with them."

He sprang to his feet crossing to the bookshelf. "I believe we have a lead here."

Holmes subscribed to a number of periodicals of a specialized nature, and I noted that he selected the latest "Lloyds' Shipping Guide" from a shelf. As Gilligan and I exchanged puzzled glances, my friend leafed rapidly through the pages, then read intently for a moment before turning to us with a triumphant smile.

"This tells a story. *Asian Star* out of Hong Kong. Ports of call: Colombo, Alexandria, Constantinople, Trieste, Venice, Lisbon, and London. Constantinople is the clue, of course, since it was the last-known locale of the Golden Bird until it appeared here in London."

"You associate a common seaman with the theft of the Bird?" I fear my voice and expression registered disbelief, a fact that did not bother Holmes.

"My dear Watson, reproductions of the god Buddha can be considerable size. Being a religious piece, it would arouse no suspicions, especially from customs. But suppose within this Buddha figure was the relatively small Golden Bird?"

Holmes's logic had an immediate appeal. "Of course, the Oriental seaman was but the means to bring the Bird into this country." Then another thought forced itself upon me. "But what is the significance of the Chinaman, especially since Dowson's gaming house suffered a full-scale attack from Orientals?"

"Let us construct a hypothetical situation," said Holmes, rather smugly I thought, "though I'll wager it turns out to be very close to the truth. The Golden Bird was stolen in Constantinople at the same time that the *Asian Star* was in port. The Bird, secreted within the Buddha, came by sea, a trip that would require considerable time. We must assume that the robbery was engineered by an Oriental or someone who employs Orientals. When the *Asian Star* arrives in Southhampton, another factor is introduced. The messenger is murdered and the Buddha disappears."

"Dowson's gang," I exclaimed.

"Employed by someone else, also after the art object."

"The man with the lisp?"

Even the imperturbable Gilligan registered surprise at this remark of mine.

"I doubt it," responded Sherlock Holmes. "I rather picture him as an emissary. He was in Dowson's headquarters with a large sum of money and the possibility of double-dealing is to be considered. As an employee, if mischance befell him Dowson and his crew would be open to retaliation. But that's is not of importance. What does seem obvious is that the original instigator of the robbery in Constantinople learned that it was Dowson's gang that had hijacked the Bird. Hence, the attack on Dowson's establishment."

"You've got it, Holmes," I stated with pride. "Two gangs are involved in this affair."

"There's little doubt about that," admitted my friend. "But again the haunting question. Such elaborate machinations. So much planning and manpower involved. Why? I will admit that twenty-five inches or so of solid gold is worth a tidy sum, but surely not enought to warrant the efforts so far expended. Dowson's organization is for hire but they command a heavy price."

Remembering the valise full of currency on the Baron's desk, I could well agree with that statement.

Holmes continued and I sensed his mercurial brain was racing ahead of his words.

"It was a small scale war we were involved in tonight. Surely there were thirty or so Orientals in action. The whole affair was much more reminiscent of an American criminal conflict than anything we are familiar with in England. What is the unknown value of this product of an ancient goldsmith's art that prompts such actions?"

"Could the Golden Bird have some religious significance?" I guessed, somewhat desperately.

Holmes registered a negative. "To my knowledge, the roc is simply a figure in mythology and plays no part in an organized religious movement. No, Watson, we are faced with a problem here that indicates deep water indeed. Possibly, Barker's last message will reveal a factor that we have not considered."

He paced the room thoughtfully for a moment and then came to a decision.

"We do know the Golden Bird is in London and an important, nay vital, question is whether it remains in the possession of Baron Dowson or if the man with the lisp departed from the Nonpareil Club before or during the outbreak of violence. Slim, best to learn what you can about the Nonpareil affair with particular attention to anyone carrying a black attaché case."

Gilligan nodded. I knew that his lock and key establishment had been financed by Sherlock Holmes and suspected that the detective paid him a monthly retainer as well for his unique abilities. Rising to his feet, he had but one question.

"Any description of the cove?"

"Alas, no," replied Holmes, with distaste. "We did not see him, but he was closeted with Dowson and Sylvius prior to the attack and may well have left with the Bird in his possession."

As the cracksman departed, Holmes turned his attention to the letter that Gilligan had delivered. After reading for some moments, his eyes found mine briefly. "This should interest you, Watson: 'My dear Sherlock Holmes: Having long been an admirer of your career, let me send this message for your consideration. Your faithful biographer, Dr. Watson, makes frequent reference to the fact that you delight in puzzles and I have composed this to provide you with mental stimulation.'" Holmes looked up with approval in his eyes. "You will note that Barker's introduction is written as though we had never met. A clever touch, that, to allay

36

suspicions should this fall into other hands. He now lists a series of questions," he added, returning to Barker's words:

" 'One: What was of Agra?' "

"That's simple enough," I said. "The Agra Treasure. I well recall that, Holmes, since it was the second of your cases that I revealed in print."

"With the melodramatic title of 'The Sign Of The Four,' " agreed Holmes. " 'Two: The Yoxley Case was?' "

"The Golden Pince-Nez."

"I believe we can accept *golden* as the key word," said Holmes. "Our knowledge of the Lindquist case makes our reading of this cryptic letter considerably easier. Consider the third clue. 'Three: Wilson dealt with? . . .' "

"An easy one," I said, triumphantly. "The reference has to be to Wilson, the notorious canary trainer."

"With what we already know, the meaning is not *canary* but rather *bird*. We now have: treasure, golden, bird, which certainly fits. The fourth question, however, puzzles me. See what you make of it, Watson. 'Four: What gave the tadpole fever?' "

"Good heavens, that's a strange clue. But wait . . ." —I almost shouted with excitement—"Tadpole was the schoolboy nickname of Percy Phelps."

"Good show, Watson! Phelps had brain fever because of the theft of the Naval Treaty. Obviously, the key word is *theft* since it fits so nicely with the next one. 'Five: From Trincomalee to? . . .' "

I thought for a moment. "The reference must be to the singular adventure of the Atkinson Brothers at Trincomalee . . . but . . ."

"But do recall that, following exposure, the brothers fled to Constantinople."

"That's it, Holmes! Treasure . . . golden . . . bird . . . theft . . . Constantinople . . . what's next?"

" 'Six: Eduardo Lucas and Milverton.' "

I gazed at Holmes in astonishment. "But they are both dead."

"True, but they certainly had something in common."

"They were both blackmailers. Lucas came within an ace of ruining the Secretary for European Affairs in that 'Second Stain' affair, as you well know."

"And Charles Augustus Milverton was an even greater and more heartless rascal, if that is possible."

"But, Holmes, it was coming along swimmingly to this point. Now we have two deceased blackmailers who could not be involved."

"But you will accept two. I think that is rather important. Let us look deeper, ol' chap. What do blackmailers do?"

"Extort money, bleed their victims dry."

"Agreed. And they are able to ply their nefarious trade because they are collectors."

I did not follow this at all so Holmes elaborated. "Both Lucas and Milverton collected indiscreet letters, proofs of crime or infidelity, knowledge of sordid episodes in their victims' lives. What Barker suggests is that two collectors are involved in the pursuit of the Golden Bird. It being an art object, we must assume that both are collectors of art. Now our adventure of this evening reveals that one of these collectors could put his hand on a very large sum of money."

"The payoff to Baron Dowson," I said, mechanically, and was rewarded with a nod.

"While the other could command a sizeable group of henchmen. Is it not obvious that these mysterious collectors are men of wealth and power?"

As I nodded, Holmes referred to the letter again.

"Here you must help me, good fellow. 'Seven: The birth of Mary Morstan?'"

"My dear Mary was born in 1861," I said sadly. "Of course, the date may not have been what Barker was referring to."

"Possibly the next clue will give us an indication. 'Eight: Victor Hatherley was? . . .'"

"He was an engineer," I said, promptly. "He was young."

Holmes puzzled on this for a moment. "He was also unfortunate."

"I would certainly say so having his thumb chopped off like that."

"I note," said my friend, "that Barker seems partial to the titles of your stories and 'The Engineer's Thumb' was the name you gave it."

"Hmm . . . Victor Hatherley was without a thumb? Missing a thumb?"

"Wait," said Holmes. "Possibly a number is our seventh clue. Would not the word *minus* go along with that?"

"Victor Hatherley was minus a thumb. He certainly was. What is the next clue, Holmes?"

"Here is an easy one and I think a picture is coming into focus. 'Nine: The objects in Holder's security.' "

"The Beryl Coronet," I said, hastily.

"And there were thirty-nine Beryls in the Coronet."

"Why, Holmes, it's obvious. 1861 minus 39 gives us 1822."

"Indeed, it does and that is the last clue. Does it have any significance to you?"

I tried, dear me how I tried, but my efforts were fruitless. Holmes was obviously stumped as well.

"What do you make of all this, Holmes?"

"Two things. 1822 is the prime bit of information. Note that the rest of this message relates to matters we have already learned about. I believe the date was the information that poor Barker was taking to Lindquist when he met his fate."

"What is your other conclusion?"

"Simply that Barker was a devoted reader of your printed words, my good Watson."

5

To Berlin

It was coming on to ten of the morning when I descended from my bedchamber to find that Holmes had preceded me and was with company. Inspector Alec MacDonald was enjoying a steaming cup of coffee with the great detective, but considering the suspicious glance he fastened upon me as I entered the sitting room, I sensed that this was not a social call.

"Ah, Watson, you come at an appropriate time," said Holmes, pouring from the great silver urn. "I'm just learning about a singular event that occurred in Soho last night."

Accepting a cup from Holmes, I tried to look interested and startled at the same time. My innocent expression did not seem to register on the dour inspector, what at this time was just beginning to build the formidable reputation that he later enjoyed at Scotland Yard.

"Knowin' your sources of information, Mr. Holmes, 'tis surprising to me you've not already heard of it."

"Tell us all," I said, sitting alongside the desk with what I hoped was a relaxed manner.

"The Nonpareil Club was hit last night by a whole gang of Chinese. Pitchin' battle, it was, too."

"Any casualties?" queried Holmes.

"A couple of the Orientals were wounded. We've got them down at the Yard but they dinna speak a word of English or wouldna' admit to it. Several of the Baron's lads got hurt as well. That's all we know. It's possible

41

that there were more either wounded or killed but the bodies were removed before we got there."

"This certainly sounds like a large scale affair. Can you divine a reason?"

"Not offhand, Mr. Holmes. Dowson has his finger in a number of sticky pies, we ha' known that for years. Since the passin' of Professor Moriarty he may well be the leading criminal of London. We've found it convenient to let him run his gaming house since we generally keep our eye on the place and sometimes secure valuable information. The Chinese element have numerous fan-tan houses but Dowson's clientele wouldna' patronize them so it doesna' add up as some territorial dispute."

The dour Scot, who had been gazing into the hearth fire, suddenly threw a shrewd glance at the great detective.

"I was rather hopin' you might shed some light on the matter."

"It is singular, Mr. Mac that you should come to me about the Nonpareil Club since Watson and I were there but recently."

Surprise blossomed on MacDonald's face and he quickly surpressed it.

"I had wanted to give the place a looking-at," continued Holmes, "and Watson and I left the losers. Not from the games of chance, which I suspect do not provide the player with the true gambling odds. My sword stick was missing when we departed from the premises and also Watson's army revolver, which he had left in his greatcoat pocket."

Fortunately, I was able to suppress my astonishment at this pure fabrication on the part of my friend.

"I was in hopes," continued Holmes, "that the two items would be recovered and, in the normal fashion of things, posted a letter only this morning to Lestrade reporting the missing articles."

MacDonald's lips were compressed in a firm line.

"Well, they are missin' no longer, sir. A cane sword

was found on the stairs of an adjacent warehouse, stained with blood. And a Smith-Webley army issue was found at the head of the same stairs with all chambers fired. I might add that there was blood in the vicinity but no bodies were found. Some bits of clothing indicate that the victims were Oriental, as were the attackers of the Nonpareil Club."

Holmes did not carry his pretense of innocence too far. He had a hearty respect for the acumen of the Aberdeenian.

"It would seem that the attackers were familiar with the history of the club and the fact that numerous hidden exits exist from it. Some, if memory serves me well, involving the adjacent warehouse."

MacDonald knew when he was licked. "Well, Mr. Holmes, I'll see that the articles are returned to you. I'm disappointed, for a fact, since had you been on the premises during the fracas, you might have provided us with a key to the affair. We're baffled."

"Perhaps I can uncover something," said Holmes. "I gather that this battle was not an attempt by one criminal group to demoralize or displace another. It seems reasonable to assume that Dowson had something that the Oriental group was after."

The police inspector nodded.

"Have you any idea what this might be?" continued Holmes.

"No, sir. There's been no big robbery on the docks, or anywhere else, that I can associate with this."

"Then let me take another approach. Who, in your opinion, Mr. Mac, would have had the organization, the manpower, to attack the Nonpareil Culb?"

"Assuming it is an Oriental, and that seems indicated, it could only be one man."

It was Holmes's turn to nod. "Chu San Fu."

"Aye," agreed MacDonald. "That tiger can wave one of his fingers and there's a hundred to do his biddin'."

"I have heard," said Holmes, slowly, "that Chu is not as active as he once was."

" 'Tis an impression he's most anxious to create. I can recall times when he was crossed and there were bodies for sure and no doubt as to how they met their end. Warnings of his power."

I could contain myself no longer. "Good heavens, who is this Oriental monster that you both discuss so calmly and how is it that I have never heard of him? Chu San Fu, indeed."

Holmes's eyes were on the fire and his voice had a dreamy quality. "The Chinese are an inscrutable and unobtrusive race, my dear Watson, completely devoted to the customs of their homeland. Their entire strata of society is a secret closely guarded. They remain completely enclosed and while we see them, know they exist, we really know little about them."

MacDonald was nodding and chose to add to Holmes's words. "For years, Chu has been the power in the Chinese community. All the opium dens, the gambling houses, the drug traffic, have been under his thumb. He also runs a sizeable import-export business that is legitimate, as far as we know. Of late, he's gone underground, as far as his illegal activities are concerned. Oh, he still wields the power of life and death, but his enemies just disappear now. Into the waters of the Thames estuary, nae doot."

Holmes's dreamy thoughtfulness had disappeared. He was regarding the Scot intently.

"Do you have some theory regarding his change of *modus operandi*?"

MacDonald nodded. "I also have a fear of a gang war and an intense int'rest in last night's battle at the Nonpareil Club."

Holmes rose and knocked the dottle out of his pipe and into the fire. "Could it be that you are suggesting a trade, Mr. Mac?"

The Scot didn't hesitate. "That's exactly what I'm doin'."

"You may be the loser. I've not much to tell and

your sources in the Chinese quarter are undoubtedly superior to mine."

"I'll take me chances."

"Very well." Holmes's fingers reached into the Persian slipper for more shag. "I think that Dowson was hired to secure an ancient *objet d'art* and Chu wants it."

The Scotland Yard inspector digested this. "Would this object be of great value?"

"Not of the type you're thinking of. It's no *Mona Lisa*, or even close to it."

"Very strange, Mr. Holmes. But your theory is provocative since Chu San Fu has one of the largest collections of Oriental art in the wurld."

I have seldom seen Holmes register surprise, but he did now. "Does he indeed? But the object I have in mind is not Oriental."

"Hmmm. Well, there's no tellin' what else Chu has in his treasure chest. 'Tis me feelin' that collectors are a breed apart."

"A very sage observation, Mr. Mac," said Holmes.

"I've a wee bit more for ye, but tell me, if Dowson had this object and Chu was after it, who has it now?"

"That I don't know," said Holmes, with regret.

"But ye'll certainly be tryin' to find out?" MacDonald was answered by a quick affirmative nod from Holmes.

"Well, sir, herre's a bit of social news that int'rests our lads in the limehouse squad: Maurice Rothfils, related to the famous international bankers, is to be married come spring."

"I've heard of that," I said, glad to have a hand in the conversation. "It's something of a nine-day sensation in Mayfair since his bride-to-be is a Chinese princess."

"Aye, Doctor," said MacDonald. "Now Rothfils just may have a title by the time he's married and there could be a presentation at court involvin' his wife. So the special branch has been quite concerned. For there's a whisper that this Chinese princess is the daughter of Chu San Fu."

Holmes stopped filling his pipe. "You are a treasure trove, Mr. Mac. This puts a new light on things and explains why the tiger is trying to sheath his claws." Noting my puzzled look, Holmes added to his statement. "The more dastardly the brigand, the more precious the cloak of respectability. You may recall, Watson, that Henry Morgan, who sacked Panama and was the terror of the Caribbean, later became the Governor of Jamaica."

"Not a very respected one," I said, somewhat stiffly.

"*Touché!*" responded my friend.

MacDonald, sensing that the well of information had dried up on both sides, rose to his feet.

"I'll not be takin' up any more of your time, Mr. Holmes." As I handed him his coat, he regarded the great sleuth shrewdly. "I'll be hearin' from you, sir?"

"I hope very soon," responded Holmes.

Then the official and unofficial detective did a strange thing. They shook hands—a social formality I had never seen them indulge in before. But then, a bargain had been made.

The next three days provided no further information regarding this strange case that Holmes and I had become involved in. I saw little of my friend and surmised that he was tapping his sources of information and frequenting strange places in any one of the variety of disguises that he affected with such expertise.

The journals had a short-lived romance with the battle in Soho. Then the matter disappeared from print. The management of the Nonpareil Club claimed they were victims of an attempted robbery. Since the authorities had been unable to locate gambling devices or prove that the club was a haven for it, Dowson and his crew were officially blameless. The two wounded Chinese claimed, through an interpreter, that they were making a delivery to the club and just got caught in the

46

middle of hostilities. A reputable Oriental merchant appeared to identify them as employees and produce a delivery order for two Chinese rugs. The Orientals were released for lack of evidence and the entire affair collapsed in the hands of the police. Everyone involved knew the gunfight was no small thing, but no one could prove it. It was as though nothing had happened.

The morning of the fourth day brought a sparkle to Holmes's eyes. He had been chafing under the strain of inaction or, at least, action that was non-productive. As usual, this had not improved his sometimes brusque and preoccupied manner. But it was the old Holmes that greeted me at the breakfast table with a smile of relief.

"I do hope you are free to take a trip, my good Watson."

"I can be."

"Then we are off to Berlin."

He handed me a cablegram, which I eagerly scanned.

MY DEAR MR. HOLMES

LETTER FROM LINDQUIST INFORMS ME OF ARRANGEMENT HE MADE WITH YOU. AGREEABLE ON THIS END. CAN YOU COME TO BERLIN AS THERE HAS BEEN RECENT DEVELOPMENT HERE RELATIVE TO THE BIRD. I WILL ASSUME RESPONSIBILITY FOR EXPENSES INCURRED BY YOU AND YOUR COLLEAGUE, OF COURSE. WILL MAKE MYSELF AVAILABLE AT ANY TIME.

VASIL D'ANGLAS.

I experienced a nervous moment. From time to time, I have been accused of being deficient in imagination and, compared to Holmes, it is possible that I am. What imagination I did have was now working overtime.

"How embarrassing," I said, "if this complex matter is resolved by the owner of the Golden Bird."

Holmes chimed in with my thoughts. "Lindquist gone, Barker as well, and we have gotten ourselves deeply involved to no avail." He indulged in a chuckle.

"It would be bitter tea indeed, but a reminder, ol' chap, that no one is indispensable."

Holmes was a fast packer, rapid departures being no stranger to him, and my experience with the Fifth Northumberland Fusiliers stood me in good stead in this department. It was only a short time later, having notified Mrs. Hudson that we would be off the premises for a few days, that we caught the boat train and were on our way to the Continent. Doctor Vernier had readily agreed to assume my duties until we returned. It was a situation he was very familiar with and I do believe that he considered my patients as partially his. In a year's time he certainly saw as much, or more, of them as I did.

The channel passage was stormy and rail connections were delayed. As a consequence, we arrived in Berlin in the late hours but had no difficulty securing a suite at the Bristol Kempinsky Hotel, where Holmes stayed when in Berlin. The night manager, Klaus, always grew loquacious at the sight of my friend.

"Ah, Herr Holmes, you have returned to make dose clever deductions of yours, *nicht war*?"

Invariably, this was Klaus's greeting and some time was spent reassuring the excitable Bavarian that the fate of Europe did not hang in the balance. Finally, we were comfortably ensconced in most satisfactory quarters and our beds were a welcome sight to me.

The following morning, I awoke to find Holmes gone. Not a new experience, of course, but at least I could assume that he had secured some sleep. Without his endless files, chemical apparatus or extensive library, he had no toys to while away the night hours. My friend did have a built-in alarm in his splendid brain and on more than one occasion I had known him to fall into a deep sleep and will himself to awaken at a certain hour. I know of no scientific proof that this is possible but I also knew that he could do it.

* * *

48

It was mid-morning, after I had enjoyed a large breakfast, when Holmes returned.

"My dear Watson, I trust you have recovered from our travels."

"Indeed, only to find myself abandoned."

"Good chap, you were sleeping so soundly that I had not the heart to awaken you. In any case, some dry research was called for, so I saved you the searching of the Meldwesen files."

I recalled that most effective tool of the Berlin police force, which Holmes had such a hearty respect for. At the police headquarters in Alexanderplatz were the one hundred and eighty rooms that housed the meticulous card catalogue on criminals and crimes.

"Who were you checking on?"

"D'Anglas, naturally. We know nothing of the man save what Lindquist told us. Possibly, our employer has a dark past indeed. If he does, it is not known to the Berlin police. By the way, Inspector Schmidt sent you his cordial good wishes."

I recalled the Inspector well. A short man with a scar on his right cheek and uncomfortably bright blue eyes. Chap had had the effrontery to laugh at a deduction of mine in connection with the "Midas Emerald" affair but his tune had changed when Holmes upheld the rationale of my thinking. I muttered something and then, with a glance at my watch, suggested that we'd best leave for our appointment with D'Anglas.

6

Our Singular Client

In a carriage directed to the West End address of our client, I recalled again how much Berlin's tree-lined boulevards dotted with striking street cafés and coffee houses reminded me of both London and Paris. The craftsman talents of the Germans kept their metropolis ultramodern, but it was delightfully punctuated with ancient, grandiose, and historical buildings with a plentitude of parks and gardens to say nothing of sophisticated nightclubs and gourmet restaurants.

Driving along the Unter den Liden, the capital did seem on this shiny day to have put its best foot forward and adopted its most pleasing face. But there was work to be done and this fact was brought to my attention forcibly when Holmes, in excellent German, directed our carriage to come to a halt at a convenient open space by the curb of the busy avenue not far from the Emperor's palace.

"Let us remain calm, ol' fellow," said the detective as I registered surprise and a question formed on my lips. "We shall discuss, apparently, our route: a soupçon of make-believe that will allow me to solidify suspicions." As he spoke, Holmes extracted the golden cigarette case with the great amethyst, which had been given to him by the king of Bohemia. But the king had had no knowledge of the mirror surface inside the case, which had served the detective well on a number of occasions.

Offering me a cigarette, he held the case in such a

51

manner that he secured a good view of the area behind us. I made as though to refuse his offering and then, with gestures, apparently changed my mind. My mummery was designed to give Holmes additional time to check our back trail, of course. Something that Holmes saw must have been humorous since he was chuckling.

"It is a covered carriage, Watson, and the driver is somewhat embarrassed since, halted in the street, he is blocking traffic. However, I catch fleeting glimpses of two Oriental gentlemen within who are obviously keeping track of us and have been doing so since we left the hotel. They are ordering the driver to remain where he is until we show a disposition to move again."

Holmes consulted his watch and then regarded me with that mischievous expression which overran his features much more often than most people realized. "We have a bit of time to spare, ol' fellow. How about some sport? There's a policeman approaching and this is too rich a situation to miss."

Stealing a glance over my left shoulder, I saw the scene just as Holmes had described it. A member of the Berlin police force was addressing the driver of a large carriage to our rear. A Chinese face appeared reluctantly from the interior of the carriage to remonstrate with the officer who in turn looked quizzically at the driver. My knowledge of German was extremely sketchy while my understanding of Chinese was nonexistent. Yet, the exchange of words, even in unknown tongues, was crystal clear. The passenger of the covered carriage was hoping to confuse the officer with a flow of Chinese and the upholder of the law was regarding the driver as though he could act as translater. However, that worthy, who must have wished he had never risen from bed on this day, disclaimed any connection with the matter via an expressive shrug of his shoulders. The policeman had an equally expressive gesture to climax the situation and he pointed down the avenue with finality.

Gigging his horse into motion, the driver maneuvered

the closed carriage past us despite verbal protests from within. Now Holmes rapped an order to our man and we swung away from the curb and proceeded sedately in the wake of the covered carriage. I joined Holmes in a hearty laugh. Suddenly, the pursued became the pursuer and our merriment increased as two heads appeared in the aperture in the rear of the carriage and regarded us balefully. The conveyance increased speed and, at a word from Holmes, so did ours and both vehicles were soon progressing at a good rate.

Holmes finally tired of the game and as we came to one of those delightful squares that dot the West End, he issued another order to our man who, suddenly took a turn to the left preserving his horse's fast trot. The other carriage was already committed to its course and we lost it with no difficulty.

Shortly thereafter, we alighted on a street corner and Holmes presented our driver with his fare and, judging from the man's expression, a most generous addition. No doubt the driver wished that he could pick up a couple of crazy Englishmen every day.

I was not surprised when we completed our trip on foot, a matter of several blocks. My friend seldom went directly to an address, feeling that information of any kind was a commodity to be secured, not given away. As we made our way down a tree-lined street, Holmes voiced the thoughts coursing through his agile mind.

"Orientals are not commonplace here in Berlin, which makes things simpler for us if we are being followed."

"Obviously you spotted the two quite readily."

"As we left the Bristol Kempinsky. I will confess their presence was a surprise, Watson. It would seem reasonable to assume that they followed us from London. The puzzling question is where did they originally pick us up!"

I was baffled, nothing new to Holmes, and he continued. "Considering recent events, had the two Chinese been watching Baker Street I would have certainly become conscious of their presence."

"I don't see what you are getting at."

"Simply that it is almost as if they knew we were coming to Berlin. I'm most curious as to how they, or more realistically the man giving them their orders, were privy to that information."

Holmes's musings came to an end as we were at the door of a fairly sizeable residence. We were in a good neighborhood, but this domicile in comparison to its neighbors warranted the rating of modest, a fact which Holmes seemed to find strange as he activated the ornate knocker on a stout oaken door.

"Watson, I expect a little more than this. Collecting objects of art is an occupation reserved for affluent members of society. Possibly, the gentleman is a dealer though I think we should have been given a business address were that the case."

A fairly young man with burly shoulders and a swarthy face, who was dressed in livery, answered the knock and Holmes presented his card. We were ushered into a small main hall area. The beamed ceiling was two stories high, the walls were paneled in dark wood, and candlelight was necessary since the windows of the residence were small—not unlike those of a monastery or, indeed, a Rhine castle.

Having secured our coats and hats, the butler absented himself, mounting curved stairs that led from the hall to the second story area. He reappeared shortly thereafter to usher us up the same stairs. It occurred to me that the man might not speak English since he had not uttered a word since our arrival. His features were broad and, in conjunction with his swarthy visage, gave me the feeling that he was Turkish or Croatian.

A door on the landing led to a sizeable room in which a large fire was burning brightly. Though the day was sunny, the air was cold and I welcomed the heat provided by the burning logs.

A figure arose slowly from a tapestried chair by the

fire as the silent retainer closed the door behind us. The man was at least six feet tall with craggy, overhanging features. Dark eyes were sunk deep in a face that seemed oversized and out of proportion. His nose was thick and his lips were broad and pendulous.

"Ah, Mr. Holmes," he said, in a very low but pleasant voice. "When Achmet brought your card it was a surprise indeed, though a welcome one. This, of course, is Doctor Watson," he added, as his dull eyes swiveled toward me. "Do be seated, gentlemen, and tell me what brings you to Berlin."

As he waved us toward available chairs, I noted that his hands were very large and knobby and his feet were oversized as well. He was terribly stooped and presented a brooding, almost ominous picture, which was belied by his cordial manner.

While his question as to our presence must have puzzled Holmes, as it did me, the sleuth gave no evidence of it. He was intent on sizing up the man and his surroundings and I knew that every wrinkle in that seamed face was being printed on Holmes's photographic mind. He certainly knew, as did I, that D'Anglas suffered from a serious ailment. The man's unusual appearance was not natural, nor was the effort that every movement seemed to cost him. He did not give one the impression of weakness but rather seemed like a wounded elephant. Suddenly, I thought I knew the source of his suffering.

Comfortably seated, Holmes approached the question in both our minds in a circuitous fashion. "As you were informed in a letter from Nils Lindquist, I have . . ." —Holmes corrected himself with a gesture to include me—"we have taken over the search for the Golden Bird."

D'Anglas was nodding slowly. "The gentleman explained the situation to me in detail as well as his ill health. I was most unhappy to hear of his death." He paused for a lengthy moment as though in deference to the departed and then continued in a brisker tone. "However, I would be hypocritical if I did not admit to being delighted that you, Mr. Holmes, and your associate have accepted the case. With all deference to Mr. Lindquist, had I felt that I could afford your not inconsiderable fee, I would have approached you originally."

"In the field of art objects, Nils Lindquist was most qualified, as I'm sure you know," responded Holmes promptly.

Our host nodded in a ponderous manner and then a spark of cunning crept into his deep-set eyes. "I was given to understand that your services are included in the original financial arrangement I made with the late Lindquist."

The man's tone was tentative but Holmes waved the matter aside with an impatient gesture. He hated to discuss business and while he had the reputation of charging enormous fees for his incomparable services, I well knew of the myriad cases which he had undertaken simply for the interest that they prompted in him.

"Nils Lindquist had made some discoveries in the matter of the missing golden object and I have been able to pick up parts of the trail he was following."

For reasons of his own, Holmes did not choose to mention Barker, the Surrey investigator, and his sad end.

"No doubt you can fill in a few pieces in this puzzle," continued Holmes. "But, first, do we understand that our visit today surprised you?"

"I guess not," was the reply. "Correspondence can hardly equal a personal confrontation. Do allow me to provide any facts at my disposal."

Holmes leaned back in his chair thoughtfully and directed a quick glance in my direction. Evidently, a suspicion of his had been confirmed.

"Mr. D'Anglas, did you not send me a cable in London requesting Dr. Watson and myself to come here to Berlin?"

The thick skin of the man's face twitched and his expression of surprise was a quick thing in comparison to his previous ponderous movements.

"I certainly did not, sir."

"There has been no recent news, no event that has cast light on the disappearance of your possession?" persisted Holmes.

"None at all. But this telegram? . . ."

"Was signed with your name. No great problem, that. But it presents interesting grounds for speculation. I must assume that Doctor Watson and I were decoyed away from London. Therefore, something is going to happen there, probably already has, that is connected with this case."

D'Anglas was nodding again. A sharp note of interest livened his slow and pedantic speech. "This bogus telegram, if it was to serve the purpose you suggest, certainly indicates that the Bird is in London."

"And that someone involved with the Bird knew not only that you had instigated a search for it, but that I was involved."

"My interest in locating it is obvious since I am the legal owner. However, before you ask, let me state that I have not mentioned your taking over the case to anyone."

"Yet someone knew," I said.

D'Anglas looked at me in surprise as though he had forgotten my presence.

"An immediate question," said Holmes. "After the Bird disappeared in Constantinople, you secured the services of an art expert in England. What prompted that move?"

"The current market in art. The Golden Bird is a well-known piece. The finest private collections these days are in England. I assumed that the Bird was stolen not for the worth of the gold but for its appeal to a collector."

"Which answers, in part, another question," commented Holmes. "An object of that size would weigh, I assume, in the vicinity of three pounds."

"Two pounds, seven ounces."

"Hmmm," said Holmes, calculating mentally. "Thirty-nine ounces, then."

"Actually thirty-one, Mr. Holmes. Troy ounces are the weight measure used for gold and there are twelve troy ounces to a pound."

"Interesting," commented the sleuth who was seldom corrected on a technical matter. "With the finest gold at certainly no more than six English pounds per ounce, we have an object whose metal value would be around one-hundred and eighty-six pounds. Less than a thousand American dollars."

Something kindled for a moment in D'Anglas's lackluster eyes and then disappeared. "You wonder at the great interest this object, whose intrinsic value is limited, stimulates. But consider the workmanship. There is another factor, of course. Collectors are generally romanticists. If an object has a colorful history it has additional appeal."

"If there is a story that goes with it," murmured Holmes, almost to himself. "Well, the Bird has been much-traveled. The Tartar capital of Samarkand, the Russian and French court, Napoleon, then the Dutch bankers. Lindquist outlined some of its history and left other details in his case report. I note that its presence was known for a considerable period and then it began disappearing."

D'Anglas was obviously dealing with a subject of fascination to him and, not surprisingly, was well-informed.

"Following the fire in the dealer's shop in Amsterdam, the Bird did disappear. But it is definitely known that it was displayed in the museum in Dubrovnik around 1810. You will recall that the walled city blunted the sword of Islam when the muslem tide engulfed other parts of the Balkans. It is reasonably well-established that the Bird was given to the Turks as part of a peace offering. Then it vanished again."

"Until it turned up in a shop on the Island of Rhodes and was stolen. Then it vanished again, resurfacing in

Constantinople." Holmes's voice dwindled away and he seemed in a deep brown study.

"Obviously, something intrigues you about this series of events, Mr. Holmes."

The sleuth nodded. There was a touch of irritation in his manner, indicating that a thread of thought was proving annoyingly elusive.

"The Tartars probably gained the Bird as a prize of conquest. After all, they systematically looted a large portion of the civilized world of their time. It's progress from the Russians to the French and, finally, the Dutch bankers is reasonable. The fact that it disappeared after a fire is not unusual. It might have been discovered by almost anyone in the ruins and its worth not realized. Its passage from the Serbians to the Turks is also straightforward. But then something happened. It appears in Rhodes and is stolen. In its long history this is the first definite indication of criminal involvement and quite a criminal at that. As soon as it appeared in Constantinople, it was stolen again."

"Your facts are accurate, Mr. Holmes, but what thought do they prompt?" D'Anglas's elephantine face was regarding Holmes intently. Had a tinge of alarm crept into his manner?

"The facts warrant an assumption," said Holmes. "Between the time the Bird was in the possession of the Turks and its appearance on the Island of Rhodes, something happened. Something made the statue more valuable."

D'Anglas permitted himself a smile. "The interest in collections grew, Mr. Holmes. Also an appreciation of fine craftsmanship and ancient artifacts. With the coming of modern times, art objects are not as plentiful as in times gone by."

"And your interest in the Bird, Mr. D'Anglas?" Holmes's tone was casual, but I had a feeling that this was a major piece in the puzzle he was fitting together.

The man spread his large and knobby hands. "Call it a compulsion, sir. I am a goldsmith by trade as was my

59

father and his father before him. It was my grandfather who first fell under the spell of the Bird. Drawings of it exist you know. He felt that the ancient object was the finest example of his art in existence. His passion for the golden roc must have been communicable, for my father was equally obsessed with the desire to possess it. Being without family, I am able to indulge myself somewhat and the pursuit of the Bird has become the driving force in my life as well."

The man's dull eyes had been sparked with an inner light for a moment but now the mental fire was banked. "For a wondrous moment I felt that the quest of three generations was ended and that the Bird would be mine before my time had come. Now, alas, I'm not so sure."

My medical training would not let this ominous remark go unchallenged. "Surely, you are a man not beyond the prime of life. Your *magnum opus* still lies within your reach."

D'Anglas's face slowly registered appreciation for my encouragement. "*Nils desperandum*," he muttered. Then his mood shifted and became grim. "However, my family is short-lived on the male side. Unless . . ."

His ponderous jaws snapped shut and he summoned a smile that was more an exercise of his facial muscles than any reflection of mirth. His massive head shifted toward Holmes. "My general health and longevity potential are of no assistance to you in your search. Tell me, sir, is there any other information regarding the Bird which I can furnish you?"

Holmes, who had been listening intently to my words with D'Anglas and not drifting off into his own mental kingdom as he sometimes did, signified that he had no additional questions.

"Then, perhaps, you'll answer one of mine." The man seemed determined to preserve a businesslike facade and I sensed that he regretted his foray into family history. "If your visit here was arranged to remove you from London, what do you deduce might be happening there?"

Holmes took his time in answering, probably debating as to how much he wished to reveal to our unusual client at this time. "I have good reason to assume that two prominent collectors are after the Bird and one has secured possession of it. Therefore, the next move will be an attempt to recover the object."

D'Anglas gave another display of native shrewdness. "Your words indicate that one of the collectors had possession and then lost it to the other."

"I suspect that is the situation," replied Holmes. "Whatever countermove has been planned, I imagine it is now a *fait accompli*. Therefore, rather than rush back to London to tilt at unknown windmills, I propose to continue our journeys."

"Constantinople," said D'Anglas, nodding.

"Possibly, the art dealer, Aben Hassim, can provide some additional information," said Holmes.

"He is honorable and enjoys a fine reputation." D'Anglas rose from his chair and moved slowly to a desk in the corner of the room. "Let me pen a brief note to him requesting that he be of assistance to you."

As his quill pen slowly scratched on parchment paper, Holmes posed a query. "Actually, Mr. D'Anglas, you are not a collector in the true sense?"

The oversized head shook negatively. "Nor in any sense. The Bird is my sole passion."

"Since it has produced such interest from other sources, I'm puzzled that you were able to secure it."

D'Anglas looked up from his writing. "When Hassim placed the Bird on the market, he sent a notice to collectors who would be interested in such an object. He included me in the list since I had approached him previously relative to the object. In addition, Hassim knows me personally. Possibly, my competition delayed in responding. Rest assured I made a bid immediately and Hassim accepted it. The agreed sum was received by him and the bill of sale mailed to me. I will show it to you, if you wish."

My friend waved this aside as unnecessary and

D'Anglas folded the note he had written and sealed it with wax, using a signet ring on his right hand for identification.

Holmes and I had risen and as D'Anglas crossed to hand the missive to Holmes, the detective looked at him with those piercing, all-observing eyes of his.

"One of the collectors so enthusiastically pursuing the Bird is an Oriental. Does this surprise you?"

Possibly, it did. Or, possibly, it was some other emotion that made the massive man sway for a moment. Instinctively, I started forward to lend him support but halted as I realized it was but a momentary reaction.

"Chinese, no doubt?" inquired our client. He continued almost before Holmes nodded. "A rare puzzle, for you are speaking of a man with one of the largest private collections of art in the world. Why would the Golden Bird mean so much to him?"

"A thought that puzzles me as well," said Holmes.

There seemed little else to say and our client showed no desire to continue our conversation so Holmes and I departed from the strange house in the suburban West End of Berlin and its even stranger owner with whom fate had placed us in contact.

7

The Hatchet Men

We had little trouble hailing a carriage and I was surprised when Holmes did not direct the vehicle to our hotel but rather to the Alexanderplatz.

"We are under surveillance, my dear Watson," said Holmes, by way of explanation. "Our movements should not be so obvious that the two Chinese gentlemen become bored. Therefore, some official assistance will prove advantageous."

In previous cases, I had been made conscious of the efficient workings of the machinelike Berlin police department with its brain core of the Meldwesen located in Alexanderplatz. Holmes maintained a friendly association with Wolfgang Von Shalloway, the chief of the German police, and I deduced that he intended to involve his friend in our proposed trip to Constantinople. I was right.

Progressing through busy streets, the detective explained that the Orientals, having lost us, would doubtless return to the Bristol Kempinsky to pick up our trail when we returned. What surprises he had in mind for the Chinese, he did not go into.

A presentation of the simple card with the name of Sherlock Holmes transformed a stiff, formal sergeant of police into a somewhat flustered and excited servant of the people.

"Herr Holmes . . . but, of course, sir. Would you kindly be seated. Hein! Hein!" he almost shouted to a passing policeman.

Crossing, he whispered to the surprised man, fiercely and with effect since the policeman hastened from the main reception room towards the lift.

Somewhat recovered, the sergeant resumed his post behind his desk. "It will be but a moment, Herr Holmes," he explained, with rare deference. The great detective nodded calmly and, turning to me, the sergeant said, with a stiff smile, "Doctor Vatson, I presume?"

Never having received attention like this at Scotland Yard, it crossed my mind that Holmes and I should travel abroad more often. But the sergeant, whose name proved to be Dienstag, was not finished. Obviously, he felt that a heaven-sent opportunity for criminal research had presented itself and was loath to let the great moment slip away.

"Doctor Vatson," he continued, "in your masterly account of the case of 'The Speckled Band' . . ."

"Another of those overly melodramatic titles," interjected Holmes with disdain.

"Der speckled band vas from India und a swamp adder. But der is no svamp adders in India, vich has puzzled me greatly, Herr Doctor."

Since Sergeant Dienstag was, to my delight, directing his question in my direction, I hastened to clear the matter up. "Your confusion is understandable, Sergeant. However, when I first made that adventure available to the reading public . . ."

Alas, my explanation could not be completed since Wolfgang Von Shalloway appeared and advanced upon Holmes with his hands outstretched.

"Ach, Holmes! And Doctor Watson? Such a happy surprise. Come . . . come, my office is yours."

Murmuring greetings, we were escorted to the lift with much pomp and Sergeant Dienstag remained confused since more important matters had to be dealt with.*

In but a short time we were in the office of the chief of the Berlin police. Von Shalloway shooed out members of his staff and ordered a cessation of all other business during the visit of his illustrious friend.

Holmes protested that he did not wish to intrude on official matters but Von Shalloway waved his objections aside. I did not take my friend's disclaimers at face value and was quite certain that the sleuth was secretly delighted at the furor that his appearance had caused. Now Von Shalloway exhibited the sagacity that had made him one of the most famous man-hunters in the world.

"To see you out of your beloved London, Holmes—that is rare indeed. So something has taken the British lion from his lair and it could only be a case."

"We are involved in a trifling matter," admitted Baker Street's most famous resident. "A theft which did not occur within the borders of Germany. In connection with the matter, I had reasons for coming here to Berlin and, in the process, seem to have acquired some unwelcome company."

Von Shalloway regarded him blankly and then his large head shifted to me. "Surely, not the good Doctor Watson?" he said, attempting a joke.

"We are being shadowed by a couple of Chinamen," I said instinctively and, perhaps, defensively, then wondered if I had said too much.

"You are now leaving Berlin?" questioned the police chief. When Holmes nodded, Von Shalloway smiled, like a Cheshire cat. "Well, we shall arrange for some difficulties with these Orientals' passports."

"No! No!" protested Holmes. "Actually, we have no proof about the two Chinamen. However, they do know

* The loathsome serpent in *The Adventure of the Speckled Band* was, by most herpetologists' judgment, the Russell's viper.

65

we are staying at the Bristol Kempinsky. Doctor Watson and I wish to proceed with all possible speed to Constantinople and, as a precaution, would prefer to leave the Chinese in the dark as to our plans and destination."

"Ah, Holmes, it is so simple. You give me no problem whatsoever. I will have some of my men remove your baggage from the hotel. The Chinamen will be awaiting you and Watson and will be sadly disappointed. Now, let us consider your fastest route to Turkey."

Von Shalloway took railway schedules from his desk and, with them in hand, consulted a large-scale wall map.

"Fortunately, there is a fast train to Stuttgart which leaves in an hour. There, you can board the Orient Express. Sometimes, the Stuttgart Special is a little late but I shall make sure that the Express does not leave until you are aboard. Now let us see—we can get you to the Friedrichstrasse Station . . . No. Let us put you on the Special at the Zoological Gardens."

Holmes, whose knowledge of trains was positively uncanny, interrupted his friend's precise planning.

"The Stuttgart train does not stop at the Zoological Gardens station."

"It will this trip," said Von Shalloway, significantly. "But a moment, my friends," he added, crossing to the door of his well-appointed office. Opening it, he barked some staccato orders, which I could not decipher at all.

"Wolfie believes in quick action," said Holmes, laconically. "Our luggage will be retrieved from the Bristol Kempinsky in short order. This is being carried off in such a grand manner that I begin to feel like the King of Bohemia incognito."

"And enjoying it to the hilt," I muttered, drily.

"What was that?" said Holmes, sharply.

"Don't deny the good man his delight in exhibiting German efficiency. You have made him most happy."

While Holmes was considering this thought, Von

Shalloway's short legs returned him to the wall map. "The Orient Express is by far your most rapid connection, gentlemen. But let us see. There are two possible routes available. One section runs to Friedrichshafen, crosses Austria and, with stops at Zagreb, Belgrade, Nis, then Sofia, Bulgaria and then into Constantinople. The other route goes to Vienna and on to Constanza, Romania where a boat train takes you to Constantinople. You have a choice."

It crossed my mind that the Orient Express had become most prestigious since its first trip from Paris to Vienna in 1883.

"By all means, let us go by land," I said, firmly, remembering our stormy channel-crossing to Calais with regrets.

"It is the fastest route," admitted the German policeman. Since Holmes made no comment, Von Shalloway continued. "So it shall be. Your tickets will be available at the stations."

Holmes was extracting his billfold, a gesture which provoked an expression of horror on Von Shalloway's face.

"Old friend, surely you would not insult me. Your hotel accommodations and transportation comes courtesy of the German government as a mere gesture of services past rendered." Sensing that Holmes would protest further, Von Shalloway overrode him. "From long experience we both know that sometimes crime does pay. Those of us dedicated to curtail it must stick together, *nicht war*?" A sly smile crept across his face. "Besides, I have not forgotten that Bessinger affair. You showed me a few tricks there.*

Holmes had said we wished to proceed to Constantinople with all possible speed and Von Shalloway had taken him at his word. With hurried farewells, we were ushered downstairs and into the private carriage of the police chief which whisked us to the Zoological Gardens

* Refer to *The Secret Files of Sherlock Holmes.*

Station. Our luggage was on the platform along with two of Von Shalloway's taciturn mechanical men who made themselves known to Holmes, handed him our tickets, and saw that we had a compartment to ourselves when the Stuttgart Special came to a brief stop. As soon as we were aboard, the train puffed into motion after its unscheduled stop. High, dirty red chimneys ambled past the windows to be replaced soon by great houses and gay gardens as we departed from greater Berlin.

As we passed through Luckenwald, Holmes and I felt in need of sustenance and made our way to the dining car, where I did quite well with the menu, washing the rich food down with most excellent German beer. Evidently, our travels plus a substantial meal made sleep easy for Holmes informed me that we were beyond Wurzburg when I awakened in our compartment, slightly fuzzy-headed. The situation was agreeable to me since our journey through Anhalt and into Hesse provided no sights that I wished to view.

Things did get more interesting at this point since the Special progressed westerly to stop at Heidelberg. Though darkness was falling, I was able to view the beautiful approach of the "Jewel of the Nekar" and caught a glimpse of the spectacular fourteenth-century castle on the hill of this famous university city. From there, it was but a short run to Stuttgart, where again we were met by emissaries of the German police and escorted aboard the famed Orient Express.

I noted, when we were comfortably ensconced in a lavish compartment, that the attendant on our car was observant of our every wish. I later learned that this most posh of European trains had been delayed for fifteen minutes in its departure from Stuttgart to await our arrival. The French attendant must have thought we were Krupp munitions tycoons or possibly members of the Hohenzollern family!

Neither Holmes nor myself felt hungry and I made haste to take advantage of our most comfortable berths.

The rattle and click of the rails, the gentle sway of the great train as it hurtled through the night, made sleep easy. I remember thinking that sharing the adventures of the supreme sleuth did lead to hectic situations, precipitous departures, and a series of events far removed from the normal existence of a general practitioner. However, apart from the matchless experiences, there was certainly the advantage of traveling in style when travel we did. And it all began with those famous words: "You have been in Afghanistan, I perceive." That was my last thought before the coming of day.

It was Holmes who awakened me the following morning and, my mind clouded with sleep, I was not conscious of the fact that his expression was grave.

"Where are we?" I mumbled.

"Zagreb," he stated. "We have company again."

Struggling upright in my berth, I gazed at him with a mixture of surprise and concern. "Not the Chinese?"

Holmes nodded. "I took a brief walk along the station platform when we arrived and spied them in the dining car."

"But how could they have followed us from Berlin?"

"They couldn't. I can only assume that they anticipated my next move—a visit to the art dealer, Hassim, in Constantinople. No other explanation is possible."

"What are we to do?"

"Act as though nothing has happened. Get into your things, ol' fellow, and we shall breakfast. If our Oriental friends are still in the dining car, so much the better.

As I struggled into my clothes with all possible speed, Holmes had a cautionary thought. "For all they know, we never saw them in Berlin or even suspect that they are on our heels. Therefore, don't stare at them as though they were international spies. Just ignore them completely and allow me to take care of the surreptitious observation."

On occasion, Holmes could be infuriatingly patronizing and I implied as much with a swift rejoinder.

"Really, Holmes, we have been through situations like this before. You infer that I am a rank beginner in matters of this sort."

His eyes softened in his disarming manner and a smile with a touch of sentiment curved his thin lips. "Perish the thought, my good fellow. Just remember that subtlety has never been one of your strongest points."

Thoroughly silenced, I followed Holmes from our compartment.

In the dining car, I deliberately avoided looking at any fellow passengers. My friend made casual small talk and selected a table that afforded him a view of the Orientals, whom I had spotted on our arrival. I ordered rather mechanically and applied myself to the passing countryside. We were well out of Zagreb and passing through the mountainous terrain of northern Serbia with frequent breathtaking views as the great train roared in a southeasterly path. My answers to Holmes's casual conversation were monosyllabic until I realized that some sham on my part might serve the purpose of allowing his eyes to stray to good purpose. Somehow I began to recount a cricket match and I'm sure my description made little sense, but then no one was listening to our conversation anyway.

Midway through our meal, I was conscious of two men passing our table. Their figures were briefly reflected in the window at my side and I realized it was the Chinese. No doubt my eyes widened for my friend's voice came to my rescue before I made some foolish reaction.

"Gently, gently, ol' chap. They are almost gone and we can dispense with deception, so onerous to you. But do have a quick glance as they leave the car. Our expedition has not been fruitless."

I looked in the direction of the departing men with what I hoped was a casual air. Even to my eyes, not noted for acute observation, an incongruous situation was evident.

"Why, they are each carrying what looks like small attaché cases. Whatever for?"

"Tradition, among other things." Holmes's words were delivered in a casual manner, but his next revelation had a jarring effect. "I have tended to consider our shadows almost in a humorous vein. I may well have underestimated the situation. Those cases they carry are never out of their reach, if they can help it. To one with training in criminology they pinpoint our secretive escorts as hatchet men."

My jaw must have dropped and Holmes continued with a merry smile to calm me. "A hatchet man is a most respected professional in the Oriental world. An efficient killer usually representing a Tong or faction. In our mechanical age, their methods may seem antiquated but let me assure you that their traditional weapon, plus their skill at throwing it, rivals the effectiveness of a soft-nosed bullet at fairly close range."

When we returned to our compartment, I made haste to open my valise and extract the Eley .320, which I had chosen to take on this trip because of its convenient size. I vowed to have it on my person till this confounded case was resolved.

Our quarters had been serviced by the train attendant but Holmes assured me that our luggage had not been touched. He made a habit of leaving little tell-tale signs that would alert him if hands other than ours had been tampering with our belongings.

Under different conditions I would have enjoyed our trip down the eastern length of Serbia, but the specter of two Chinese assassins lurking on the train had a depressing effect. Between glances at the door to our compartment, I tried to lose myself in the passing scenery, to little avail. Conversation with Holmes was nonproductive simply because he had no clear idea of what he might learn in Constantinople and I was already privy to as much information regarding our quest for the Golden Bird as he was.

We were across the Danube and in Belgrade before

noon. Holmes and I decided to remain in our compartment so the only glimpse I got of the ancient city was the marriage of narrow Turkish streets and nineteenth-century palaces with a heavy larding of Byzantine architecture as we arrived and departed.

As the Express ran down the hundred miles or so between Belgrade and Nis, Holmes was either deep in thought or asleep. I could not determine which. It crossed my mind that to the west on the Adriatic was Montenegro, certainly a familiar area to my friend. I had always entertained the thought that during his absence from London, following the Reichenbach Falls episode and the end of Moriarty, that he had spent some time in this district; but I had never been able to entice the information from him and now certainly was not an appropriate time. Instead, I grimly clutched the butt of the Eley in my pocket and determined to guard the bastions should Holmes, indeed, be in the arms of Morpheus.

But, alas, it was I that courted sleep and when my head jerked erect found Holmes regarding me humorously.

"No danger, old friend. We are approaching Nis and are on the final leg of our journey. We might stretch our legs a bit. It has been a long trip."

Feeling cramped I fell in with Holmes's suggestion readily. However, I was never to visit the station of this Serbian city. Holmes prudently awaited the halt of the train and surveyed the platform before making a move to alight. As a result, we did not move at all, for his keen eyes noted something and he drew back from the window of our compartment quickly.

"Now that is odd," he said. "The two Chinese gentlemen have alighted from the train with their luggage. Stay away from the window, Watson. I have a good angle on them and I doubt if they can see me."

"What in heaven's name are they doing?"

"Merely collecting their luggage. Ah, they have placed it in the hands of a porter. The porter is carrying

72

their possessions into the station, but they seem more interested in observing their fellow passengers."

"You mean they are just watching the train?"

"Unobtrusively, but that's what it amounts to. It would seem that they expect us to alight."

When the Orient Express pulled out of Nis, our Orientals were still on the platform. Holmes had some words with our attendant, whom he addressed in his impeccable French. Shortly thereafter, he learned that the Chinese gentlemen were only ticketed as far as Nis.

Holmes was as puzzled as I was. "It makes a hash of my theory, Watson."

"How so?"

"The Chinese were set upon our trail to find out what we were up to. There can be no doubt about that. However, I felt that they anticipated our going to Constantinople, hence their presence on this train. Now it would seem that they expected us to get off at Nis. What possible interest could we have in this city in lower Bosnia? Well, Watson, when something proves completely baffling, 'tis best to dismiss it till additional information presents itself.

8

In Constantinople

The remainder of our journey to Turkey seemed rather stale. It was as though the opposition, as I categorized the sinister Orientals, were not interested in what we might discover in Constantinople, which did not bode well for our inquiry.

Through we arrived quite late of the evening, Holmes easily secured accommodations at the Golden Horn Hotel and, though I had slept considerably during our trip, I had little difficulty in quieting my thoughts and drifting into the refreshment of unconsciousness. Holmes did not pace our suite nervously as was his frequent custom when on a case. Possibly the departure of the hatchet men had been a letdown for us both.

The next morning I was impatient to see the fabled city, which had been the center of so many civilizations dating from the seven Troys, with their ruins atop one another. The meeting of East and West, jewel of the Eastern Roman Empire as well as the Ottoman, junction of three continents and three seas—Constantinople had intrigued me since childhood. But could I feast my eyes on Hagia Sophia or wander through the Topkopi Palace? Certainly not, for Holmes was intent on a case and even the Blue Mosque to him was just a background building, nothing more.

Since the shop of Aben Hassim was on Istikial Caddesi near Taksim Square—a fashionable address, by the way—we walked to it. I did get a taste of the city with its mosques, palaces, crowded bazaars and beautiful shops. I had viewed the Galata Bridge over the Bosporus from our hotel window.

It did not occur to me at the time, but Holmes directed our steps unerringly. The man's knowledge of cities and geography in general was, as I have mentioned before, uncanny.*

Hassim's place of business was relatively small but tastefully furnished, with the quiet and affluent atmosphere that frequently sedates the visitor into paying considerably more for an object than intended. Again, Holmes's card provided instant action and a salesman escorted us to the small office adjacent to the showroom, which was the lair of the owner.

Aben Hassim was a small man with a Vandyke beard, the swarthy complexion clued by his name and, of all things, a monocle. Somehow it seemed out of place next door to Asia, but he twirled it in his right hand when talking and was as at home with it as a French diplomat. I grew interested in the eyepiece, especially since he did not choose to use it when reading the letter from Berlin that Holmes presented to him after we had exchanged customary greetings. Closer inspection convinced me that Hassim's monocle possessed a powerful lens and I realized that he used it to inspect *objets d'art* without resorting to the pocket or desk glass of common usage. No doubt he had garnered a considerable reputation for instant appraisal in this manner.

"D'Anglas's letter explains your presence, Mr. Holmes, though a visit by such a famed criminologist would naturally be in connection with the Golden Bird. Its disappearance is the only incident in the history of my establishment that could pique your interest."

"Could you tell us how you came upon the piece and how it was removed?"

---

* It is interesting to note that a latter-day detective of widespread fame and girth who was born in Montenegro spent a great deal of time studying maps.

"Happy chance allowed me to acquire it. A woman was cleaning her attic in a house that, in times gone by, had served as a modest lodging place. Her mother and grandmother as well had rented rooms. In the attic was an old trunk and when she succeeded in opening it she found the Bird. There was nothing else of value in the trunk. I inquired as to that, but the most untrained eye detects gold, Mr. Holmes. The lady brought the object to me and I recognized it immediately." Hassim's monocle was twirling in his hand. "It is the eye that does it, always. Just as a book-lover can recognize that rare first edition on some second-hand book-shelf, so the art dealer must be able to capitalize on that rare moment when serendipity graces his door. I will be frank. It was with difficulty that I suppressed my excitement. The workmanship of the Bird certainly rivals that of Cellini or Lorenzo Ghiberti. I informed the woman that the piece was indeed gold and weighed it, referred to the present gold price on the international market, and made her an offer which she accepted. Now my problem was not to dwell overlong on my acquisition since, if I fell in love with the piece, it might prove difficult to part with it."

Hassim paused to regard us with a wry smile. "An industrial disease native to my calling, gentlemen, and a most unprofitable affliction. When a dealer falls prey to the avarice of the collector, he ceases to function as a cog in the commercial world. True, gloating over his treasures provides an inner reward but does not place food on the table. I have seen cases . . ." He broke off with an apologetic expression. "But that is another story and not of interest to you. I immediately took steps to affirm my legal ownership. No problem since, though the Bird has had many owners, I had purchased it from a source that had, however unwittingly, held possession for forty years or better. With the necessary paperwork effected, I made known to the world of art that the piece was for sale. D'Anglas made an immediate offer by post, which I was glad to accept. Considering the

Bird's history, I was rather relieved to sell the object while it was still in my hands."

"Your concern indicates that you took pains to secure the golden roc while you had it," said Holmes quietly. "A bank vault, perhaps?"

The dealer indicated the wall behind his desk. "Fortunately, the house of Hassim has a number of valuable objects from time to time and I have installed the latest in modern safes."

Holmes was viewing the squat strongbox in the wall with interest. "Mills Stroffner, I see. That model was manufactured three years ago and they haven't improved on it."

"Quite right, Mr. Holmes," replied Hassim, with some pride. "But then, Sherlock Holmes would naturally know about the best in safes. As would Doctor Watson," he added, quickly.

I found the attitude of the Continentals that we had met on this trip quite delightful. Long association had placed me on friendly terms with Lestrade, Gregson, MacDonald, and others at the Yard, but they never considered me as an expert on criminological matters. However, the police sergeant in Berlin and Hassim viewed matters differently. Obviously, my writings relative to Holmes had led them to misjudge my fund of information and aptitude. Notwithstanding, having played such a distant second fiddle for so long, it was charming to be clothed in the garment of expertise even though the material was spurious.

"You accepted D'Anglas's offer and then what happened?" asked Holmes. "I don't recall that the Bird was lost in the mails."

"No, sir. It was packed and ready for shipment. I placed the container in the safe and was ready to take it the next morning to supervise the shipment. During the night something must have happened since the Bird was gone the next day."

Holmes regarded the art dealer for a long and thoughtful moment, certainly not, to the normal observer, unusual for one hailed on all sides as the finest mind of England. But to one who had been associated with him for so long, the orchestra was playing a more sprightly air. The hawk was prepared to swoop on the wings of logic and drive an unsuspecting pigeon to the ground.

"The statue was taken, then, from your safe?" A nod was Holmes's answer. "Surely," continued the sleuth innocently, "someone other than yourself has the combination?"

Hassim shook his head with an air of protest.

"We of more peaceful pursuits are not familiar with the criminal mind or intricate subterfuges but there are certain necessary precautions that are obvious. Even my family do not know the combination of that safe."

Holmes rose to move closer to the strongbox, which he inspected briefly with his pocket glass.

"No marks of any kind. How was it opened?"

The dealer spread his arms and shrugged his shoulders expressively, but there was a sudden flicker of worry in his eyes. Holmes's question seemed naive, a quality at variance with his worldwide reputation.

"How else but by a skilled burglar? Do not the Anglo-Saxons refer to them as 'master cracksmen'?"

Holmes's manner hardened. He was ready to spring the trap.

"I know this Mills-Stroffner design well and there are four men in the world who could open it in one night without using explosives." His eyes swung to engage mine for a brief moment. "One is now in Dartmoor where I put him a short time ago.* The second, a blind German mechanic named Von Herder, is dead. The third is a trusted employee of the British Special Branch, while the fourth, Jimmie Valentine, is in America."

A thin sheen of perspiration appeared on Hassim's forehead.

Holmes continued with that inexorable doomsday fi-

* *The Case of the Soft Fingers.*

nality that had struck terror in harder cases than this Turkish dealer in art. "The crib was not cracked, to use a colloquialism cherished by the ha'penny dreadfuls."

Hassim, visibly wilting, tried to rally a protest of denial but was not given the chance.

"I picture a different scene," continued the detective. "You had concluded your arrangements with D'Anglas in Berlin and the bill of sale was mailed to him. No doubt his payment was banked. Then an unexpected visitor appeared. Oriental, of course."

Hassim winced as though in receipt of a sharp blow. The panic of defeat flooded his eyes.

"The Chinaman presented himself as an emissary possibly using the overworked and ubiquitous title of 'Commision Agent.' He stated that his client had to secure the Golden Bird and offered a sum beyond your expectations." Holmes surveyed his victim with a more mellow manner. "I suspect that ethics compelled you to refuse but it was pointed out that, should the Oriental not depart with the object he wished, certain things would happen to you, or possibly to your shop or your loved ones."

As though to escape from Holmes's compelling, almost hypnotic gaze, Hassim's eyes sought mine. "It is as though he had been here," he said. "In the next room listening."

I believe I shrugged. I know I tried to preserve a stolid expression. The poor wretch was suffering as my friend's recreation had been a dead-center hit.

"You admit it, of course," pressed the detective.

The Turk buried his face in his hands. His urbane, man-of-the-world manner was a thing of the past and he was but a poor, harassed individual sadly beyond his depth.

"Yes . . . yes . . . I refused the offer, as you said. I wanted no part of such dealings, but when . . . when . . ."

The instinct of self-preservation stilled his tongue. His dark face was now ashen.

Holmes completed his thought. "A name was mentioned. It had to be, so that you knew the threats were not idle bombast. It was the insidious Chu San Fu."

A shudder passed through Hassim's frame. Then a strange thing happened. The dealer's face rose from his hands and a fatalistic calmness spread over his features. It was as though he had thought: "One can only die once." His backbone regained rigidity.

"That is correct, Mr. Holmes. The name is known to me and to any other art dealer as well. A shadowy figure headquartered in London who has invaded, nay assaulted, the art world. His Chinese collection, especially the Tang vases, is common knowledge and parts of it have been exhibited." His voice faded for a moment and Holmes turned to me with a nod, a reminder of our conversation with Inspector MacDonald.

"A gesture toward respectability," I said, by way of indicating that I was tuned to my friend's thoughts.

"Correct, Doctor Watson," said the Turk. There was added respect in his eyes. "The man has to be a criminal. He has no rating in international banking circles, but his funds seem unlimited."

"A modern Monte Cristo" commented Holmes.

His remark served as a prod to Hassim's thoughts. "He has a collection of Eastern art that would rival the possessions of the fictional count. He has outbid the market and, when that is not expedient, I'm given to understand that blackmail and theft are not beyond him."

I shook my head in despair. "For what purpose? Currency notes are anonymous and surely preferable to one on the opposite side of the law."

Hassim's vitality seemed to return as the subject of the conversation gripped him.

"There, gentlemen, I can speak with authority for I have seen and I know. Some men grow beyond the thirst for money because they have so much. Some outgrow the more driving compulsion for power, for one man can have just so much of that. Then they are susceptible to a malady that can be diagnosed as an attempt by each to satisfy his severest critic, which is himself. They sit in a room, possibly a secret room, regard a piece of green quartz, and say, 'Only I in all the world possess a piece of jade of this size and quality. I am superior in this respect to those who rival me in wealth and power.' "

The Turk was sincere. His words rang with conviction but I found it hard to follow his reasoning.

"Should I possess the finest-known piece of jade," I said, "I would surely wish to show it to friends, possibly have it exhibited occasionally as the property of J. H. Watson, M.D."

"But you are delightfully normal, ol' chap," said Holmes. "Hassim speaks of a rare breed, but they do exist."

The dealer's words tumbled forth in response to the irresistible stimuli of attentive listeners. "Hypothetically, Doctor, let us imagine you are still normal but with far greater assets. Might you not will a priceless collection to one of your many British museums, providing that it was displayed as the Watson collection? Or might you not endow a university with a library to be known as the Watson Library?"

As I shifted somewhat uncomfortably in my seat, Holmes painted another fanciful picture. "Or you might finance an expedition if you were assured of having a mountain named after you. You will recall, ol' fellow, that even Moriarty could not resist displaying that genuine Greuze painting in his study."

"And look where it got him," I argued. "That was the clue that set you on his trail. All this perpetuation of a name does strike me as ostentatious."

"But normal, Watson, and we could hardly give you ten lashes for that. Many museums couldn't exist without private collections or objects on loan for showing."

Hassim, obviously charmed to find a kindred spirit in rapport with his thinking, ploughed ahead. "As you say, normal, Mr. Holmes. But the abnormal . . . the elusive few who do not seek to impress their associates, for they care not what others think. A perpetuation of their name may be impossible if their history is too infamous to bear inspection. Pride they have, possibly more than anyone, but they only crave to impress their demanding inner voices.

"What of all the rare paintings, the statuary, the draperies and rugs and snuff boxes and jewels that have disappeared? If they were exhibited many of them would be recognized and rapidly, too."

"You feel they are residing in one of those secert rooms you spoke of," said Holmes, obviously intrigued.

"They have to be somewhere. They are displayed in a sense, but only to an audience of one. The ultimate hoarder who sucks up their beauty, delights in their irreplaceable value and silences his inner voice by saying: 'These are mine. I am unique.' "

Hassim's convincing words conjured up in my mind a Scrooge-like character in an ancient attic, cackling over a secret trove by the light of a flickering candle. I fear my expression still reflected disbelief. The Turk was immediately sensitive to this.

"Doctor, the ultimate hoarder is nothing new in history. Recall, if you will, the Pharoahs of Egypt who, like most absolute rulers, took much and returned little. They carried a great part of their wealth with them to their graves."

"But that practice had religious overtones," I said, quickly.

"As it did with the Thracian chieftains who were buried with their gold," said Holmes, "but the parallel is still valid. Of course, what the Pharoahs had buried with them, to the later delight of grave robbers, was theirs to do with what they would. But the ultimate hoarder, a nice phrase that, secretes much that is not his for his ego satisfaction."

Holmes's eyes returned to the art dealer.

"You feel that Chu San Fu is one of this type?"

Hassim's reply was prompt. "I'm sure of it. There are

others, of course. Basil Selkirk of England; Ruger of Sweden; Manheim of Germany. There are several Russians, one who collects watches with no questions asked. The Americans are rather new to the game but they will produce some of the breed."

The Turk exhibited a wan smile for us both. His sigh was a deep one. "Gentlemen, an interesting conversation and a subject which fascinates me, but now does not the piper have to be paid?"

Since Holmes merely looked at him quizzically, he continued, though the words came hard: "One has to circulate if only for business reasons. I am acquainted with Colonel Sakhim of the Turkish Secret Police and know that he corresponds with you, Mr. Holmes. He is quite an admirer of yours, by the way. Is it to him that we go?"

"You refer to your selling the Bird, an object which no longer belonged to you, to the Oriental intermediary. Hmm! A problem, indeed!"

Holmes indulged in a weighted pause but I suspected what his next move would be. My friend was never averse to playing the role of prosecutor, judge, and jury simultaneously and his record of leniency was rather good, a fact known to readers of "The Adventure of the Blue Carbuncle." He did not disappoint me.

"I am not a family man, but it takes little to realize the pressures that you were subjected to. So, Mr. Hassim, we shall not visit the esteemed Colonel and, instead, mark this down as a most instructive happening in your life. One that will underscore the value of scrupulous honesty."

The art dealer just stared at Holmes in complete amazement. Then tears welled in his eyes and, following creases, slowly moved down his face; but he made no movement to brush them away. His voice was that of a somnambulist.

"My great grandfather cut rare stones. My grandfather, and father, dealt in art objects, as do I, and dur-

ing this near century the House of Hassim has preserved the highest reputation. Only I transgressed."

Holmes was showing signs of discomfort, a rare thing
for him. He had an intense aversion to any display of
feeling, especially one of deep gratitude.

"Come now, let us not be emotional," he said. I was
prepared to rise, sensing that Holmes would beat a
hasty retreat, but he surprised me. "Is there not something else you wish to tell me about this unusual affair?"

The question so startled Hassim that his flow of tears
terminated abruptly. "I . . . I was about to mention it.
How did you know?"

"It had to be." Holmes shot a glance in my direction.
"Missing piece, you know."

I nodded with counterfeit certitude, not having the
faintest idea what he was thinking of.

Hassim, who now regarded my friend with complete
awe, spoke rapidly: "The very next night another man
came to my shop. He also wanted the Golden Bird and
did not choose to believe that it was gone. He felt I was
haggling for a better price. With him was a very large
man who spoke with a strange accent, though he was
English."

"Cockney," I exclaimed, automatically.

Hassim shook his head. "He was, I believe, from
what you call the section of Lancashire. When I kept
insisting that the Bird was no longer in my possession,
the large man grabbed me by the throat. I still have the
marks."

Loosening his collar, Hassim exposed part of his
throat on which there were three livid marks that I
could see, possibly more.

"When I blurted out that the Bird had been bought
by a Chinese, both the men lost interest in me. The
smaller man informed me that I had never seen them,
that they had never been here or it would not go well
with me. Then they departed, to my great relief."

"You feel that the smaller man was the leader of the

85

pair?" asked Holmes, as though he already knew the answer.

Hassim nodded. "The large one was, as you might say, the enforcer."

"Describe the smaller man as best you can."

This proved difficult for the Turk. "He was nondescript. Thin. Fairly old. Medium height. He had trouble with his speech. A lisp."

"The man with the lisp," I burst out in a most unprofessional manner.

Holmes rose. He had learned what we wanted to know.

9

Back to Baker Street

Our departure from Constantinople was almost as rapid as our exit from Berlin. Upon leaving the shop on Istikial Caddesi, Holmes made haste to return to the Golden Horn Hotel, where he booked us on the Orient Express to Calais. Much to my displeasure, the fastest connection involved taking the boat train to Constanza, Romania, where the Express made up to return through Vienna to Austria and Germany with the special section continuing to the French coast.

Fortunately, the Black Sea was calm and we made connections without incident or without arousing the curiosity of any fellow passengers. I must have let my irritation show somewhat and while Holmes could not conceive of my interest in the historical city we were leaving with hardly a glance, he did show compassion during our long return journey by relating various historical facts about Constantinople.

He did not dwell on ancient Troy since, as he put it, "That story was clouded by time and legend," though he did state that he felt there must have been a factual basis for the recounting of the Greek and Trojan war immortalized by the *Iliad*. Of King Byzas of the Megarians, who expanded the city seven centuries before Christ, my friend was most fluent. He was also versed in the reign of Emperor Constantine who changed the city's name from Byzantium to Constantinople and proclaimed it the capital of his Holy Roman Eastern Empire. Possibly, dry history teachers had tried to inculcate me with these facts but they did not have Holmes's colorful delivery. Then he progressed to the reign of Suleiman the Magnificent and really hit his stride. I had not realized that this greatest of Ottoman rulers had besieged Vienna and was beaten back in defeat by Sobieski of Poland. Soon, my friend's graphic recreation of history was explained, in part, when he dwelt at some length on Suleiman's invasion of Rhodes and his defeat of the Knights of St. John who retreated to Malta.

"An interesting situation here, ol' chap. The Knights of St. John, using the strategic position of Rhodes, had been pillaging Mediterranean shipping for years. When the island fell, Suleiman must have captured an immense amount of booty. But it has never been found."

Since the sleuth had fallen into a thoughtful silence, I was able to express a thought that came to mind. "Good Lord, Holmes, you don't think some private collector got his hands on that?"

"Hardly. I imagine the Treasure of Suleiman is, like Morgan's Pearls, hidden somewhere awaiting that astute visionary capable of deducing where the ancient wealth is secreted. Possibly, when I hang up my shield, I shall not devote my time to bee-keeping at all but embark on a search for the famous and undiscovered caches."

"You mentioned Morgan's Pearls," I said, questioningly. Holmes had referred to England's famous, or infamous, pirate on more than one occasion.

"Henry Morgan's most famous coup was his attack on the Spanish settlement of Panama. He used an overland route to strike at the treasure port, by the way, unusual for a seafaring man. Having sacked the city, Morgan is reputed to have secretly taken the pearls, the most valuable part of his loot, and buried them somewhere on the Isthmus of Panama. Evidently, he never returned to recover them for they have not appeared to this day."

"But they are known to have existed."

"Oh yes. Pearls were Panama's chief contribution to

the swollen coffers of the Spanish crown. It took money, Watson, to support the Spanish armies in Europe and to build the great Armada."

I must confess my friend's intimate knowledge of history proved somewhat surprising, but then I recalled that he could remember obscure items in his newspaper files years after filing them away. How reasonable that colorful incidents of mankind's background should be at his fingertips, especially if they touched upon unsolved mysteries.

Naturally, our somewhat one-sided conversation during the trip across Europe turned to the case at hand. Holmes drily observed that our extensive travels had contributed little that we had not already known.

"However, Watson, we have met two of the principals in this search of ours, something that would not have occurred had we remained in London."

"Do you accept Hassim's theory of the ultimate hoarder?"

"In part, if not in whole," was his reply. "I can name any number of known objects of value which have simply disappeared. And, though Hassim did not refer to them, there are some very well-known masterpieces about which rumors have circulated. The *Mona Lisa* is one. There is a school of thought that the painting in the Louvre is not the Da Vinci original but a masterful copy."*

My expression of amazement prompted a laugh from my friend. "Can you imagine one of the men Hassim mentioned with the original in his hands. He could certainly laugh at the world and yet, though I don't deny the possibility, I find it a little difficult to swallow. What good is a supreme joke if the world cannot enjoy it as well. To laugh alone is a solitary sport indeed."

I must have looked vague since Holmes backtracked

---

* How interesting that this theory was revived and much bruited about after Vincenzo Perrugia stole the *Mona Lisa* from the Louvre in 1911 and the painting was not recovered until twenty-eight months after the theft.

to alleviate my confusion. "We have come across situations akin to what I'm referring to. The affair of the 'Ruby of Alkar' and the matter of the 'Midas Emerald' to name but two. In each case, the missing gem was too well-known to be sold legally and, like the *Mona Lisa*, was unalterable. Diamonds are a thief's best friend, ol' fellow. Being such a hard substance, they can be cut and lose their identity. Two of the crown jewels of England were once a single stone. But were you in possession of a painting as famous as the *Mona Lisa*, you certainly could never show it to anyone. Surely, that removes some of the joy of acquisition. I contend that Selkirk or Manheim or any of those *sub-rosa* collectors mentioned by Hassim would really move mountains to secure an unidentified masterpiece."

"Like Morgan's Pearls."

"Exactly. Their size and luster would be proofs of their value but they were never weighed, no description of them exists, and in fact they had no owners. Morgan stole them from the Spaniards, who had squeezed them from the suppressed native population who knew where they were to be found in their virginal state."

"The same situation existing with the spoils of the Rhodes campaign."

"Of course. There are others, Watson, undoubtedly more than we imagine. Hassim mentioned the Pharoahs. Our archeologists haven't uncovered one tomb so far that wasn't looted rather thoroughly."*

Tales of history and hidden treasure, coupled with speculations on the case involving us, helped hasten our trip but as the Calais coach approached the channel, I could sense Holmes urging it forward. He was eager to return to our abode and resume the chase of the Golden Bird, which interested at least two shadowy individuals, only one of which was known. I rather suspected that Holmes would center his energies on uncovering the

---

* Holmes was correct since this adventure predated the Carter expedition which discovered the tomb of Tutankhamun.

employer of the man with the lisp and voiced this idea.

"Quite right, ol' chap. However, we have another thread in this tangled skein to consider. We were decoyed from England, of that I am sure. What has happened in our absence? What incident prompted someone to remove us from the scene of action?"

At every station, my friend secured newspapers, which he eagerly scanned for mention of some event that might have an association with the golden statue, but his diligence was not rewarded.

When we finally arrived at 221B Baker Street, it was with delight that I surveyed familiar sights. Mrs. Hudson made much of our return, though, in truth, we had not been absent any great length of time despite the fact that we had crossed Europe twice and had been but the length of a bridge from Asia.

Holmes immediately resumed investigations, or at least tried to, but he encountered unexpected difficulties. Mrs. Hudson insisted that we consume some good English fare after all that foreign food. Our concerned landlady was a great believer in the health-giving properties of British provender, and, consuming her rare roast beef and Yorkshire pudding with gusto, I readily concurred in her theory.

There followed what I have always considered as the difficult period in any case. One day crowded upon the heels of another and Holmes's manner became increasingly brusque while his hawk-like face seemed even thinner under the stress of frustration. He was in and out of our Baker Street chambers at all hours, scarcely touching the meals which Mrs. Hudson repeatedly prepared to tempt him from his monastic fast. Each morning he feverishly searched the journals for some item to buttress his theory that we had been lured from London by the spurious cable. Unrewarded, he would disappear, with scarcely a word, to haunt the byways and shadowy corners of the great metropolis and to query the army of contacts and informers at his disposal. That he used one or more of the secret quarters that he maintained in the City, I know for a fact, for he returned to Baker Street on several occasions in some strange garb, looking nothing like the famous resident who had departed. Holmes stated on more than one occasion that the brain needed facts to chew on and masticate. While Mrs. Hudson worried unceasingly about his stomach, as did I, the truth, made obvious by long experience, was that it was his superb mentality that was suffering from malnutrition. However, years of association bred patience on my part and that of the other members of the Baker Street establishment.

It was a bright morning four days after our return from the Continent that I descended from my bed chamber and found a smiling detective voraciously devouring rashers of bacon along with two coddled eggs.

"Ah, Watson. You are in time to join me in that mainstay of the British Empire—a stout breakfast," he said, with a smile that belied his dark mood of recent days.

"I am delighted to see that you are partaking of one," I replied, gratefully accepting a cup of steaming coffee which he poured for me.

"Your concern for my nutritive needs could not go unnoticed, ol' chap. I fear this matter of the elusive art object has affected me considerably." An expression of irritation crossed Holmes's drawn face. "Alas, Watson, it is the flow of the inexorable tide that is called *time,* which defeats the investigator. For a rapid solution, give me the event which occurred within the hour. Clues have not yet been sullied by clumsy hands. Descriptions and recollections are clear and accurate. The *now* situation is child's play compared to the *then* one. And the *way back when* is the most difficult of all. Spinning in the undertow of time, fact and fantasy become entwined in an embrace that baffles. The truth is reflected in a misty mirror and becomes conjecture, not fact. This matter of the Golden Bird extends over three generations and that is what makes it such an obstinate nut to crack."

"From your manner, I would infer that you have come upon news."

"Let us say that since no information came our way, I went in pursuit of it."

"Oh, come now, Holmes. I am familiar with your methods. For nigh on a week you have been haunting London in pursuit of a clue—a thread of information."

"Agreed. But it was an aimless quest. Finally, I allowed reason to shine upon my despair. I have been lame of brain indeed."*

My expression of disagreement prompted Holmes to go into detail as I hoped it would.

"Consider that in the matter of the Golden Bird and the rival collectors . . ."

"Mere conjecture," I said quickly, as the great detective had frequently said to me.

"Nonsense! Their footprints are everywhere. If we were lured from England, and I can see no other reason for that counterfeit message from Berlin, then something was planned and, considering those involved, I see no reason for the event not happening. Ergo, it did, but did not cause sufficient interest for the news to reach us. It was not a robbery for I have been in close contact with Scotland Yard and there has not been a reported crime that I have not considered with care. A fatality, then. But we cannot scan the journals of every city in England. Therefore, I finally did the obvious."

"Which was?" I prompted. He did seem to gain enjoyment by leaving me on tenterhooks.

"I went through the files of various insurance companies. We have discussed the dedication of the Egyptian Pharoahs in taking their worldly goods with them on that final journey into the unknown void. It is a custom

---

* This particular remark of Holmes gives rise to an interesting possibility. Did this see the birth of the much-used colloquialism "lamebrain"? I must allow those more versed in the history of figures of speech to decide the matter.

of the Anglo-Saxons to make detailed arrangements for their final resting place. The most common means of assuring their burial in other than potter's field is insurance. You will recall that Lindquist remarked that when the end grows near there is a desire to tidy things up. 'Clean the slate' were his actual words, I believe."

"Never mind, Lindquist," I said, biting my lips. "What did you learn?"

"In the hamlet of St. Aubrey one Amos Gridley died a week ago. The name is unfamiliar to me, but I found it quite interesting to learn that the late Mr. Gridley had a pronounced lisp."

"Of course," I said, with elation in my voice. But second thoughts dispelled it quickly. "Surely, Holmes, that is a thin reed you are grasping. How many are born with a speech impediment?"

"I really don't know. However, St. Aubrey is but thirty miles away and if you are available for the journey, we can satisfy our curiosity."

"Let us do so. How did this Gridley die?"

"Ostensibly from a fall but there seems to be some confusion regarding the matter. Enough to make the insurance people wish to take a second look."

This set well with me, since if the death was by mysterious means, it gave credence to Holmes's fastening on this particular matter. I could not picture him dashing away from his beloved London merely to follow the trail of a man with a lisp, even if said gentleman was now a corpse.

I had but to throw a few necessities in a light valise should we find it necessary to stay overnight, though my friend anticipated that we would be able to return to Baker Street that evening.

At St. Pancras Station we caught a train, and were soon headed north of London to the ancient city of St. Aubrey. Holmes did not seem disposed to discuss our journey or the case, but I would have none of that, still being most ignorant of the reason for our trip and what we expected to find at the end of it.

"How did you happen to chance upon the matter of this Amos Gridley, Holmes?"

"Elimination. I had to wade through the case of a manufacturer in Liverpool, who slipped getting into his bath and died from a fractured skull. Then there was a woman in Leeds who drowned while taking a hot bath. She had a medical history of minor heart murmurs and her death was listed as drowning due to syncope. She had white foam at her mouth, certainly a sign of drowning."

I confess I had grown somewhat excited as he recounted in his matter-of-fact manner these two fatal accidents. "But, Holmes, surely this goes beyond coincidence. Two deaths both involving bathtubs."

"The number of deaths which occur in bathrooms might well stagger you, ol' fellow. But those cases did not interest me. Gridley's death did."

"Because he had a lisp."

"You must admit that it does have an association with the matter of the Golden Bird."

Somehow Holmes's explanation did not satisfy me, but I had little choice but to accept it. Holmes, as he frequently did, discussed matters alien to our case of the moment, dwelling on the fact that the files of an insurance company provided a treasure trove of information. This did give me an opportunity to return to the Amos Gridley matter.

"You mentioned that there was some mystery regarding the death."

"The possibility of suicide which, if true, would relieve the Trans-Continental Company of their obligation. As a gesture of appreciation for the use of their files, I promised to explore the matter for them."

"Surely, there is some other peculiarity that would prompt the insurance people to secure your services."

My friend's smile was on the sardonic side. "Insurance companies do not lean toward deduction or intuition or what you might call 'feel,' ol' chap. They are governed by averages. In a manner similiar to a gambling casino."

This analogy must have elicited a look of surprise from me so he continued the comparison.

"A gaming establishment, from time to time, may incur heavy losses due to a run of luck by a player. But they adopt the long range view based on the fact that in games of chance, the odds favor the house. In a similar vein, our great insurance institutions issue coverage and govern premiums according to averages of what has happened over a period of time. In general, things follow a pattern. Men tend to die at an earlier age than women. Of total deaths a certain percentage are accidental, another percentage due to cardiac disorders, and still another, to epidemical diseases, and so on. The actuary tables have become a science. If something upsets the balance or seems to run counter to the norm, a sharp eye spots it and questions are asked."

Holmes's mercurial mind fastened on a new topic and he proceeded to regale me with facts regarding our destination, St. Aubrey. Really, the man's knowledge of geography and history was amazing. I was unaware that the city was ancient, indeed being built on the site of a Roman camp which dated back to 40 A.D. The area had once been rich in tin, which explained the presence of the Romans. It boasted some ruins that had provided a tourist attraction at one time. But this had died out and the tin mining had petered out as well.

10

St. Aubrey

Instead of contacting the local authorities upon arrival at St. Aubrey, Holmes marched me to The Crossbow, a pub whose fame was more than local. Since Holmes was seldom concerned with the inner man, I was much surprised at his opening move. However, the mystery was rapidly solved when we were taken to a table and greeted by one Harold Witherspoon, M.D., who was obviously awaiting us. I was not surprised to learn that my fellow member of the medical profession served as the medical examiner of St. Aubrey. Obviously, Holmes had laid the groundwork for our investigation in advance.

After suitable greetings and small talk, Dr. Witherspoon was persuated to order some bitters and I joined him with a draft of stout. Holmes requested a gin and lime and guided the conversation to matters of business.

"It is fortunate that you could join us, Doctor."

Witherspoon waved this aside. "No problem, Mr. Holmes. In fact, a necessity since I was not only contacted by an Inspector MacDonald of the Yard, but also by an officer of Trans-Continental Insurance. *Le roi le vent,*" he continued, with a smile, but then tempered his statement. "Actually, there is little official work here in sleepy St. Aubrey. While we are not far from London, it would seem that we are shielded by the veil of years." He threw a glance at me. "I retired from my private practice before assuming the duties of medical examiner."

"The matter of Amos Gridley is fresh in your mind?" Holmes was surveying the doctor keenly.

"Indeed, sir. Bit of a surprise, that. Amos was a loner. Ran an antique shop here. Single man all his life. Parsimonious, you know, but necessity may have cast him in that role. His line of work is not noted for financial rewards and people don't come to see the Roman Ruins as they once did." Witherspoon flicked his eyes toward me. "Have you ever visited our local landmarks of history, Doctor Watson?"

"As my mouth opened to respond, Holmes overrode me. "Possibly we can both view them, after our business here." There was an echo of impatience in his manner. "The body was discovered outside his cottage, I believe."

Witherspoon was evidently sensitive to nuances. Suddenly, he did not look as bucolic or benign.

"Right below the porch, having fallen from the roof of it, you see. Cause of death was a broken neck. No doubt about that."

"Any bruises or lacerations?" inquired Holmes.

"A number. It was assumed at the inquest that Amos was on the shingle roof of the porch of his house. A slanting roof, by the way. A slip, followed by a slide down the incline and over the edge and . . ." Witherspoon spread his hands expressively. "The drop was certainly great enough to break his neck." The doctor regarded Holmes for a brief moment, then continued: "But I did not answer your question. The body had a considerable abrasion on one leg. There were wood splinters indicating that it was caused by friction with the shingles. The top of Amos's head was badly lacerated and bruised, though not as much as might be expected. Possibly, the fact that his neck snapped cushioned the effect of the fall."

Holmes was still regarding the medical examiner. Evidently, he did not feel this subject had been exhausted.

Witherspoon shifted uncomfortably in his chair and, after a pregnant pause, a sigh came from his lips. "There was one bruise, Mr. Holmes, which puzzled me. Behind the right ear of the corpse. By its color it was made before death. I brought this to the attention of the authorities. However, we could draw no conclusions from it."

"And the verdict of the inquest was accidental death," concluded Holmes.

At this point, our waiter arrived. During the discussion we had regarded the menu and Holmes surprised me by ordering substantially. He seemed familiar with the specialties of the house and requested Eggs Flan with a side order of Potatoes Lyonnaise. Doctor Witherspoon settled on steak and kidney pie with some peas and a bottle of Bass ale. I chose Dover Sole with asparagus, along with a second draft of stout. As our orders were completed the table was graced by another presence.

"Ah, here's Constable Dankers," said Witherspoon. "This is Mr. Sherlock Holmes of London and his associate, Doctor Watson."

As Holmes and I murmured greetings I sized up the representative of the local guardians of the peace. Dankers was a portly man with a grizzled face dominated by a thick moustache, which he obviously waxed. He regarded both Holmes and myself with a frosty glare and his manner was almost truculent, fairly shrieking that his territory did not need the aid of some consulting detective from London, famous or otherwise. Holmes, who had dealt with small town officialdom before, was most urbane.

"Do sit down, Constable, and join us in luncheon."

Dankers gave no indication of accepting this invitation. "I'm a very busy man, Mr. Holmes. My duties . . ."

He got no further for the open palm of Holmes's left hand fell flat on the table with a crack that made the condiment cruets jump.

"Surely this cannot be!" My friend's voice was as solemn as I had ever heard it, as though he were announcing the return of the black plague. "Do you mean, Constable Dankers, that you have allowed the loose ways of the metropolis to invade this rural hamlet? What have we in this fair garden spot? Crime rampant in the streets?"

Dankers's ruddy color faded somewhat and he was regarding Holmes with startled eyes. "Why no, sir. Nothing like that. A missing bicycle is a big thing hereabouts."

Holmes's stern manner mellowed. "Capital! With nothing but mundane matters on your mind, you will benefit by a moment of respite from your duties. Do sit down, Constable."

His voice had the steely ring of authority and Dankers occupied a chair with commendable alacrity. His bluster having disappeared like air from a punctured balloon, he became quite deferential. Holmes signaled for the waiter, but Constable Dankers said he could not take any food at the moment. The waiter suppressed a smile and disappeared only to return shortly with a bottle of Guinness, which Dankers did not refuse.

"Doctor Witherspoon has been bringing us up to date on the death of Amos Gridley," said Holmes.

"We've gotten as far as the inquest," confirmed the medical examiner. "Why don't you take it from there, Dankers?"

The constable obliged. "Accidental death seemed pretty obvious, gentlemen," he said. "Amos's only relative is a nephew, Lothar Gridley, who is a sailor by trade."

"And was at sea when his uncle died, I believe."

"That's right, Mr. Holmes. *Pacific Queen* out of Melbourne. She arrived two days after the death. Lother was willed the antique shop and what money Amos had at hand. The total couldn't come to much."

"Lothar Gridley is in line to receive five hundred pounds of insurance money," stated Holmes.

Dankers rubbed his chin thoughtfully. "That's right,

sir. A good thing, too. Certainly, the antique shop and goods don't amount to much in hard currency."

Since the constable lapsed into silence, my friend also took a moment for reflection, which resulted in a nod of approval.

"I can see where you would abandon the thought of murder for gain. What about the deceased's relations with others hereabouts?"

"Well," said Dankers slowly, "I'd never accuse Amos of being popular. A loner, you see, and, generally, people distrust that kind. A bit gruff but not a mean or resentful man. Close with a shilling he was."

"Of necessity," interjected Doctor Witherspoon, "as I've mentioned. I knew Amos as well as most. He was in hopes that his nephew, Lothar, would give up the sea and live with him here. He seemed to feel that a younger man around the shop might aid business."

"Even had his cottage painted," added the constable in a reminiscent manner. "I've no wish to speak ill of the dead, gentlemen, but he hired Molton Morris for the job. The two of them had some arguments about price that might have been heard as far as Kensington. Finally, Molton refused to finish the job until he was paid the agreed sum. Old Amos came through eventually but Molton had to walk off the job to get him to pay up."

"Bad blood between the two?" I questioned.

Witherspoon and the constable exchanged smiles. "Mostly talk, Doctor. I think Molton has a mite of Arab blood in him somewheres, for he loves to haggle better than most."

Dankers centered his gaze again on Holmes. " 'Twas at the inquest that the thought was advanced that Amos might have done himself in. Lothar demanded to testify and brought out a strange thing."

"The fact that his uncle suffered from acrophobia," said Holmes, calmly.

Both the residents of St. Aubrey regarded the great

detective with amazement and, despite our long association, I did as well.

"How did you know that, Mr. Holmes?" stammered Constable Dankers.

"You both told me," was the reply.

Our meal arrived at this moment and while it was being served, Holmes pressed the constable to join us. After a moment, Dankers admitted he might try some "bangers and mash."

"You see," Holmes continued, "you established that Mr. Gridley was loath to part with coin of the realm and yet he contracted to have his cottage painted, a job certainly not beyond his own abilities. When the painter, Mr. Morris, walked off the job, an argumentative soul like the deceased would surely have completed it, if capable. What made him incapable? A fear of heights."

Dankers and Witherspoon were regarding Holmes with admiration.

"Well, sir," said the constable, after a moment, "when you explain it, the matter does seem obvious."

"And leads us to another obvious thought. If Amos Gridley had acrophobia, what was he doing on the porch roof?"

As the constable's veal sausage dish arrived with another bottle of Guinness, Dankers shot a worried glance at the medical examiner.

Witherspoon picked up the conversational ball. "An acute observation. However, Amos's nephew did prove that his uncle had sought medical aid for his phobia at one time, and to no avail," he added, as an afterthought.

"Lothar Gridley would want to scotch any thoughts of suicide since that verdict would have removed any necessity of the insurance company making payment," said Holmes.

"And he would have been out five hundred pounds," commented Constable Dankers. "But his information was correct for we checked it out."

My friend's eyes were dancing. "Here we have a type of oddment which frequently proves so fascinating. A man with a morbid fear of heights who seeingly goes onto a roof of his own volition. There was a ladder, I assume?"

A faint sheen of perspiration was evident on Constable Dankers's brow. "Actually, no."

At this point, my own curiosity knew no bounds. "Good heavens!" I exclaimed. "The man did not fly there!"

Holmes speared me with a frigid glance, but Dankers patiently explained. "The roofed porch is but one story, Dr. Watson, where the cottage is two. There's a dormer window opening directly on the slanting roof of the porch."

Witherspoon interrupted with some excitement. "A fact which might explain an apparent contradiction. Most sufferers of acrophobia fear open heights. I mean to say that Amos Gridley climbed to his second-story bedroom for years with no fear at all. Possibly he opened the window and, still in contact with the main house which lent him a sense of security, stepped out on the porch roof to check its condition. I do know that he contended that the painter, Morris, had tramped over his shingles in such a fashion as to cause leaks. In any case, possibly his fear of heights caught up with him or perhaps his foot just slipped and he slid to his death."

Holmes closed his eyes for a moment of reflection. When they flashed open in but a moment, he seemed disposed to accept Witherspoon's pat explanation.

"In any case, Doctor Watson and I shall have to take a look at the premises," he said, casually. "Do have another Guinness, Constable," he added, signaling the waiter.

"Don't mind if I do," replied Dankers, promply. He drained his glass and wiped his moustache carefully. There was a shrewd look in his eyes.

"Pardon my asking, Mr. Holmes. Truly, no death is a small matter, but what be there about the Gridley matter that brings you from London?" Again, the constable shot a quick look at Witherspoon. "Would you be representing the insurance company, perhaps?"

The waiter arrived at this moment and Holmes ordered a refill all round along with a tot of brandy for himself. "As Watson can attest," he said, somewhat airily, "I have an overdeveloped interest in those matters that present interesting angles. So frequently it is the less celebrated affairs which provide fascinating sidelights to the true devotee of ratiocination."

And that, I thought to myself, is as elaborate a way of admitting to nothing as I have ever heard! There was some doubt in my mind that the constable or medical examiner were hookwinked by Holmes's flow of words, though they had the good grace not to exchange a telling glance or elevate their eyebrows in disbelief. To my surprise, Witherspoon seemed to fall in with the idea.

"Since a visit to the scene of the crime does seem in order, let me run you over to Gridley's cottage. 'Tis no more than the further side of the valley and my carriage will get us there in short order."

Holmes was happy to accept Doctor Witherspoon's offer and soon thereafter we bid Constable Dankers farewell and were headed for the outskirts of St. Aubrey.

11

The Famous Chair Fighter
of the Andaman Islands

It was a pleasant afternoon and Witherspoon's horse set a good pace with no urging. For several miles the road was level, though winding, with low hills on either side.

We began to progress upward toward the end of the valley and our speed diminished. To our right was a low-hanging building with a sod roof that displayed a ramshackle sign announcing THE HAVEN. Witherspoon indicated it with a gesture of his hand and a grimace of displeasure.

"The local den of iniquity. It does have the good grace of being removed from St. Aubrey. Bit of hard drinking goes on there. Constable Dankers keeps an eye on the place just as a matter of procedure."

The Haven, being on the crest of a small hill, we swept down a gentle incline and Witherspoon negotiated a right-hand turn onto a narrow lane, which brought us, in short order, to a small cottage but recently repainted. The building was two stories' high and of Queen Anne design, being flanked by a porch of modest proportions that was roofed as we had been led to expect.

Having piled out of the carriage, Witherspoon indicated the porch. " 'Twas from there that Gridley fell." He crossed to indicate an area under the eaves. "The body was found right here."

Holmes surveyed the ground with no more than a cursory glance. Because of the passage of time, there were no revealing clues to engage his attention. Rather, he moved back from the dwelling to survey the slanted porch roof, which formed an angle with the side of the main building. The dormer window was of fair size and I could readily see that, in addition to providing ventilation and light, it could also be a means of access to the porch roof.

Holmes was studying the dormer with interest. "Locked, I judge," he said, almost of himself.

"The house has been sealed until the matter of the estate is settled," explained Witherspoon. "There's also the question of the crown tax," he added.

Holmes's quick steps took him to where he could view a side of the house. "I wonder if there might be a ladder around?" he asked.

"Don't know as Amos had one. His little tool shed is locked, though we could get Dankers to open it and the house as well."

Holmes responded to Witherspoon's suggestion with a negative gesture, crossing to a barrel placed under a downspout leading from the wooden rain gutter beneath the eaves.

"This might serve the purpose, gentlemen. Empty, I note. Lend me a hand, if you will."

It took but a moment for the three of us to upend the barrel, obviously used to collect rainwater, and position it at a corner of the porch. Holmes surveyed it with satisfaction.

"This should serve my purpose admirably and permit a closer look at the shingle roof, which proved fatal to its owner. Watson, good chap, if you would hold the barrel and stabilize it, possibly I can, with the aid of Doctor Witherspoon, boost myself up on it and scramble onto the porch roof."

Witherspoon promptly gave him a leg up and, standing on the barrel, Holmes quickly secured a firm handhold and raised his lean and wiry form up to the porch roof. Walking with some care, he made his way to the dormer window, which he subjected to a close scrutiny.

Both Witherspoon and I had stepped back from the house to view his actions and, after exposing the window to the revealing lens of his ever-present pocket glass, Holmes began to walk down the incline of the porch preparatory to descending and rejoining us. Something caught his eye and he regarded a wooded area close to the cottage for a moment.

"I say," he stated, casually, "it would seem our activities are of interest to someone else."

Witherspoon and I spun around to look in the direction indicated by his gaze. "I see no one," said the medical examiner.

"He's dodged behind some foliage. Black-haired chap. Quite large. From the coppery color of his skin, I'd judge him to be a seaman."

"Lothar, without a doubt," stated Witherspoon. "Strange his being secretive, but no loss to us." As Holmes scrambled down from the roof, the medical examiner adopted a confidential tone. "Frankly, gentlemen, though his uncle thought highly of him, Lothar is not one whose company you would welcome. Like many who go down to the sea in ships, he displays an alarming thirst when on land and I do not mean for water."

Holmes exhibited a thin smile. "From your tone, I might judge that he is a frequenter of The Haven. He might well have seen us pass by it and decided to investigate."

"Well, he's not thought well of by the townspeople," stated Witherspoon. "Not overly intelligent and an awkward hand in a row." The medical examiner seemed nervous. "If your survey is complete, Mr. Holmes, possibly we should return to the village proper."

As we started toward Witherspoon's carriage, I threw a quizzical glance at my friend and companion.

"You seemed more interested in the dormer window, Holmes, than the roof itself."

"And a good thing, too," was his response. There was a trace of that complacency in his words that so

107

often proves grating to one like myself who lacks his unique abilities. "I presume," he continued, "that the house painter, Morris, was eager to finish the job and his arguments with the deceased. His work on the window was slapdash indeed. The paint around the window frame was certainly applied with more speed than dexterity. Though not obvious from the ground, the paint was allowed to run from the brush and cake around the window slide. I can assure you, gentlemen, that said window was not opened following the repainting of the building."

Holmes's surprising statement was allowed to stand unchallenged for a moment as we were all distracted by a sound in the nearby underbrush.

"A dog, probably," guessed Witherspoon, "or more likely, a possum." The medical examiner's attention returned to Holmes. "If what you say is true, sir, how did Amos Gridley get on the roof?"

Holmes looked solemn as he assumed his seat in the carriage and I sat alongside him.

"Gridley's being on the roof to begin with never seemed right to me. Another, and more sinister, theory regarding his death presents its grim face. That bruise you noted, Doctor Witherspoon, which was acquired prior to death fits into it rather neatly. A strong man, adept at such questionable practices, could well have sandbagged the old fellow and, while unconscious, carried him to the roof. A shove and the body slides down the incline and falls to the ground. The neck is broken and we have an accidental death as a convenient cloak for murder."

Witherspoon flicked his reins and the powerful gray set out at a spanking pace, anxious to return to his stall and some oats. There was a silence as we progressed through the peaceful countryside. It suddenly occurred to me that this was unusual. That I would not challenge Holmes's deductions was acceptable, for I had good reason to know of their unerring accuracy through the years. But Witherspoon advanced no objections to my

108

friend's recreation of events even though they would prove most difficult to sustain in a court of law. Actually, I realized that as Holmes had, step by step, delved into the death of the St. Aubrey resident, the doctor had become more and more silent and his somewhat hearty manner had disappeared altogether.

Holmes was not averse to silence. The sleuth's face was placid and I sensed that his mind was happily sorting out random pieces and fitting them into a mosaic of fact. Witherspoon was involved with thoughts of his own and his face seemed strained. I fell victim to the silence and tried to evaluate the incidents uncovered in our journey to this rural hamlet.

That Amos Gridley had been killed, I accepted. Holmes would not have expounded his theory in such detail, if in doubt. But what in the antique dealer's passing by violence had captured the interest of Holmes? Could he have been in Constantinople in the shop of Aben Hassim? It did not seem likely, yet the man had had a lisp, though I did not recall anyone making mention of it in sleepy St. Aubrey.

We were at the top of the rise when Holmes roused himself from his thoughts with a request that startled me indeed.

"Could we stop here a moment, Doctor Witherspoon?"

The medical examiner instinctively reined in his horse with a questioning glance at Holmes.

"Watson and I are, by force of circumstances, much chained to the city. It being not more than three miles back to St. Aubrey, I wonder if you might continue alone. A constitutional in these peaceful surroundings would benefit us greatly."

Had not Holmes placed me on the alert with a surreptitious nudge, I might have burst out laughing. Bucolic surroundings held scant charm for my friend, but obviously he was up to something and I tried to be of help.

"Capital idea, Holmes. An hour at a brisk pace will stretch our legs."

Witherspoon had a worried look about him and made an effort to erase it.

"If that is your desire, gentlemen, I'll meet you at The Crossbow on your return."

When Holmes and I had descended from his carriage, Witherspoon allowed his horse to resume motion. As the vehicle departed down the road, I noticed Witherspoon throw several glances over his shoulder back in our direction. Then a dip in the hill took him from view and Holmes came to a halt.

"Now, Watson, we shall backtrack a bit. The Haven, referred to by the helpful medical examiner as the local den of iniquity, is of interest to me."

Mystified, I could but follow as his long stride ate up the ground between the road and the country pub.

Its interior was unprepossessing. At one end of a long, much-scarred bar, two rough-looking individuals were engaged in a mumbling conversation and paid us no heed at all. Behind the bar was a short, squat, heavy man with a bald head adorned by several scars of a permanent nature. He had a dilapidated shirt buttoned at the neck. His face was round and jowls hung over his collar. A dark vest, shiny with wear, did not totally conceal the stains under his arms. He was chewing on a short cigar with dirty, yellow teeth as he aimlessly polished a glass. He regarded Holmes and myself with small, somewhat bloodshot eyes.

The sleuth had registered on the two customers at the end of the bar and evidently dismissed them.

"Has Lothar Gridley been here today?" he asked the barkeep.

"Who wants ter know?"

"I do," replied Holmes, in a very quiet tone.

As the worthy removed his cigar from his mouth with a purposeful manner as though eager to stipulate how little importance he attached to that statement, Holmes stepped closer to the bar, his face becoming more visible in the dim exterior. The man surveyed him again and evidentally suffered a change of heart. His raspy voice became almost cordial.

"He be here but awhile ago. Sittin' by the window." A thumb indicated a grimy frame of glass and a table in front of it. "Then he ducked out, he did."

"Possibly to return," commented Holmes. "We'll see."

I followed my friend who crossed to the table and secured two chairs from an adjacent one. Since there was a half-way filled bottle and a tumbler on the plain wooden surface, I felt the seaman would return all right. We were not seated for long before the creaky door behind us opened and a broad-shouldered man with raven hair entered, marching with purpose toward us and then halting as he became aware of our presence. He was tall and his clean-shaven skin was weathered and of that burnished brown produced by sun and salt. He regarded us with a scowl.

"Who be you?" he said, after a pause.

"Two of those just at your late uncle's cottage," said Holmes. "We would appreciate a moment of your time."

"Time's cheap," was the response.

"You are Lothar Gridley?"

"I'm not ashamed of it." Gridley resumed his chair and splashed whiskey into his tumbler. He did not offer us any. Considering that our surroundings were far removed from the Criterion Bar, I approved of this lack of hospitality.

"You were watching us a short while ago," said Holmes.

"And if I was? The cottage will be mine shortly."

"I fancy so," replied the sleuth. "There will be no trouble about the insurance money by the way."

"Aye, I gave a guess that's why you was nosin' 'round. The idea . . . thinkin' that Amos would do hisself in. Life was dear to him and that's a fact." With our presence apparently explained, Lothar Gridley un-

111

bent and signaled with a hand gesture. The barman materialized with two additional tumblers, which he thumped on the table. I declined somewhat hastily though Holmes allowed a sizeable pouring into his glass. I noted that he did not drink it.

"Will you be returning to the sea?" he inquired pleasantly.

Downing a massive swallow, Gridley shook his head as he wiped his mouth with the back of one hand. His palm was horny with callous. "No chance, mate. I'll find me a little place like this, though a mite more shipshape, and it's the easy life for me. If I drink up some of me profits, what's to worry?"

Holmes looked dubious. "Five hundred pounds might not go that far."

Gridley snapped his fingers with a loose laugh. "The insurance money, you mean. We'll nay worry 'bout that."

"I'm glad you are well provided for."

There was sudden suspicion in the sailor's eyes.

"Did I say that?"

"You did not. But it's another matter I would have words with you about in any case." Gridley's manner did not indicate that he would appreciate words on any subject but Holmes caught his attention quickly enough.

"We're agreed that your uncle's death was not a suicide. I'm not of a mood to accept it as accidental either."

There was a pause broken by the sound of Gridley's tumbler coming down on the table.

"Finally, somebody with a smidgen o' sense. I've been tellin' 'em old Amos would never ha' been on that roof."

"I heard about your testimony at the inquest. Now your ship did not make port till after the fact, but do you have any thought regarding the matter?"

The man's truculence had disappeared and his manner seemed frank and open. "Someone done fer him, 'tis a fact. I be hearin' talk 'bout some Chinee nosing around the shop but, of a sudden, they come out with the accidental death palaver and everybody's hushed up, mum as oysters."

"Strange." Holmes sat in silence for a moment. "Save for mischance, you might have joined your uncle in his business."

The sailor regarded Holmes as though he had lost his senses. "Business? If you be meanin' the shop, you're off course fer fair, matey. Amos needed no help from me."

Holmes kept probing. "There were those trips." His tone was casual but I knew where he was leading the conversation.

Gridley shook his head. "I'll nay be knowin' 'bout that, but then St. Aubrey has seen little o' me. 'Twill be seein' less when the estate's settled. They do say he hied off at times, lookin' fer antiques but that's bilge water. Whose to buy 'em if he had 'em?"

I found the conversation of the deceased's nephew a series of contradictions but Holmes indicated intense interest in his words.

"You have," he persisted, "no inkling as to who did your uncle harm?"

" 'Twas no one from these parts," replied the seaman. "They could nay ha' handled him fer he was a tough old marlin spike. 'Tis me thought that in his youth he was a wild one fer fair."

"Ahh," said Holmes, "that long scar on his right arm."

"How be yuh knowin' o' that?"

"I think the medical examiner mentioned it."

I was glad that Holmes and Gridley were intent on each other for I must have registered some surprise knowing full well that Holmes's statement was pure fabrication."

The door to the pub creaked open again and I was vaguely conscious of another man entering the establishment as my friend turned to me with satisfaction.

"Well, Watson, we'd best be back to town now."

"Watson, he said!" It was the newcomer's voice that rang out in the dim interior. It was harsh with anger and grew in volume as he continued.

"That's him fer sure. The prince of nosey Parkers. Sherlock Holmes, the detective."

The two customers in the corner pivoted toward us and moved closer. The fat barkeep reached for a bung starter.

"So, Dave 'the Dirk' Buckholtz," said Holmes. I noted that he gathered his legs under the table, ready for action. "Somewhat removed from your haunts, aren't you, Dave?"

"As be you, Holmes." The newcomer's gaze included the others in the tap room. "Not a year since he sent me brother, Mack, to Princetown. Here's a chance I canna' miss."

The man's right hand was moving toward his belt as he rushed toward our table. Judging from his name, I felt he was reaching for a knife, but did not wait to have the matter proven. Jumping to my feet, I swept my chair aloft and swung it in a half-circle, aiming the legs at the oncoming man. They caught him full on the shins and his feet came out from under him but his rush carried his body forward and his chin came down on the table top with an alarming sound. I was staggering off balance, the chair still in my hands, and the bottom of one of its legs caught the fat barkeep full in the throat. Dropping his bung starter, the man wheezed in pain and fell to the floor clawing at his windpipe. Thrown further off balance by this completely accidental collision and still clutching the chair for what reason I know not, I spun to my left on one leg and the wooden seat of the chair caught one of the two customers full in the jaw. He fell like a log. His companion, who had been closing in on us as well, suddenly backed off as I regained my balance with a desperate effort and stood breathing heavily in the middle of the room.

"Hold on, man, fer I'm wantin' no part of the likes of you," he shouted and suddenly turned and bolted through the front door. Not knowing quite what to think, I turned and surveyed a stark tableau.

Holmes was standing behind the table, his back to the window, with as close to a startled expression on his thin, aquiline features as I had ever seen. Beside him, Lothar Gridley was regarding me with a slack jaw. Dave the Dirk had fallen half under the table and was motionless. The bartender still lay on the floor gasping, his legs twitching spasmodically. The unidentified customer was on his back, inert, a thin trickle of blood coming from his open mouth. Possible concussion, I thought automatically.

"I've always said, " muttered Lothar Gridley, " 'Tis the quiet ones you watch fer."

Still breathing heavily, I regarded him with, I hope, some dignity. "I beg your pardon?"

His face turned toward Holmes. "Not a word has he said since I come in and of a sudden there's three men laid out."

"Quite," replied the sleuth. "My associate, Watson, is a famous chair fighter, you know. A method of mayhem much practiced in the Andaman Islands."

"I've never sailed to the Andamans," said Gridley.

I found myself most grateful for this information. Holmes, possibly because he could think of nothing else to say, was indulging in one of his little jokes and I speared him with a glance of reproof. My censure seemed to curb his impish humor.

"Prior to this brief interruption, we were ready to leave. I see no reason to delay, do you?"

Holmes was looking at Gridley who shook his head, indicating the bodies on the floor.

"What they got, they asked fer. Are you really that detective, Sherlock Holmes?"

Holmes indicated this was so. "Currently conducting an investigation for the Trans-Continental Insurance Company."

Gridley was regarding me with a wary air.

"Well, I'm not knowin' much about detectives, Mr.

Holmes. But it's happy I am that your associate here seems kindly disposed toward me."

I could hardly contain myself as we left The Haven and resumed the road back to St. Aubrey.

"Really, Holmes. Chair fighting! The Andaman Islands! Such nonsense. How shall I ever face my patients or dear Mrs. Hudson again with a reputation as a barroom brawler?"

"My dear Watson, I doubt if this tale will spread beyond The Haven and you were quite magnificent, you know. It is the result that counts and you certainly extricated us from a sticky wicket in there. Now let us hasten our steps back to St. Aubrey, for there are some fish that must be swept into the net."

Holmes set a brisk pace back toward the town and, though pressed to keep up with him, my natural curiosity would give me no peace.

"But of what use was this foray into that shoddy pub? Lothar Gridley's words did not jibe with the facts."

Holmes's lips were compressed in a thin line. "It depends on what facts you accept. The nephew was most casual about the insurance money, which leads me to believe that Amos Gridley had income other than his antique shop. Penurious he might have been but not without assets. Lothar also admitted that the old man took trips, a fact not brought to our attention before. Therefore he could have been the man in Constantinople and at the Nonpareil Club as well. Also we know that the deceased had a scar on his arm."

"What prompted you to guess that?"

"It pays to be well-versed in the history of crime. A retentive memory is also of assistance."

Though I made several more overtures, I could not extract further information from my friend who seemed to be intent on planning his course of action. Frankly, I had had enough of action for the time.

* * *

When we reached the head of the town's main street, tree naved with ancient oaks, the porch of The Crossbow was visible. I noted Witherspoon and Constable Dankers standing there evidently watching for us. Witherspoon acknowledged our arrival with a wave of his hand and the two local residents descended to the street and walked to meet us.

"We were beginning to worry about you," said the medical examiner.

"Watson and I took time to admire the countryside," replied Holmes. "Now if I can view Gridley's place of business, we might close the book on the late antique dealer."

"We are almost opposite it." Constable Dankers indicated an early Georgian edifice on the other side of the street. He seemed grumpy and sleepy-eyed but made for the door, beneath an ANTIQUES AND REFURNISHING sign, readily enough, extracting a key from his pocket.

As we entered a large, dark room, Dankers crossed with familiar steps to open the curtains of the two deep bay windows, which faced onto the street. The afternoon sun revealed cabinets and cupboards that seemed repositories for a goodly collection of tools. I noted an absence of period pieces, knickknacks and bric-a-brac and wondered if the antique dealer had kept his inventory elsewhere.

Holmes gave the room no more than a brief glance and then turned to face the constable and medical examiner. There was a crispness in his manner, previously unrevealed.

"So much for the late Amos Gridley who, it would seem, did little business in antiques but a great deal of refinishing, framing and reconditioning."

Dankers nodded. "Amos was handy."

"He would have to be. Twenty years ago in Devonshire there was a man called Garth who succeeded in unloading a number of art forgeries on unsuspecting collectors. Like all who plied his questionable trade, he had to be adept at framing and the composition of

117

paints to allow his bogus masterpieces to pass muster. Such a man would be valuable to a great collector like Basil Selkirk, would he not?"

The name rang a bell with me but I could not recall where I had heard it. Danker's mouth hung open and he seemed to be having trouble breathing. Witherspoon's brow was furrowed and there was a resigned expression in his eyes as though he had feared the falling of the axe and was not surprised when it happened.

"The man, Garth," continued Holmes, "was known to have a long scar on his arm. You did not mention that Amos Gridley had a similar marking, Doctor Witherspoon."

"It did not seem important," mumbled the medical examiner.

"Garth also had a lisp as did Gridley. There are a number of things neither you nor the constable chose to reveal. Doctor Watson and I have been treated to a pleasant view of a slack-water hamlet at peace with the world. Indeed it is, but the picture is out of focus. The tin mines and the tourists are long gone, gentlemen. Nowhere do we see tilled fields and there is not a factory in sight. What do people live on hereabouts? The streets are well-tended, the houses in good repair, so there has to be a source of income somewhere. And we know where, do we not? That notorious recluse, Basil Selkirk, the eccentric millionaire collector. Selkirk is St. Aubrey. Conveniently close to London, but outsiders journey *through,* not *to.* A little kingdom to preserve peace and tranquility around Selkirk Castle, which neither of you so much as mentioned. Selkirk wants the peace and serenity of other years safe from the inroads of developers and the encroachment of the masses of the metropolis. He wants it; he pays for it; and you preserve it for him."

Suddenly, I had it. It was in Hassim's shop in Constantinople and the dealer had mentioned the famous collectors of the world. Basil Selkirk of England had been one of them. Now I knew what had drawn Holmes to St. Aubrey, the site of the millionaire's country estate. Small wonder that the death of Gridley had sparked him into action.

Constable Dankers showed signs of argument, but he evidently was taking his lead from Witherspoon who had, mentally, thrown in the sponge.

"What now, Mr. Holmes?" asked the medical examiner.

"We're no part of any crime," added the constable.

"Agreed," replied Holmes. "I'll not deny Selkirk's right to the haven of his choosing. But the facade you men are paid to preserve does not fit into my plans so I had to shred its fabric. What does suit me is an interview with Selkirk. And you are going to facilitate it for me."

"I'll be damned if I will!" remonstrated Dankers.

It struck me that the bumptious, bleary-eyed country constable was with us no more. Dankers's eyes were sharp and he had a hard core of toughness not apparent before. Play-acting, I thought. It has all been a well-rehearsed entertainment with the performers concealed behind the masks of mummery.

"Things might be worse, if you don't," was Holmes's cool response. "I've no doubt you both realized that Gridley had been murdered. But there could not be anything so *gauche* as a homicide in the private kingdom. Therefore, the cover-up, though I doubt if you know the guilty party or even the reason for Gridley's death."

"That's a fact," agreed Witherspoon wiping his brow with a handkerchief, though the thick walls of the old building preserved a cool interior.

Holmes's piercing eyes were fastened on Dankers, certainly the more truculent of the two.

"Much better a consulting detective than a batch of Scotland Yarders to deal with. Think of that. I can advise Trans-Continental Insurance to settle the Gridley claim. Murder still makes them liable. For the nonce, the death can be listed as accidental for I care not a whit about that either. But I will see Selkirk."

119

As Witherspoon and Dankers exchanged another nervous glance, Holmes moved inexorably onward.

"There are two ways of playing it. Either I have become suspicious through some careless remark that one or both of you made and now consider Basil Selkirk to be an important cog in the mysterious death of Amos Gridley . . . that is one story we might pursue. The alternate will prove more palatable. Mr. Sherlock Holmes, while in St. Aubrey, is deeply desirous of speaking with the famed collector, Basil Selkirk, in connection with some *objets d'arts* that have figured in cases in Mr. Holmes's files. Do mention the Beryl Coronet and the Midas Emerald, two pieces certain to whet the appetite of a man like your employer. Make your choice, gentlemen."

Again, the constable and Witherspoon exchanged glances. The medical examiner's shrug was expressive and I could deduce their choice before they revealed it.

12

The Meeting with that Frightening Man

Not long thereafter, Holmes and I were again leaving the center of St. Aubrey, though this time we followed a road to the west. Witherspoon had made his carriage available to us and the necessary directions were simple enough. Constable Dankers had used the station phone to contact Selkirk Castle. Evidently, its owner was disposed to see the famous detective, though Dankers did not go into detail regarding his conversation with the millionaire. Possibly, the matter was arranged through intermediaries. In any case, we set a good pace. The road we were to follow to our destination was now winding up a grade and I assumed Basil Selkirk's residence was over the rise ahead of us, which proved to be true.

At the top of the hill, Holmes drew the carriage to a halt to allow the horse a moment of respite. I took a deep breath as well. The ground ahead sloped gently down into a tree-studded valley. A small river curved in from the north following a serpentine course until it terminated in a considerable body of water. In the center of this lake was a mound and on it were towering battlements, looking for all the world like a miniature Dubrovnik.

My lips pursed in a silent whistle and even Holmes looked impressed. A mountain some considerable distance beyond the stout stone walls provided a rock-strewn and bleak backdrop. The scene would have been well-suited to a Graustark melodrama.

"No fairylike cupolas and spires like those fancied by the Mad Bavarian," said my friend. "An ancient feudal keep augmented by modern workmanship, for you will note, Watson, the appearance of concrete where the ancient walls have crumbled with age."

"Impressive," I mumbled. "I rather fancy us as adventurers intent on the rescue of the Prisoner of Zenda."

"Not a bad comparison," agreed Holmes, urging our horse into motion again. "But rather than use a fictional castle, allow me to suggest the city of Bar."

This meaning nothing to me, I questioned Holmes.

"A ghost town on the Montenegrin Littoral," he explained. "The stern scene before us bears a remarkable resemblance to the ancient Serbian ruins. Bar, of course, has not benefited by a modern Croesus intent on restoration."

As we drew nearer to the castle, I noted that the road terminated at the end of a promontory, which extended into the moat. Our presence had been noted for there was a creak of a windlass and the heavily timbered drawbridge was lowered ponderously to allow us to progress between massive walls and into the courtyard beyond. As we rode across the drawbridge, I noted the color of the water and drew Holmes's attention to it.

"Twenty feet deep or more," he commented. "No wading pond like the moat at Birlstone, which you recall, old friend. I note the presence of finny inhabitants. I would not be surprised if a man so preoccupied with privacy as Basil Selkirk, has not stocked his first line of defense with piranha. But no, it's doubtful that such a tropical fish could live in our latitude."

We were now passing through the walls, which I estimated to be ten feet thick, and Holmes drew our carriage to a halt before the stone stairs leading upward to the massive doors of the medieval establishment.

Basil Selkirk might well cherish his privacy but he was well-attended in his seclusion. Two dark-haired grooms were there to attend the horse, which they led away as soon as Holmes and I had alighted. A thin, fair-haired man with pale and delicate features appeared at the main door and, greeting us both by name, ushered us into the massive pile of masonry.

As we followed our guide from room to room, I felt like I was in Buckingham or the British Museum. That we strode over priceless Persian carpets past rare furniture and walls filled with masterful paintings I had no doubt, but there was not time to inspect individual pieces and my mind's eye recorded a kaleidoscope of matchless works. As we were led down a long hallway, its floorboards polished like a mirror, there was the sound of a door opening and a craggy face viewed us. Mounted on a heavily built, muscled body, it seemed familiar. A gentle pressure of Holmes's fingers upon my arm cautioned me and I did not take a second look at the silent observer. It was Sam Merton, the heavyweight fighter, and I puzzled at his presence until it occurred to me that his function was that of a bodyguard. Probably not the only one, for Selkirk might well have an army in his huge and ancient keep.

Finally, we entered what must have originally been the dining hall, and in centuries gone by I could well-imagine armored knights quaffing mead at the long table in the center. A huge chandelier threw light on the ancient festive board, but such was the size of the room and height of the walls that deep shadows curtained the corners.

In a fireplace in which four grown men could have stood with ease, a massive single log blazed without a fire curtain, for there was ten feet of stone apron between the flames and the beginning of the polished floor.

At the head of the table, with his back to the fire, sat a figure. I would not have been surprised if he turned out to be the Black Prince, but it was, in fact, the least martial figure I could imagine. Huddled in a wheelchair, surrounded by a thick blanket, sat a very old man. His features were thin and his bloodless lips revealed large teeth, which I judged to be false. But his hair was real and in profusion, combed back in a careless manner that lent a touch of madness to his appearance. Heavy bushy eyebrows topped two of the keenest blue eyes I had ever seen. The face was a thing of age and decay, but those eyes rivaled the dancing flames of the Yule-size log behind him.

As our pale young guide led us closer, the old man's scrawny neck seemed to extend in a reptilian fashion and his hunched shoulders made an effort to straighten somewhat as he forced his wasted frame backward in the chair to regard us more closely.

"Ah, Mr. Holmes. You have been to Constantinople, I perceive." His lips curved and a dry chuckle burst forth, which grew in intensity. Suppressing his merriment, he flicked a handkerchief from his sleeve, wiping spittle from his mouth. Then, those protruding, intense eyes shifted to my direction. "And this can be none other than the famous Doctor Watson."

I must have mumbled something but it is doubtful if Selkirk heard me. His attention was now elsewhere. His scrawny arm rose in a shaky and somewhat erratic gesture and I sensed that the blond young man, who had guided us through a veritable museum to what seemed like a mausoleum, was withdrawing. There was a sound of a door closing in the background and then silence. The frail figure stared intently at Holmes who was returning his gaze. There was the faint twitching of a smile on my friend's lips and it occurred to me that the two were sizing each other up like a pair of master fencers ready to reach for naked steel.

I know not what Basil Selkirk found in Holmes's manner or appearance but he seemed satisfied. Another shaky gesture indicated adjacent chairs.

"Come, come," he said. "We must talk. I entertain few visitors and my people are always after me with medicines. Foul-tasting stuff, but it keeps this ruin you see fueled for another day."

As we seated ourselves, Basil Selkirk's head cocked to one side as he regarded Holmes. It was almost a boyish movement and I felt it incongruous from one so aged.

"So you're the one that exposed that idiot—that fool involved with the Beryl Coronet . . ."

"Sir George Burnwell," prompted Holmes.

"One of the most dangerous men in England," I added.

"Stuff and nonsense," was Selkirk's acid retort. "Fool stole three of the beryls when he might have had all thirty-nine. Had I been after the Coronet you can wager I would have gotten it all."

"Not legally, it being a public possession of the Empire," replied Holmes with a touch of severity in his tone.

"Be that as it may," said the millionaire, nodding as though to confirm his statement. "There's many ways of doing things. But enough of that. Now tell me"—he leaned forward in his chair eagerly—"it's the emerald I want to know about." The old man was rubbing his hands together and his eyes glistened with excitement.

"The Midas?"

"Of course. There is no other emerald. Not really. But I have never seen it and you have. What was it like?"

Holmes chose his words carefully. "When I first saw the Midas Emerald it was in a jeweler's box in my hands. I opened the lid and. . . ."

"Yes? Yes?"

"Green light seemed to explode into the room."

"Ah!" The old man's sigh, almost of ecstasy, came from deep down in his frail and wasted body. "You describe it well. I can almost see it myself." He threw a quick, penetrating glance at me.

"From Cleopatra's mines in Upper Egypt, you know. Egyptian emeralds are better than those Central American ones."

He seemed to ruminate a moment. His face lowered and then it rose again to view us with those birdlike eyes.

"Smart woman, that Cleopatra. I have a lot of Egyptian staters in my coin collection, you know."

A twinkle appeared in Holmes's eyes. "In deference to your business acumen, might I deduce that your staters are the old Ptolemic ones and not those issued by the Queen of the Nile."

Selkirk burst out in his high cackle again and laughed till tears came to his eyes. Finally, he dabbed at them with his handkerchief. The great door in the background opened and the old man waved at it with irritation.

"Out! Out!"

"But, Mr. Selkirk . . ." protested the voice of the blond young man in the shadows of the huge room.

"Leave, I said. I'll ring for you."

As the door closed slowly, the old man had recovered, though his toothy mouth was still stretched in a grin somewhat like a death mask.

"Young fool! But I suppose he serves a purpose. In any case, Mr. Holmes, you've made your point. I heard you were sharp." Suddenly, his eyes swiveled to me as though detecting my puzzlement. "Cleopatra lowered the silver content of the stater from ninety percent to thirty-three percent. Not too many people know that. But you did," he added, spearing Holmes again with his disconcerting gaze. "Do you have a cigarette about you?" he asked, abruptly.

Holmes nodded, reaching for the gold case in his pocket, but then his hand slowed in its progress.

"Are cigarettes bad for you?"

"Of course, they are. Why do you think I'm asking you for one."

Holmes passed his case to the old man and helped him light a Melachrino, which he inhaled with gusto.

"All the things one loves are bad for them. But don't be concerned," he added, noting my medically conditioned frown of disapproval.

"I'm such an old rascal that it doesn't matter at all."

I noted that the cigarette held between overly thin

fingers was steady as he shifted in his chair and regarded us with a trace of cunning.

"Now, let's be at it."

I could think of nothing to say and looked at the silent Holmes helplessly.

"Come, come, I'm not completely a doddering idiot. What you're here for. It's not to see a relic of the past or to brighten an old man's moments with a few words about the Midas Emerald. You want something."

"I want the Golden Bird," said Holmes, simply.

"So does everyone else."

"A fact that puzzles me."

The millionaire took a deep puff of the cigarette and his head cocked sidewise again in his peculiarly elfin manner.

"You're sharp for a fact."

"Do you have it?" persisted Holmes.

"I might have an idea where to lay my hands on it."

"I represent the legal owner. If necessary, I can secure a warrant of search."

"You're whistling in the wind, Holmes. When I cornered the Canadian wheat market, three nations couldn't stop me. If I've a fancy for that gold statue, I'll have it and that's a fact."

Obviously, Selkirk's interest had been aroused. Suddenly, he looked younger and seemed to sit more erect in his chair.

"Do you have a fancy for it?"

"I'm intrigued. Not for its value, which is no great thing."

Holmes's eyes were half-closed in thought. "Because somebody else is so anxious to get it," he said.

Selkirk cackled in delight. "You do know about the matter. You're right, of course."

"The Oriental." Holmes made this a statement rather than a question.

"The bloody brigand!" There was steel in the old man now and his thin lips were twisted in a grimace that was frightening. Then his slight figure relaxed.

127

"How strange that despite the prattle of pious churchmen and do-gooders, it is hate that can make the blood run faster, if but for a brief moment. And I don't even hate the Chinaman. It's jealousy, gentlemen, for 'tis said that he is a bigger rascal than I am. Or was," he added, with a tone of regret. "In any case, you are right."

One cannot associate with another for so long without becoming attuned to his moods and I sensed that Holmes had decided on his approach. The fencing was over.

"Let me advance some thoughts," said my friend. "The Chinaman is after the Golden Bird and you don't know why?"

Selkirk nodded briefly, gazing at Holmes slyly as though awaiting further revelations from the known master of deduction and rather daring him to produce them.

The manner of the aged financier, which I found disconcerting, did not phase Holmes in the least. He continued: "The Oriental located the Bird in Constantinople and sent his men after it. You sent Gridley on their heels for obvious reasons."

The somewhat taunting manner of the financier had disappeared and there was admiration in his bright eyes. "I respect a man who does not waste time with usless questions, Mr. Holmes, but I've seldom been thought of as obvious. What prompted you to divine my move?"

"You told me. You said the Bird was of no great worth, at least not enough to excite your interest. Obviously, you learned that your Oriental rival was going to great lengths to secure the statue. You felt, of course, that he knew something you did not and joined in the chase."

Selkirk was nodding in satisfaction. "You say it as it was. I believe, Mr. Holmes, that we should strike a bargain, for you might be of use to me. Tell me what you wish to know. If I choose to answer, I will do so truthfully."

This surprising reaction seemed what Holmes expected. He attacked the matter in his usual methodical manner.

"You don't know what prompts the Oriental to covet the Golden Bird but could you hazard a guess?"

A negative movement of the head was his answer.

"Is the name, Vasil D'Anglas familiar to you?"

"A worker in rare metals, living in Berlin. Proficient. I know he bought the Bird from the dealer in Constantinople. He is not known as a collector."

"Possibly not in your segment of the spectrum," said Holmes, drily. "He informed me that the Bird had become a passion with his family and himself."

Selkirk shrugged. His manner indicated that he could accept this explanation as reasonable so Holmes switched to another tack.

"I find the history of the object interesting. Through the ages knowledge of its existence has persisted."

Since my friend's voice trailed off, Selkirk filled the void of sound. "Gold will always command respect. From the graves of Scythian chieftains to New York's East River."

My face, which Holmes often accused of being a ready mirror of my thoughts, must have registered confusion. Selkirk seemed to have his attention centered on Holmes, but his next words were to me.

"There is a British frigate sunk there, Doctor. It carried the payroll for the British army fighting the War of Independence in the Colonies. There have been many attempts to reach the sunken vessel for the pay was in gold. Alas, the currents of Hell's Gate have defied the searchers. I merely use it as an instance. Gold is forever the magnet of mankind. As regards the Bird, there is the craftsmanship to consider. It is an object of value and I would welcome it to my collection though I would hardly take elaborate steps to secure it."

"As yet . . . there are those who did, and before the Oriental."

Holmes had risen and was staring into the great fireplace. As a result, he may not have noticed the sudden shift in the birdlike eyes of the financier. Selkirk's lips parted for a moment as though a question trembled upon them, but he suppressed it. Quiet settled over the cavernous room, broken only by the snap and crackle of the flames in the hearth that sent dancing shadows into the room. Holmes began to list facts, as though their voicing would allow him to inspect them with greater accuracy, to search for a flaw or inconsistency that would lead his mind to hidden truths.

"Your man, Gridley, was a day behind the Oriental's emissaries in Constantinople. But he, or you, figured that the statue was to be transported to England aboard the *Asian Star*. When the Chinese sailor reached London, the statue concealed in his personal Buddha, it was your hirelings, members of the Dowson gang, who took the statue from him. Frustrated, Chu San Fu ordered an attack on Dowson's stronghold, the Nonpareil Club. But Gridley preceded them, paid Dowson the arranged fee, and either departed from the club just before the attack or, more likely, succeeded in escaping during it. In any case, all signs point to your having the Golden Bird, Mr. Selkirk."

Holmes turned from his scrutiny of the fire and faced the financier, loosening the power of his commanding personality as he did so.

Selkirk again exhibited his death-mask grin and his face was nodding excitedly with what seemed like satisfaction or possibly gratification.

"Better and better. In truth, Mr. Holmes, you do amaze me and that is surely not the first time you've heard those words. You have recreated a chain of events which certainly fit the facts at your disposal. Like a glove, they do. Not that I'll admit to any of it but we'll let your recounting stand as a basis to work from. Indeed we shall. But did you not mention that others had pursued the Bird with more than the usual persistence?"

Holmes recaptured his quiet smile. "You know all

130

the facts relating to the Bird's history. If the signs are as I read them, you would learn everything about the object if only to frustrate your opponent."

"For a fact," agreed Selkirk. "But perhaps I have not benefited by your interpretation of them."

Holmes chose to acquiesce. "We shall not speculate on the Bird's unknown origin or its equally unknown creator, a fact obscured by the mists of time. Its passing from the Tartars to the French court and then into the hands of Napoleon is, in my opinion, not relevant to the problem. But I do find the Bird's being stolen from the Island of Rhodes of great interest indeed."

This time Selkirk could not smother a question. "Why?"

"Because it was stolen by Harry Hawker. During an infamous, though successful, career, Hawker was the tool of Jonathan Wild, a master criminal of the past century. Was Wild intrigued by this art object that had gone from hand to hand through the years?"

Now it was Selkirk who was gazing thoughtfully into space. "If he was, we must ask why? The Bird passed from the Tartars to the Russians and then the French always as a gift, a gesture, a device to lay the groundwork for goodwill."

"And, later, as collateral" added Holmes.

"Yet, at a certain point it became the object of criminal pursuit. You know, Mr. Holmes, that the Bird reappeared in the court of the Ottoman Sultan and was stolen from there around 1830 only to disappear again until Harry Hawker found it in Rhodes."

Obviously this was news to Holmes and he said so.

"Then," continued Selkirk, "it fell out of sight again for forty years."

"I think fate played a hand there," said Holmes. "Conjecture, of course, but suppose Hawker went to Constantinople with his prize. He died before disposing of it and the statue remained in a trunk belonging to him for four decades."

Selkirk seemed as happy as a small boy hearing a

fanciful story of derring-do. "While that thought does not shed light on the matter, it does fill out the canvas. Here, sir, is another tidbit for you. Prior to its appearance on the Island of Rhodes, the Bird is rumored to have been in Albania."

Holmes thought for a moment. "It was stolen from Rhodes in 1850. Would it have been in Albania, say in 1822?"

Selkirk shrugged and for a moment his intense eyes closed as though from weariness, but they snapped open again almost immediately.

"Perhaps we should return to the present," suggested Holmes. His tone hardened. "An inquiry agent, a Chinese seaman, and one Amos Gridley have died within the month. All because of the Bird. Gridley was an employee of yours. What do you intend to do?"

"Must I do something?" replied Selkirk, but these were only words. The financier's mind was racing, a fact obvious even to me.

"You should," replied the detective. "Chu's men picked up Gridley's trail and it led them here. The man's fall from the roof of his cottage was no accident. He was murdered, probably because of his loyalty to you. Doctor Watson and I benefited from information Chu did not have. Gridley was not only the man in the Nonpareil Club who came for the Golden Bird. He was also the man in Constantinople on its trail. Therefore, I deduced that he was an emissary of yours. How long do you think before the Oriental arrives at the same conclusion?"

Again Selkirk cackled and my fingers twitched with nervousness. "Not long, sir. I'll give you that. Of course, his reaching me is another matter. A visit by his underlings and dacoits would not find a warm reception."

"And yet," persisted Holmes, "it is a wise man who knows not to underestimate a resourceful enemy. You have been warned."

"And by an unimpeachable source, Mr. Holmes.

Your words will not go unheeded. For this, I am in your debt. I shall repay you, of course. You said you wished the Golden Bird. You shall have it in due time. You have my word on that."

By what means the financier effected a signal I do not know, but the door to the huge room opened and our pale guide reappeared.

"I tire, gentlemen," said Selkirk, and there was a note of apology in his voice. "You will be contacted shortly. Before departing, may I extract one promise? This matter has a way to go yet or I miss my guess. When it is over, return and we shall exchange words again. I do believe this has been one of the most pleasant days I can recall."

The pale blond man was beside him now. With regret, Selkirk gestured to him.

"Show the gentlemen out, Cedric."

Silently, our guide ushered us from this *outré* room and away from one of the strangest interviews I had ever been witness to in my many years at the side of Sherlock Holmes. As we reached the door, I threw a glance over my shoulder at the frail, dried-up figure, huddled in his robe beside the blazing fire. It was the last time that I ever saw the frightening Basil Selkirk.

13

Our Quarters Under Seige

When we had regained the road outside the feudal
establishment of the financier-collector, Holmes set the
horse to a good pace. He seemed distracted and showed
no signs of voicing his thoughts but I could not preserve
our silence, which was out of step with the mood I had
anticipated.

"My dear Holmes, surely you are not disappearing
into that mental world of yours. The old man said that
you would have the Golden Bird. Your promise to
Lindquist will be fulfilled. If you believe Selkirk, that is,"
I added.

"Oh, I believe him, Watson. Which is why I am
sorely puzzled. Consider, if you will, that we were not
engaged in a fishing expedition. Actually, we were attempting to land a whale with no line at all."

Holmes consistently referred to his adventures using
the plural, which was gratifying but had no basis whatsoever in fact. I seldom knew what was flitting through
his massive intellect and could certainly divine no reason from his last remark. But I knew that he would relieve my befuddlement if it suited his fancy, which it
usually did.

"All we did, Watson, was drop a little bait into the
water. A consulting detective and his associate acting in
the interests of a metal worker in Berlin are hardly capable of mounting an offensive against one of the most
powerful men in the world. So I hoped to tempt the old

rascal with a colorful tale that might brighten his existence and, in return, gain some information which he might see fit to throw us in the manner of a king throwing a bag of coins to traveling minstrels."

"Instead of which he promised to solve the matter for you."

"I don't recall his saying that," replied Holmes. His small smile had a grim quality to it. "Actually, he suggested that this matter had a way to run yet. But he did promise us the Bird, that I cannot deny."

"What is nagging at you, Holmes?"

"What did I do for him? He said that possibly I could be of use. Evidently, I was. True, he used my mention of Chu as an excuse to repay me but I'd told him nothing he did not already know. Watson, somehow I benefited the old brigand in some way. The Basil Selkirks of our world never give something without full value in return. He used me in some way and for the life of me I cannot fathom how." The clip-clop of the horse's hooves was the only sound for a considerable period of time. "Did Selkirk seem intrigued when I mentioned the year of 1822?"

"I can't say that he did," I said, trying to recall that moment in the baronial surroundings we had just left. "What prompted your remark, by the way?"

"It was the final clue given to us by the departed Barker."

Following our return to St. Aubrey, we left the four-wheeler with Doctor Witherspoon and bade a rapid farewell to the rural hamlet. Fortunately, a train to London was due soon. Evidently, Holmes found no answer to the question plaguing him for our trip to the metropolis was made in silence.

The following morning, when I descended to the sitting room of our chambers, Holmes was not in evidence. This came as no surprise. The smell of tobacco was strong in the room and I sensed that my companion had spent much of the night ruminating on the strange collection of facts so far unearthed in this most unusual case. It took but little imagination to picture Holmes's tall, thin frame pacing the floor and arranging bits and pieces into various patterns only to sweep them aside like a mental jigsaw and begin all over again. That his restless disposition would cry for action and drive him elsewhere in search of a wisp of information which "had to be" was in accord with his mode of operation in previous cases.

Mrs. Hudson, when serving breakfast, did reveal that he had departed at an early hour. In response to a question, she stated that he was clad in his familiar deerstalker and not decked out as an aged sea captain or any one of the myriad disguises which he could assume on short notice. This, of course, was no indication of where he had gone. I well knew that Holmes had other hideaways in the great city to which he could retire and clothe himself in a false identity to prowl the shadowland of the lawless. It had often crossed my mind that he might have established domiciles under false names and recognized personalities with which to pursue the information, the whispers that often guided his precise mind to a solution. The thought of three or four Holmes in one city was, in my mind, a frightening concept for anyone bent on preying on society and I thanked my stars for a good honest upbringing among law-abiding people, the immunization from the plague that was the sharp and piercing eyes of Sherlock Holmes.

Since he had left no message, I devoted the day to catching up with my much-neglected practice, ably handled by Vernier or Goodbody during my frequent absences. It was in the early evening hours that I returned to Baker Street, where I found Holmes, in his familiar dressing gown, attended by familiars of our residence.

The bony figure, topped by the large cranium of Inspector Alec MacDonald, sat in our visitor's chair, while lounging in a straight-back was the almost skeletal form of Slim Gilligan. The master cracksman had removed his cloth cap, but the unlit cigarette dangled from his lips as it had on so many other occasions.

"Ah, Watson, you time your arrival well," said Holmes, genially. "It seemed appropriate that we have a council of those directly involved in this matter and your presence completes the circle. I have related to Slim and Mr. Mac something of our trip to rural surroundings and we were just considering the next step."

"I have a thought regarding that," I said with determination, placing my medical bag by the cane rack and divesting myself of my coat and bowler. "Does not a summation seem in order? This case has led down so many paths that I am hopelessly mired in a sea of confusion."

Gilligan's toothy smile was immediate. "It's sometimes wiser, Doc, not to know too much."

"But Watson's point is well-made," said Holmes, somewhat to my surprise. "Our interests are identical here since Mr. Mac is officially involved in the death of Barker, a matter in which we have considerable interest as well."

"What about the Chinese seaman on the *Asian Star* or Amos Gridley?" I asked, quickly. If answers were forthcoming, I had a number of points that required clearing up.

"The mystery of the Golden Bird is interwoven inextricably with the homicides," said Holmes.

"But if you come into possession of the Bird," I began, but was interrupted by Holmes.

"There is more to the puzzle of the elusive statue than simple possession."

I hoped the detective would continue to explore this vein but he shifted his tack.

"Have there been any recent rumblings in the underworld?" he asked our visitors.

MacDonald placed his Irish whiskey on the occasional table by his side. "You are thinking of Baron Dowson and his boys. No, they havena' made moves toward Chu San Fu in retaliation for the fracas at the

Nonpareil Club. I had pictured a gang war breaking out but there are no indications of it."

"Exactly the opposite," commented Gilligan. Slim was not loquacious by nature, so when he made a statement, there was reason behind it. Three pairs of eyes swiveled in his direction and he elaborated. "Whitey Burke an' four of his best lads left London this mornin' bound for St. Aubrey, of all places." My breath came in suddenly but neither Holmes nor MacDonald reacted to this news.

"I'm thinkin' that if Dowson was gunnin' fer the Chink, 'e'd 'ave use fer Whitey. Burke bosses the Lambeth Duster Gang and they 'ave a sorta workin' arrangement with Dowson."

"Now that's interesting," said MacDonald, ponderously.

"And very logical," commented Holmes. "Watson and I know that Dowson is in the pay of Basil Selkirk. The industrialist may be anticipating the attention of Chu and his people."

MacDonald absorbed this news for a moment. "Then Burke and his men are goin' down-country as mercenaries."

"That is my thought," agreed Holmes.

"So, as you intimated before Doctor Watson's arrival, 'tis Selkirk and the Chinaman. Dowson's gang is the army that the financier is puttin' into the field. Well, I wouldna' welcome bein' quoted, but if they have at each other a bit, 'twould be no loss to the Yard."

"Save that we have no guarantee that only their blood will be split," remarked Holmes, with his quiet smile. "There was a certain efficiency in the manner of the Italian city states, which hired their mercenaries and fought their wars with a minimum of loss to the civilian population. However, back to our problem: Watson and I have been fortunate enough to discover much about the history of the elusive Bird, information I consider important in attempting to uncover why this art object has acted as such a catalyst in this affair. We know who is after the statue, though not why. However, one thing remains a complete mystery: the death of Barker, the Surrey investigator. He was delving into the matter of the Golden Bird at the time of his death. He was employed at the Nonpareil Club. As I have frequently stated, premature theories are the bane of investigations but it is reasonable to assume that he learned Dowson had been hired to recover the object from Chu San Fu. It is what else he learned that is so important. Something prompted him to hasten to his employer, Nils Lindquist, and he was killed in the process. Before dying, he said one word to Lindquist: '*Pasha!*' Does that mean anything to you, Mr. Mac?"

A brief negative was the inspector's response and Slim Gilligan mimicked him when Holmes's eyes shifted in his direction.

The sleuth thought for a moment. "There may be a break in this case shortly, but because of the powerful and potentially dangerous elements involved, I doubt if a disclosure of value is due to fall into our laps. Therefore, it behooves us to concentrate for the time on Barker. If he learned something, we can, as well."

It is sticking in his craw a bit, I thought. *A fellow investigator, either by diligence or chance, has come across information that has so far eluded Sherlock Holmes. One of his greatest assets has always been his complete confidence in his ability, which precludes any possibility of negative thinking. But he's reached an impasse and he won't rest until he's thought his way round it.*

My musings were interrupted by MacDonald, who had often been the audience to one of Holmes' patented *tour de force* solutions and must have savored a *dénouement* of his own.

"Relative to Barker," said the Aberdeenian, softly, "I have a wee bit o' information. Bystanders identified the vehicle which ran him down as a hansom. So the Yard in its slow-movin' manner investigated all the public conveyances it could." There was a touch of triumphant malice in his words that had to be directed toward Holmes. "We found one not far from the furniture warehouse that housed the Amateur Mendicant Society."

Holmes was watching him intently as he paused. I recalled the Society MacDonald mentioned. It was a case my friend solved in '87.

"The front right wheel had a stain on it and our laboratory men were able to establish it as blood. They used the very reagent you discovered Mr. Holmes to establish that fact. In addition, they discovered that the blood was the same type as Barker's. The hansom had been stolen and then abandoned."

"Capital work, Mr. Mac!" said Holmes, with enthusiasm. "While we have assumed that Barker met his death by foul play, it is comforting to have a deduction verified. This evidence might not be accepted as conclusive in a court of law, but I believe we can take it as fact. Coincidence can be stretched but so far. All right then, if we have no more revelations to contribute let us center our energies on Barker and whatever he discovered. I would like to know what he was doing at the Nonpareil Club. That may have a bearing on what he found."

"Let me inquire into that," volunteered MacDonald. "In the process of investigating his death it would be reasonable to inquire into his employment. In fact, it would be strange if I did not."

Holmes nodded. "Also the fact that Barker's death has not been dismissed as accidental might make Dowson somewhat nervous, not a bad thing at all. Let me inquire into his personal life and quarters. I have some ideas regarding that, Slim, which it might be better for Mr. Mac not to be aware of. Officially, that is."

The inspector knew Holmes's methods, having been associated with him on a number of cases. His craggy face loosened to permit a wise smile. "Barker's landlady said that his lawyer had paid for the rental of his lodgings till the end of the month," he mentioned. "Strange

141

that we have found no trace of said gentleman," he added in such a manner that I was sure he knew of Holmes's involvement.

"But, as Gilligan said, some things are best not known," concluded MacDonald.

He seemed on the verge of rising when I became conscious of the sound of music on the street below. I was looking at Holmes at this very moment and saw his alert eyes flick toward the casement window. Was I right in thinking that his face suddenly hardened?

"Strange. An organ grinder on Baker Street at this hour," I commented. Instinctively, I rose from my chair by the fire, moving toward the window.

"Passing by, no doubt," said Holmes, quickly, but my curiosity was aroused and I crossed to the aperture.

From long habit, I peered out from the side of the curtains rather than opening them. Behind me, MacDonald had also risen, preparatory to leaving. Holmes's voice had a touch of urgency to it.

"Inspector, simply as matter of security, why don't you depart via our back yard," he suggested.

I looked back from the window in surprise. This was an unusual thought on Holmes's part and I could see that it puzzled MacDonald as well. However, he did not choose to comment on it.

"Vera well," said he, in his low-timbered voice as my attention returned to the street outside.

On the pavement below there was a raggedy man winding the crank of an ancient street organ. He was gazing upward at illuminated windows in a hopeful manner and, indeed, one did open and there was a flash of metal in the light of the gas jet of the street lamp and a clink as it struck the cobblestones. Like a flash, a small monkey darted from atop the musical instrument to retrieve the coin, causing me to smile, but only for a moment, for in the wavering jet of the lamp I noted another presence in a doorway opposite Mrs. Hudson's house. For but an instant I glimpsed an Oriental face peering at the organ grinder's monkey and then it disappeared into the darkness.

"Good Lord!" I exclaimed, turning back to the others. "There's a Chinaman outside and he's watching this house, I'm sure."

As both Gilligan and the inspector instinctively stepped toward the window, they were halted by a surprising statement from Sherlock Holmes.

"I know."

Gilligan, as always, exhibited no reaction but both MacDonald's and my eyebrows escalated.

"The organ grinder is an . . . associate. The possibility of the hand of Chu San Fu reaching as far as Baker Street had occurred to me."

"And the music was the signal," said MacDonald. "Then the Oriental must have arrived but recently. I see now the reason for my leaving by the back."

I had vacated my position at the window and Gilligan had replaced me there. One glance at the street was enough for the cracksman.

"Slippery Styles," he exclaimed, with a grin. "Iffen the watcher leaves, 'e won't be alone. Though 'e'll never know it," Gilligan added, with relish.

"This puts a different complexion on things," stated MacDonald, his face suddenly creased with worry.

"Come now," replied Holmes, "after Styles leaves and he will have to shortly, to prevent being conspicuous, Wiggins and a couple of his street urchin friends will be in the vicinity."

"Ta . . . a smart move, Guv," said Gilligan. "Them Baker Street irreg'lars can wander at will without attractin' notice."

"In a matter such as this, considering the forces that form the opposition, I need all the help I can get," said Holmes, and this was a remarkable admission to come from him.

MacDonald and I exchanged a significant glance. Holmes was notorious for his lack of concern about his personal safety, a fact that had prompted many an uncomfortable thought for both of us. I was reassured by the conviction that some of London's finest might soon find themselves in the area as well.

MacDonald bid us goodnight and made his way down the stairs and out the rear past the plane tree in our small yard and through the inconspicuous door that served as a seldom-used back exit. From there, he had easy access via the Mews to King Street and a route of departure safe from the eyes of the watcher without.

I wondered for a moment if the back of our residence was being watched. The Chinese crime tsar seemed to have unlimited manpower at his command. But then I realized that Wiggins and the irregulars were no doubt already on the scene and would have notified Holmes had our rear been under surveillance.

With the leaving of MacDonald, Holmes had some instructions for Gilligan. To facilitate them, he crossed to the desk and scrawled an address on a sheet of paper, which he tendered to our ally.

"Slim, here's where Barker had lodgings during his London residence, which was terminated in such an unfortunate manner. The front door has a Crowley lock. You might find the back more convenient. There are two windows to his living room, either of which will not delay you more than thirty seconds. I noted that there is convenient ivy on the back wall of the building as well. While I spent some time going through Barker's things, a more detailed search is called for."

"Right you are, Guv," replied the cracksman, with his ready smile. "It's a pleasure doin' biz wiv you. Every little caper is like a summer breeze."

"Let's hope they are all like this one." For a brief moment there was that gleam in Holmes's eyes that was reserved for very few people indeed. "But think, my good fellow, how reassuring it is to know that a complex problem would become simple in your deft hands."

Holmes was habitually sparing in his praise, and I knew of very few who commanded his respect. Not all of them, associates like Gilligan. Von Herder, the blind mechanic who had worked for Moriarty, was one. Van Seddar, the Dutch gem expert associated with Count Sylvius was another. And, of course, that late Napoleon of crime, Moriarty and his right-hand man, Colonel Sebastian Moran, were held in the highest esteem by the sleuth for their talents if not for their motives and morals. Gilligan had his place in this diverse and limited group.

Holmes and Gilligan departed together and I assumed that my friend was leading the cracksman to the upper story, where there was access to the roof of 221B. Gilligan had a pronounced preference for rooftops. How he intended to vacate our residence and reach the adjacent building I had not the faintest idea but I had no doubt that he would accomplish this feat, and with ease. Holmes had many times mentioned that the mark of the expert was the ability to make the difficult seem commonplace and, considering some of his own amazing solutions to baffling problems, I was certainly ready to agree with him.

In but a short time, Holmes returned with a satisfied air.

"It is said that one is judged by one's associates, which makes me the most fortunate of men. To secure an aide who will follow instructions implicitly is one thing and not an easy one. But to secure a Gilligan who can think on the spot and adapt himself to a changing scene, that is a treasure indeed."

Through my mind flashed a series of incidents when I had blundered on a wrong trail, and my face must have expressed this painful recollection or possibly Holmes divined the memories that his comment would awaken.

"Come now, good fellow, we all make our contributions in our particular style and where would I have been on many occasions without your invaluable presence?" Sentiment was rare for the sleuth and I could see him erase it promptly. "To prove my point," he contin-

145

ued, "do you have readily available that piece of heavy ordnance you carry on occasion?"

"I can secure it in a trice," I stammered, quickly, glad to be of some use.

"Do so by all means and check its load. I shall caution Mrs. Hudson and Billy not to answer the door below without alerting us first. Some caution from here on in will not be amiss."

When we retired for the night, I had the feeling that our cozy domicile was in a state of seige, a most unusual situation indeed.

14

The Removal of the Bird

The following morning there was no trace of the Chinaman on the street outside. Holmes, with his breakfast coffee at hand, wrote a cable to the Trans-Continental Insurance Company advising them to settle the claim of Amos Gridley, and composed another to Vasil D'Anglas in Berlin intimating that the Bird might be in his possession shortly.

This last communiqué piqued my interest, of course.

"Then you really expect Basil Selkirk to place the statue in your hands."

"How I wish I had a direct answer for you, Watson. He said he would and there was no reason for him to make an idle promise. Unless it was a ploy to gain time. But time for what? Selkirk spent a great deal of money securing the Bird for the sheer joy of foiling his rival, Chu San Fu. Why relinquish his prize at the moment of triumph? Wait!" Holmes said, suddenly.

Whatever idea had come to his mind, it was sufficiently promising to cause him to spring from his chair at the breakfast table and begin to pace our sitting room nervously.

"It ties in," he muttered, after four or five circuits of the immediate area. His thin face dominated by the famous hawklike nose centered on me and there was a realization in his piercing eyes. "Let us backtrack, good fellow. We were decoyed from London to Berlin and upon arrival were under the surveillance of at least two

147

Chinese. They stayed with us as far as Serbia and then disappeared. Upon our return to London and during our excursion to St. Aubrey, there was no sign of them. Then last night we were again under the observation of a tool of Chun San Fu. Why, it is all becoming as plain as a pike staff. The Oriental divined that Amos Gridley was the man who secured the Golden Bird from Dowson. He did not realize that the wood-worker was but an emissary and assumed that if he could find him, he would find the statue. Knowing we were also on the trail of the Bird, he lured us from London at the time that he closed in on Gridley." An added thought furrowed Holmes's brow and he resumed his pacing for a moment before continuing.

"Why his hatchet men should follow us on the Orient Express is puzzling. My theory grows thin there. However, of a sudden, we are of interest to Chu again even though he has disposed of Gridley without retrieving the Bird and has certainly realized that Basil Selkirk is the man who has thwarted him."

Another thoughtful silence allowed me to try and collect my thoughts. "Dear me, Holmes, I am more confused than ever."

"As well you might be. But consider Selkirk, the master chessman who uses men as pawns and countries as bishops. Selkirk realizes that Chu's attention will be attracted to him. In his guarded enclave this might cause him scant concern, but still, he does not underestimate Chu. Fortuitously, a splendid catspaw drops into his lap. Something to divert the Oriental crime tsar away from him."

"A catspaw?"

"That we are both looking at, my good Watson. We are the catspaw. Basil Selkirk lets it be known that we shall be in possession of the Golden Brid, which explains the Chinaman's renewed interest in our movements."

Holmes crossed to the window with his quick stride. "No watcher in evidence, which tells us nothing.

Chu's spies may have secured a less conspicuous vantage point than a dark doorway. But here come, not one, but two carriages and it seems as though they will stop outside." Turning to me with that bright, almost small-boy look of triumph, he repeated a favorite phrase of his: "It had to be."

It was. Joining Holmes at his observation point I watched two closed carriages come to a stop at the curbing adjacent to our door. There seemed to be a number of burly men in the vehicles, but only one emerged from the lead one. It was the heavily built Sam Merton. There was a box in his hand and he gave the street a rapid glance up and down before proceeding to the entrance to 221B, with that insolent grace frequently evident in the very powerful. I had last seen the professional boxer in Selkirk's castle. A known intimate of Count Negretto Sylvius, Dowson's right-hand man, I was not surprised to see the puglilist on this mission once Holmes had explained what was in the wind.

Since our dwelling had been placed on the alert the night previous, Holmes signaled to Billy, the page boy, from our landing. A sudden thought caused me to dash upstairs to my room and when I returned with the reassuring weight of a revolver in my dressing-gown pocket, Merton had already been shown up. The fighter was standing, somewhat awkwardly, beside the desk on which he had deposited the box in his keeping.

"There, Guv," he was saying to Holmes, "is the bloody box what I was tol' to give ya. No one tol' me what's in it but the big man said you would know."

"Let us say I have an idea," responded Holmes, laconically. "Sam, I had hopes for you but you're back to your old tricks, I see."

Rather than take umbrage, Merton nervously shifted from one foot to the other. Belatedly, he removed his cap and, for all the world, resembled a nervous student brought before the headmaster.

"We all gotta live, Mr. 'Olmes. Me speed ain't wot it was, ya know, but I can still drop 'em if I can get to 'em," he added, with a flash of pride. "You spotted me down at Selkirk's in St. Aubrey. You knew I was back on the shady side."

"I knew that you again became involved with Count Sylvius over three months ago," said Holmes, sternly. "I don't know what to do about you, Sam."

"Don't worry Mr. Holmes. Maybe it ain't as bad you think." Nervously, he made his way to the door.

"You take care of yourself, Mr. 'Olmes."

With that he was gone. It had been an unusual exchange, but I knew that ever since the Crown Diamond Affair, the bruiser with the slab-sided face had been in complete awe of Holmes.

My friend erased the disappointed expression from his face and turned his thoughts from the wayward fighter to matters at hand. Crossing to the box, his thin and dexterous fingers released the twine encircling it.

"Let us view the prize, Watson, but with dispatch. As our American cousins might say—we have a hot potato here."

With the lid off, he extracted the statue from the box and placed it on the desk top, stepping back to view the object which had left a trail of violence and death behind it.

To my untrained eye, it appeared identical to the Bird we had seen in Dowson's office at the Nonpareil Club. It was of a peculiar whitish gold and glistened in the morning sunlight that suffused the room. Its face was as fierce as a falcon in flight and the legs of the legendary creature seemed capable of grasping a miniature world. The workmanship was exquisite and I had never seen anything quite like it before. But then, how often does one see a roc?

Holmes gave the object a rapid inspection with his pocket glass and seemed satisfied.

"It appears genuine, Watson, though I'd like to have an art expert verify my opinion. But time is pressing."

"You feel Chu will attempt to take it away from us?"

"He ordered an assault on the Dowson gang in their

150

own back yard, you might say. Our lodgings should hold no terror for him. However, he must plan the method of separating us from the object and while the wily Oriental is so occupied, we shall take action."

Leaving the box and twine on the desk, Holmes rapidly secured newspapers with which he blanketed the small golden treasure. Tucking his precious cargo under his arm, he gestured to me.

"Come, Watson, the game is not afoot; it is on the wing."

I followed him out on the landing, up the stairs to the second story, and into the room that Holmes and I used as a catch-all, though, in truth, I could not remember the last time I had been in it. The shelves of books were as I remembered them along with several sizeable bundles of newspapers awaiting inclusion in Holmes's files. My old army trunk was in one corner along with several other pieces of luggage that we had stowed there. One wall was changed completely, however. There was a Jacobean oak bench with a back rest suitable for two to sit upon, flanked by end tables. The bench was somewhat recessed in a manner that seemed strange to me.

"I ordered a little construction work at that time, two years ago, when you felt the call of Brighton. You recall, ol' chap, the considerable tan which you acquired at the seashore?"

While speaking, Holmes gestured me toward the bench, for what reason I could not imagine. As I sat down, I recalled the brief holiday that my friend referred to along with the burn induced by the sun and saltwater that had been most painful. Holmes had by now locked the door to the storage room, a most unusual action, and joined me on the bench. The fingers of one hand fiddled with the oaken side rail and, of a sudden, we were moving in a circular fashion. The bench and the wall behind it swiveled in a half-circle and I was staring into the darkness in a completely reversed direction than a moment previous. I was too stunned to utter a sound and it was most reassuring to hear Holmes's heartening words.

"But a moment, Watson, and there shall be light on the scene."

I heard the sound of a wooden match and then there was a sulphur flame with which my friend ignited a gas jet. We were in the house adjacent to 221B. No other explanation was possible.

After total darkness, the light dazzled me momentarily, but soon I observed a room somewhat sparsely furnished but with definite indications of tenancy.

"Where are we, Holmes?" I asked, in a rather quavering voice.

"In the lodgings of Hans Von Krugg, the well-known language expert of the University of Munich. The professor is on leave from his university post to explore the link between the ancient Cornish language and the Chaldean. His theory is not without supporters in the academic field and he has printed several papers on the subject, which, translated, of course, have appeared in English journals."

"Where . . . where is the professor?"

"Standing right here with you, ol' chap. I am Professor Von Krugg. At least, I have been from time to time during the past two years. However, today the professor will experience a slight identity change. Not a noticable one or the idea is unsound."

Completely amazed, I allowed Holmes to lead me from the mechanized bench that had miraculously transported us from one address to another and, before I knew it, had me seated before a sizeable dressing table with a large mirror. On the table top were a number of tubes and jars similar to ones I had seen Holmes perform miracles with before. Various wig-holders displayed a variety of toupees, beards and moustaches. Holmes surveyed my startled features in the mirror with a professional eagerness.

"We shall have to shadow your face quite a bit, you know. The professor is on the thin side. However, his luxuriant white beard is his most distinguishable feature and it does make it rather difficult to observe his features. Very near-sighted, too, you know. Wears thick glasses. Most people who view him have their eyes drawn to his hump and then look away."

"Hump?"

"Oh yes. The professor is a hunchback, but he gets around rather nicely with the help of his cane."

Over my futile protestations, Holmes was working a dark grease paint into my upper cheeks already.

"You know, Watson, this is going to work quite well. I should have had you play the professor before this. A nice touch to have Sherlock Holmes and the professor pass each other on the street."

"Now see here, it's all very well for you to go charging off in a disguise, but I'm hardly the type for such play-acting."

"Come now, Watson, it is much easier than it might seem. Most people give others no more than a cursory glance. Have I not, on many occasions, stated that the Homo sapiens looks but does not really see. Rather good reason for that. Most people are interested in themselves. The rest of the world they see, but not too much registers. However, for the sake of the prying eyes without that I am sure are there, we shall have you tidied up in Von Krugg's beard and glasses and with his loose-fitting clothes and the rather bent way that he walks, your tendency toward *avoirdupois* will be concealed. By the way, when you walk, be sure to swing your cane somewhat erratically. You must remember that. Small boys sometimes try and touch the back of a hunchback because of an old wives' tale of its being good luck. If you flail around a bit in a short-sighted way with your cane, such miscreants will make sure to avoid you."

"But, Holmes, this is ridiculous. What, by all that is holy, gave you the idea of a hunchback?"

"The anticipation of just such a situation as we face today. The back is the least of our problems since I have a splendid hump for you designed by Daziens of New York, according to my specifications. Inside the hump, of course, will be the Golden Bird."

With my mouth hanging open in surprise, I must have looked like the dolt, indeed, but Holmes paid me no heed nor did he listen to my protestations, which grew fainter as he worked his legerdemain. Within fifteen minutes I did not recognize myself in the dressing-room mirror. I could have sworn that I could enter the Bagatelle Club without drawing one greeting.

As Holmes dressed me in a longish dark coat, somewhat shiny in spots, and the rest of the professor's regular habiliments, he cautioned me as to gestures and a shuffling walk. By this time, I was quite caught up with the idea, for the urge toward exhibitionism lurks within us all, however dormant. It was no easy job, for my friend rehearsed me strenuously like a dramatic director intent on a perfect performance for a thespian.

Some time later, I stood before Holmes with my shoulders hunched forward because of the *ersatz* hump attached to my back. Within it was secreted the Golden Bird.

"Now, Watson, should anyone address you, keep walking, by all means, and mumble something. Your German is passable enough for a few words. The professor knows very few people so there is little possibility of your being approached.

"Make your way to the Diogenes Club by the most direct route. I have a note here for my brother, Mycroft, with whom you will leave the Golden Bird. Once this is accomplished, remove the beard and make-up and the hump as well. The coat you are wearing is reversable. Pull the sleeves inside out and turn the garment around and you will find that it has a different appearance altogether. Mycroft will lend you a suitable hat. You can then return to our quarters as yourself."

"But what will you be up to, Holmes? You'll be in danger."

"Tut, tut, ol' fellow, do you think those two constables of MacDonald have eluded my notice? I shall make it apparent that I'm on the premises so that Chu's watchers will not think we've flown the coop. And I shall be available should the Oriental make some overture as regards the statue of the roc. You see that your debut in the field of drama will be most valuable to our cause."

I was buoyed up by Holmes's assurance that mine was an important task, and my determination to make it a good show had an added impetus which I did not reveal to Holmes. I was most anxious to talk to his older brother, the very capable and influential Mycroft.

While the following half-hour was nerve-wracking, matters progressed as Holmes had anticipated. Departing from the edifice adjacent to our quarters, I wandered down the street, attempting to follow my friend's instructions, and my performance must have been passable since I could detect no one dogging my footsteps, nor did anyone greet me as I progressed from Baker Street toward Pall Mall and the mysterious Diogenes Club.

In the public mind, this highly respectable and sedate establishment was the haven for elderly gentlemen devoted to silence, where members could immerse themselves in the daily journals without bothersome remarks from or to fellow members. Conversation in the meeting rooms of the establishment was strictly forbidden. The idea was sufficiently bizarre to be completely acceptable and arouse no suspicions as to the real purpose of this most impressive citadel of silence.

As I mounted the stone steps and entered between the marble pillars to present my card at the desk, several venerable members were in evidence reading the financial news or dozing with a tot of port at their side and partially smoked cigars that had grown cold in mottled, shaky hands. But one can be remarkably observant when one knows what to look for. Several of these seemingly archaic members had a shoulder breadth unusual for their age and their beards and moustaches could well have been commercially produced, just as the pallor of their seemingly lined faces could have come from a master of make-up, as my stooped shoulders and bearded visage had. Evidently, I was expected, for the club manager who knew me gave no indication that my appearance baffled him but accepted my card and retreated from the main desk for a brief moment, returning and signaling for me to follow him.

My feet sunk in the Persian carpets that formed islands in the polished oak flooring, and I crossed toward an ironwood door leading from the entrance hall of the club and into the room, which I knew from experience served as one of Mycroft Holmes's offices. The door was lined with steel from within, but swung easily on massive hinges and then I was in the presence of the second most powerful man in England.

I had shared quarters with Sherlock Holmes for some years before realizing that his older brother was not the auditor for some little-known branch of the government but, instead, had created a unique position for himself in the small group that handled the reins of the Empire on which the sun never set. Prime ministers came and went, but the meticulous mind of Mycroft Holmes continued to collate information from all over the world and evaluate it and piece it together in the series of patterns that most influenced that policy of Her Majesty's government. Be there a whisper in the Montmartre or on some remote Tibetan mountain that might prove of import to the destiny of Britain and the organization created and headed by this large, dreamy-eyed man would relay it to their chief.

Though Holmes, after the crucible of time had forged the metal of our friendship, had never been evasive regarding his brother's influence or power or abilities, he had never voiced what I suspected was the actual truth, namely that Mycroft Holmes headed up England's intelligence operations. On paper, such an organization did not even exist and, while I was certain of the man's far-flung apparatus and his commitment to our nation's

156

destiny, I had no curiosity to have my suppositions confirmed on the theory that 'tis best to let sleeping dogs lie.

The older Holmes's massive desk was, as usual, clear and tidy with no indication of the immense flow of business that passed over its surface daily. He greeted me with genuine warmth though when referring to his brother his manner, by habit, became slightly sardonic. During my association with both these quite amazing men, I had never detected the slightest rivalry or jealousy between them. Sherlock Holmes stated openly that his brother would make a superior detective if he could but pursue crime to the scene and follow the tedious paths that a thorough investigation required. Mycroft Holmes confessed himself completely incapable of doing so and contended that his brother's devious mind was better-suited to anticipating the potential paths of national policy then his own. Since each of the Holmes family offspring contended that the other could be the superior, they followed their chosen paths with a mutual respect, and I felt that their chiding of each other, on occasion, was simply a family characteristic adopted in their childhood.

"Dear me," said Mycroft, his watery blue eyes absorbing my unusual appearance. "What has Sherlock got you involved in now? Can it be that you have abandoned the role of biographer and are apprenticed to the mummer's trade?"

"My involvement is not what concerns me at the moment but rather that of your brother," I replied, somewhat testily. Handing him the message from Sherlock Holmes, I began to divest myself of my disguise with some relief. When the statesman had concluded his reading, I had the infernal hump off my back and was extracting the statue from it.

"And this is the focal point of Sherlock's latest escapade," he commented, surveying the golden roc. "A piece of considerable value. Well, I shall accede to Sherlock's request and place the statue in safety here.

157

From your unusual garb I must assume that there is considerably more to the story than just this art object."

"Indeed there is. This Golden Bird has excited the interest of two of the most powerful criminal organizations in London. It is my feeling that your brother is in considerable danger, since it surely is now known that the statue has come into his hands."

Mycroft shifted his corpulent figure and nodded with resignation. "With his usual aplomb, Sherlock is, no doubt, completely ignoring the possibility of personal danger. To his credit, I will admit that the cloak of invincibility, which he seems to consider himself enveloped in, has served him well."

"To this point," I interjected, "but there are matters here as yet unknown and the players on the stage of this drama wield frightening power."

Evidently, the concern in my manner communicated itself and for the first time since the Bruce-Partington affair, Mycroft Holmes abandoned his Buddalike calmness.

"So, Basil Selkirk is involved."

I was startled, having forgotten momentarily that the elder Holmes was reputed to have greater powers of deduction than his brother.

"Elementary," he continued. "With an art object, Selkirk's interest is a foregone conclusion. Since the shadowy financier is of concern to Her Majesty's government, I can instigate some official moves. What would you have?"

His innocence did not hoodwink me. Were his brother endangered, I knew Mycroft Holmes would employ the powers at his command even if he had to invent a reason. However, his subterfuge paralleled my interests and I was glad to humor it. I chose to confide in the espionage expert without feeling a tinge of disloyalty to my intimate friend, since his brother could well learn whatever facts I had and in short order too.

"Holmes has been after this art object for some time. MacDonald of the Yard is privy to the case since homicide plays a part in it. Basil Selkirk employed the Dowson gang to secure the Bird and has now placed it in the hands of your brother."

"And Chu San Fu is after it?"

"Why, you know all about the affair," I stated with some heat.

"I know that if a sinister criminal organization is in pursuit of this statue, it would have to be the inscrutable Chinaman. Art objects are seldom the target of smash and grabbers or the pedestrian criminal. Besides, the involvement of Selkirk clued me. The fiancier and the supposed Oriental importer have been rivals for years."

"I'm sure Baker Street is under observation by minions of the Oriental. MacDonald is aware of this and has men on duty in the area."

"Then we shall see that the diligent inspector gets no interference from the Commissioner."

"Holmes also has his Irregulars involved and, for all I know, detachments of that shadowland army that seems to be at his beck and call." I made this statement in a tentative tone, trusting that the acute statesman would divine my plea, which he, naturally, did.

"But something a little more is needed, in your opinion," he said, with a dry smile. "I agree. If Sherlock has rallied his forces, he is treating the affair with the utmost gravity and it behooves us to do as well. Fortunately, a gentleman of my acquaintance is but recently returned from foreign lands. I shall suggest that he might find this affair and Sherlock's involvement of interest. Does that satisfy you, my good Watson?"

Indeed it did. I well knew the frighteningly efficient person that Mycroft Holmes was referring to and made my way back to Baker Street minus my disguise with a much lighter heart. A knight had been added to the complex chessboard, and he was not only positioned on our side but very much dedicated to the interests of my friend, Sherlock Holmes.

15

Holmes Plans Our Defense

Upon my return to 221B, I was heartened by the obvious expression of relief upon Holmes's face. Clad in his dressing gown, he was sawing aimlessly on his violin. Seated close to one of our windows facing on Baker Street, it occurred to me that the sound of music must have been audible without, especially since the window was partially open and the room quite cold because of it.

Holmes laid aside his violin, standing and crossing before the window several times as he spoke to me. It was as though he were performing and the aperture was the proscenium arch of his theatre. While Holmes frequently used his musical moments as a spur to deep thought, the reappearance of the violin suggested a stratagem on his part.

"My dear Watson, I'm delighted to see that your performance was acceptable. Soon we shall have you on the bill at the Tivoli."

I must confess that I swelled with pride as I related my meeting with Mycroft Holmes, though I did not reveal the latter part of our conversation.

"Excellent! Excellent! Now we are assured of the safety of the art object. During your absence, there have been things stirring here as well. A cable from Berlin notifies us that our client, Vasil D'Anglas, plans to come to England."

This news fell on very welcome ears. "How fortunate! With D'Anglas on the scene, we can give him the Golden Bird and be done with the matter," I exclaimed.

Holmes regarded me with his head half-cocked to one side and a slight smile on his keen face.

"I am reminded once more of the remark of Basil Selkirk. 'This matter has a way to go yet or I miss my guess.' "

As I began to remonstrate, Holmes picked up his violin and with a warning gesture struck some authoritative notes, moving toward the window as he did so. Most of the time, his violin periods consisted of aimless wandering with no musical progression, though they were not unpleasant to the ear. But now he was obviously playing the introductory notes to a composition. Coming to a pause, he activated the gramophone, which I had not noted until this moment. The instrument began playing a lively air. Holmes made a dumb show of playing his violin as he moved past the window easily visible from without and then retreated from public view to rejoin me.

Placing his musical instrument in its case, he regarded me with an expression of sly satisfaction.

"It is my thought, Watson, that the Oriental ear is not closely attuned to the violin. Our observers without will not note the difference between my technique and that of Sarasate. At least, we hope not."

I must have exhibited my frequent expression of bafflement since he laughed softly and jogged my mind with the quicksilver of his own.

"Nothing is more reassuring to a watcher than to have the subject of their scrutiny in full view. The next best thing being a sound that indicates what he is involved in. Now we can devote ourselves in matters of importance while presenting a placid picture to the outside world. Certain allies have been busy and we now know for a fact that chambers across from us have been taken over by a supposed Russian gentleman who has had a number of Chinese visitors. You will be reassured to know that two of MacDonald's men are consuming enormous quantities of tea in Parkinson's down the street, at a table which has a clear view of our outer portal. Elements of that singular organization known as the Irregulars under the leadership of that grimy little rascal, Wiggins, are covering our back area."

"Good heavens, Holmes," I responded, with a chuckle, "don't tell me Slim Gilligan is perched on the roof."

"Hardly. Though I expect his presence. The point is, Watson, that we are under a state of siege, but we have the advantage. They—the disciples of Chu San Fu—are watching us but they don't know that we know it."

"What is your plan?"

"Fate may be forming one for me."

Holmes retreated for a moment into his inner world of contemplation, emerging from it quickly with a trace of apology in his sharp eyes.

"Let us consider the situation, ol' comrade. Chu San Fu is convinced that we have the Golden Bird in our possession. The information reaching him in his Limehouse headquarters positions us firmly in his sights. I am in hopes that this fact will not prompt any rapid move on his part but rather lull him into some carefully arranged plan to secure the object of his desire."

"Here we are then, the sitting ducks."

"But knowledgeable ducks, Watson. How much better to have our adversary come at us where we reside in strength than to go about our daily existence casting looks of apprehension over our shoulders. I well recall when Moriarty was bent on my destruction and I adopted the role of a moving target. It was a nerve-wracking time."

I nodded instinctively, remembering clearly that period immediately prior to the downfall of the Napoleon of crime, when Holmes had avoided open windows like a plague and walked in the shadows and only at night. It flashed through my mind that at that time he had mentioned that it was stupidity rather than courage to refuse to recognize danger when it was close upon you.

"You certainly expect them to make a move. Why not have MacDonald's men on the premises?"

"If we flush the grouse, they will settle elsewhere. The obvious presence of the constabulary will prompt a change of plans, which I don't want." My expression caused him to continue. "Yes, good chap, I'm inviting an attempt on our quarters."

I must say this line of thinking was wearing my patience thin.

"See here, Holmes, you preach the doctrine of rationality. If it's a confrontation you desire, I'm with you, as you know. But where is the advantage? The Golden Bird, due to your far-sighted planning, is as safe as if it were in the vaults of the bank of London. Intruders cannot gain by their efforts. But neither can we. Chu San Fu will not be present if an assault is made. The matter will be handled by his dacoits and Chinese scragmen. If we trap them, what do we gain? Suddenly, they lose any knowledge of English, respond to all questions in their native tongue and look bewildered. If I judge the hold Chu has on his followers, five to ten in Pentonville will not frighten them into betraying him."

An additional confirmation of my theorizing crossed my mind and I voiced it. "No doubt, his people have family in China on whom the master criminal could wreak vengeance. An additional guarantee of silence."

Holmes had been gazing at me with an almost beatific expression of satisfaction.

"My good chap, obviously our years together have not been wasted. You have given a surface evaluation which would command respect at a conclave of Scotland Yard inspectors."

My momentary elation was chilled by the cold water of second thought. "But where have I missed? Were I right, you would argue the point."

Holmes indulged in a chuckle. "You know me too well. In answer, let us lift the carpet of your thoughts and look beneath. Who is our opponent? How does he think? In what way will he react? Were we expecting a visitation from Count Negretto Sylvius, Dowson's chief lieutenant, I might not be sitting here so smugly. Sylvius is much inclined toward spur-of-the-moment action. He is impetuous, hence irrational and difficult to anticipate. But Chu San Fu is cut from different cloth. A planner. If lulled into the belief that we are the sitting ducks you mentioned, he will meticulously polish every facet of his scheme. Like all master criminals, he has two audiences to deal with."

"How so?"

"His first purpose is to hoodwink me. But he must do so in the manner of the magician to impress those who follow his flag. A great deal of his power is psychological. Show me the army that believes its general cannot fail and I'll show you a victorious one. The aura of omnipotence is indispensable to one like Chu San Fu."

"If so," I thought, "he's not alone in that." I'd seen many a hardened criminal fall before the name of Sherlock Holmes. Seldom had my friend been so loquacious regarding a case, but patience is not one of my virtues.

"See here, your reasoning, as always, is quite faultless but how does it affect your purpose in this matter? I'm still in the dark."

"Let the Oriental strike, Watson, since we can almost set the time. But let the results be unknown. If he tastes either victory or defeat, he will know what to do. But if he is in doubt, then we turn his intricate mind against himself. Doubt and egotism cannot coexist. We'll make him vulnerable yet, good chap."

As though satisfied with his review of the situation, for I was no more than an audience to his assessment, a background sound to provide punctuations to his sentences, Holmes rose and turned off the gramophone at a suitable point, appearing at the window again at intervals to keep our watchers assured of his presence. The afternoon wore on, though not without incident.

Several times, Wiggins slipped into the house through the back to report to Holmes and leave with written instructions for unknown destinations. As the early darkness of a winter's evening approached, Gilligan materialized. To my mind, he never appeared but suddenly became present. I assumed that he came in over the roof. Now Holmes had no time for play-acting and resorted to the most lifelike waxwork reproduction of himself created by Tavernier, the French modeler, a device which he had used to good effect in former times and would, indeed, use again.

Seated in an armchair with Holmes's dressing gown, the effigy was startlingly lifelike and could fool someone within our sitting room, to say nothing of watchers without. I was assigned the job of adjusting the moveable head from time to time and to all intents the great detective was placidly reading a book. Needless to say, I took great precautions with my job, but managed to keep my ears attuned to the animated conversation between the cracksman and Holmes.

"I went over the Barker digs and gave it the full treatment, Guv. There's nothin' wot's 'id there. That's the first thing I established. So I give 'is belongin's a real hard look. 'E weren't one fer makin' notes and 'e traveled light."

"A temporary residence," said Holmes. "Barker's home was in Surrey."

"I went over 'is books carefully, lookin' for some clue. 'E had the usual bible, a Bradshaw, Whitaker's Almanac, a 'ole batch of railroad timetables."

"Standard equipment, the last. Barker did quite a bit of traveling in his line of work."

"There wuz a complete copy of the works of Edgar Allan Poe and I went through that page for page. A bust. Then there wuz this kinda strange piece o' work."

I noted that the cracksman extracted a slim volume from a pocket. "I brung it wiv me, Guv."

Holmes seized the volume eagerly and his manner betrayed excitement as he read the title.

"*Jonathan Wild, Master Criminal.*" He threw a glance of triumph at me.

"Again Wild appears in this tangle. Let's see. Published by Leadenhall Press. Obviously, a limited edition and I would judge not well-received since it has never come to my attention. An old volume, but Wild was at his zenith in the last century and his career was not common knowledge even then." Holmes had been leafing through the book as he spoke. "Evidently, this was written by a member of the Wild gang who was apprehended and served out his time and later attempted to capitalize on the dubious reputation of his former master. It will bear close inspection."

"You feel you've stumbled onto something?" I asked, as bait to learn what intrigued the sleuth.

"Wild keeps coming up. Lindquist told us that it was Wild's man, Hawker, who stole the Bird from the Island of Rhodes. Barker had learned something that he tried to tell Lindquist before he died. Barker had this book. Surely, there is a connection." Suddenly, Holmes's lips tightened with a grimace. "It just occurred to me that I told Basil Selkirk about the Rhodes incident. I wonder if that was the service that I performed for the financier and for which he sent me the Golden Bird?"

Holmes had no time to dwell on the machinations of Basil Selkirk or the book dealing with the career of Jonathan Wild, for other matters claimed his attention.

At his instigation, Mrs. Hudson and Billy, the page boy, vacated the premises. I could hear our esteemed landlady, obviously instructed by her eccentric boarder, discussing a meeting of the Marylebone Sewing Circle with a neighbor as she departed. What Billy's connection was with this sedate group was never made clear, but my friend had removed the domestic staff from the danger area and, in the process, had made things seemingly simpler for anyone desiring to invade 221B.

A communiqué from Mycroft Holmes assured Holmes that the Golden Bird was indeed genuine or Mr. Halcroft Crouder, art expert by appointment to Her Majesty, did not know his business. I could see that the confirmation of the authenticity of the art object was no surprise to Holmes and his double-check was but one of the precautions which he took automatically. My delivering the Bird to Mycroft Holmes had served two purposes—removed it from the possible clutches of Chu San Fu, and made it available for close scrutiny by an authority in the field. What did claim my undivided attention was the fact that Mycrof Holmes's message to his brother was delivered by none other than Wakefield Orloff. This surprised Holmes, who stated that he was under the impression that the security agent was abroad. In his quiet tones, that impassive man mentioned that he had just returned from the Continent.

As this seemingly plump figure seated himself in a straight-back with the flowing grace that was his trademark, I felt much comforted. Whatever plots were being hatched by Chu San Fu, there had to be unpleasant surprises for the Oriental with Orloff on the scene. Heavens, I had no doubt that Sherlock Holmes was capable of frustrating the master criminal, but Orloff's arrival was like having a detachment of the Coldstream Guards drop in.

Seated with his back straight and his weight balanced on the balls of his small feet, the fearsome security agent surveyed the scene with his habitual half-smile and fathomless green eyes. His bowler hat, with its steel-reinforced brim, was within easy reach. Of course, there was a Spanish throwing knife between his shoulder blades, for there always was. Whatever other armament he carried was superfluous, since I had seen him, with my own eyes, totally demolish the strongest man in the world in a matter of seconds.*

If Holmes had any suspicions that I was a motivating factor in the presence of this walking arsenal, he gave no indication. He seemed genuinely delighted to see his brother's agent on the scene, for they had worked together before on a number of occasions. As for Orloff, the faintest sense of danger was like the huntsman's horn to a foxhound. A chilling man not given to jest or

* *The Case of the Mysterious Imprint.*

banter, yet I noted that whenever he greeted my friend, his green eyes kindled with a warmth completely foreign to them.

"Do I sense a pending crisis?" he inquired.

"If you do," replied Holmes, "I'm comforted by the thought that others are not as acute."

"Two emissaries from New Scotland Yard are down the street and since I know they would not have you under observation, I assume their presence is of a cooperative nature."

"If the back is clear, my Irregulars are going to spirit MacDonald in here. Best have his men maintain their posts. If they have been noticed—a possibility—it continues to draw attention to our front, obviously not the line of attack." Suddenly, his alert eyes locked with Orloff's. "You have posed no questions as to what is going on or who is behind it." His eyes swiveled quickly to me, though without irritation or accusation, then they returned to the security agent. "Possibly, you are briefed on the matter already."

Orloff was too old a hand to reveal anything. "Two members of the force outside, Mrs. Hudson and the page boy gone, Gilligan present, and Watson's pocket weighted down with his service revolver, it hardly seems that you are prepared for a pleasant evening at Simpson's."

Holmes chuckled. "As I grow older, it seems I become obvious. I assume you know about the golden statue?"

Orloff admitted as much with a nod.

"Chu San Fu thinks it is on the premises and he wants it."

Orloff's lips pursed in a soundless whistle. "That being so you can hardly turn me out. It would be the mark of an unfriendly act. What is the plan?"

"There will be a police van standing by with a flying squad of MacDonald's men. The Chinaman has his people in the building across the street. How many I

169

don't know, but I doubt if they are the strike force. I hope to bag the lot."

There was a glint in Orloff's eyes but his chubby body, which was actually solid muscle, never moved and had not since he had seated himself. The man's ability to relax completely and remain immobile as though saving himself for the critical moment was absolutely amazing to my medically trained mind.

"What makes you feel that Chun hasn't got your rear covered?"

"I've made myself conspicuously present throughout the day. No need to guard against my departing via the back when I'm ostensibly in full view. Besides, the Irregulars would know. Wiggins is no fool."

"Nor are his fellow street urchins." Orloff thought for a moment. "How do you think they'll do it?"

Holmes's reply was swift. "They might try a diversionary tactic but that's doubtful. By rights, they should have no idea that their visit is expected. Therefore, they'll wait till dark and then attempt to sneak in, feeling that there are but two sedate, middle-aged men to deal with. We will make the rear very inviting for them. Since the ground-floor windows are barred, the cellar seems their obvious choice."

"Any arrangement for an alarm?" asked Orloff, as though he knew there was.

"When they come, one of the Irregulars will be positioned in the plane tree in back. He'll signal a cohort and the alarm will be relayed around to Baker Street. Slippery Styles will appear in his organ-grinder guise to signal us."

"What if the hour is late?" I asked, voicing a reasonable possibility.

It won't be. They'll want to get inside and take care of us, Watson, before Mrs. Hudson and Billy return. Then they can start searching the premises and attend to our landlady should she arrive before they've completed the job."

170

"Good heavens, Holmes, do you think they plan to murder us in our sleep?"

"I doubt it. 'Tis the statue Chu is after. Chloroform seems more likely. When MacDonald arrives we'll be ready for them. Actually, that's more manpower than we need, but I'm quite obsessed with the idea of making this a very silent and sudden job. If we take them to the man without a fuss, Chu will be at a distinct disadvantage. Right where I want him, of course."

16

The Attack

It is always the waiting that is the worst. I am not of a buccaneering nature. My period in the service of Her Majesty involved medical duties and was not as a soldier of the line despite the fatal battle of Maiwan. But still, rather than preserve silence, endure darkness and contemplate possible disaster, give me action any time.

An early evening fog made the undetected entrance of MacDonald a simple thing. With the inspector on the scene, our force was complete and I could not think of four men I would rather stand with. The final setting of the stage was pleasing in its detail. We extinguished the light beside the wax dummy, which had served as a target for the eyes without. Another lamp was lit. Shadows moved across closed drapes, but only those of Holmes and myself.

After a suitable time, the light in my bedroom went on and I made myself visible at the window before extinguishing my lamp and rejoining the others downstairs. Holmes carried out a similar deception and 221B Baker Street was apparently dark for the night. Gilligan was downstairs in the cellar just in case the intruders slipped by the Irregulars. Orloff was observing the back yard through a darkened window. Holmes and I stood by the front door in case of a surprise move in this direction. The fog thinned and then retreated to the Thames but the moon did not reveal its presence and, save for the flickering gas jets on Baker Street, the darkness was Stygian. I steeled myself not to release nervous tension by asking my comrade unnecessary questions but it was difficult. The nearby clock chimed the hour and the next one and then it happened. There was the sound of the organ grinder on Baker Street.

I had rehearsed the next move mentally and, to my credit, did not muddle it. Following Holmes's catlike tread, I made my way rapidly to the cellar. The blackness was complete, but knowing every inch of the area proved comforting. The two half-windows opening on the back yard were faintly visible since there was dim light from the night sky now. Orloff and Gilligan stood to one side and below each window. Holmes was positioned slightly behind them ready to move toward the area of action. MacDonald and I stood at the base of the stairway with revolvers ready. We were the artillery of the miniature army, ready to fire if necessary. The sound of the street organ and the traffic on Baker Street could not be heard. The silence was oppressive. Then there was a creak at one of the basement windows and I could vaguely detect a hand applying pressure to the frame. Again silence and then the other window was tested. Holmes had insisted that both be locked. There could be too much of a good thing and he did not wish to alert the intruders. However, the catch on the second window was looser than the first, a fact detected by whoever was trying to force an entry.

The frame of the second window moved slightly and there was a rasping sound as metal was inserted in the space. The simple hook-and-eye attachment was detached easily, but the frame would not give since side bolts held it fast. There was a pause and I could picture the man without reaching for additional equipment. Then there was an irritating scratching sound that sent tingles through the short hairs at the base of my neck. A tool was working on the glass. A cutter, of course. Before its job was done, a piece of putty was applied to one portion of the glass. Then more scratching and a circle of the glass was silently removed. A thin arm reached through the opening and disengaged the side bolts. The window swung inward and a piece of wood propped it in its upright position. There was a lengthy silence as the man outside listened with care. I know not of the others, but I held my breath. Then there came the sound of tools being moved to one side and a body shifting position.

Like a shadow, Gilligan had moved to the other side of the open window, which he and Orloff now flanked. A pair of feet appeared through the aperture and then a thin body shoved itself into the air and came down on the floor of the cellar with complete silence. As the figure straightened from a crouched to an upright position, Orloff was upon it. In a blur of movement, his arm encircled the man's neck, shutting off the slightest sound. His other arm, with fist clenched, swiveled and the struggling human slumped like a bundle of rags. Another pair of legs appeared in the window as Orloff passed the inert body to Gilligan, who moved it back into the cellar away from the outer wall.

I felt as though I were suddenly deaf since there was not the slightest sound. The second pair of legs were much bigger and their owner did not choose to drop into the cellar but attempted to lower himself, and successfully, from the ledge. I judged him to be very large, possibly a Manchurian. Evidently, the same thought occurred to Orloff for he did not attempt a throttle-hold but swept his deadly bowler from his head and swung it in a murderous half-arc against the man's head. Now there was a faint sound, the thud of metal against bone. Holmes was at Orloff's side and the two of them lowered the giant to the floor.

Gilligan was back beside the window now. I sensed the faint odor of spices, possibly the sickening sweetness of opium mixed with that of sweat. It was the smell of Limehouse. Still a third pair of legs made their appearance, but the owner must have sensed that something was amiss for there was an intake of breath. Like a snake, one of Gilligan's abnormally long, thin arms reached. His hand grabbed an ankle, pulling the body downward as his left hand swung the sandbag he carried on occasion. A third body joined the others on the floor.

From without there was a faint whistle, which startled me so that my hand grasped my revolver and threatened to crack the butt plates, but then I realized that it was only a signal from our boy in the plane tree. This was the lot and we had them.

The matter was not finished but we were well on our way. Holmes and Orloff boosted Inspector MacDonald through the open window into the back yard, where he conferred with our tree-climbing ally before his police torch flashed a signal into the night. Gilligan had the three bodies, all Chinese, trussed up like Christmas turkeys in jig time, and gagged as well. Orloff began to lift the bodies, pushing them into the yard. As I followed Holmes to the ground floor, I noted that Orloff picked up the giant of the trio as though he were a baby. The man's strength was almost as unbelievable as his lightning reflexes, which I knew so well.

Holmes and I were now in the role of observers, but the operation, to this point, had progressed so smoothly that I momentarily considered writing it up for the study of students at Sandhurst. The exhilarating scent of victory does tend to make one somewhat overdramatic.

A ground-floor window gave us a good view of the street.

"Mrs. Hudson is staying the night with her sister, Watson, but we must make sure that her neighbors have nothing to comment upon during her absence. Besides, a fracas on Baker Street would be damaging to our image."

I doubt if our image was on the minds of MacDonald's squad, but they had certainly been well-rehearsed. The two men detailed as a protective measure had already vacated their latest haunt, the deep doorway of Spea and Henry's liquor store and were moving up the other side of the street. I saw a police van appear at the end of the block. Suddenly, dark shadows were everywhere. They were in the building opposite us in a trice. A window above opened suddenly and, to my horror, a man lowered himself over the ledge and dropped. But before he could regain his feet he was firmly grasped by two constables. I could not tell whether they gagged him or coshed him, but he was silent. The police van came up the street at a sedate rate and constables reappeared with two more prisoners in tow. The lot disappeared into the van, which then pulled round the block to pick up the other Chinamen in our back yard.

Holmes heaved a sigh of relief and turned to me with obvious delight. "It's as though it had never happened, Watson. No neighbors in windows. No onlookers or questions. Perfectly executed."

"Perfectly planned," I managed to say, laconically.

It was not long thereafter that MacDonald returned. I busied myself with tantalus and gasogene, and bonded spirits were passed round to join high spirits over a successful venture. Holmes toasted the Scotland Yard inspector. "Now it is up to you, Mr. Mac. If you can keep the six captives under cover, we've bought ourselves some time."

MacDonald threw a quick glance at Wakefield Orloff. "Truth is, Mr. Holmes, I planned to bury them in a suburban station and keep moving them round. I'd anticipated embarrassin' questions from the Commissioner if he got wind of it. But we had a turn of luck. The six boyos we bagged are being taken to a safe house and 'twas the Commissioner himself who informed me of the arrangement."

"So," said Holmes, also looking at Orloff, "my brother has dealt himself into the game."

The security agent was unperturbed. "Mycroft Holmes knows most of what goes on, you know. At the moment, the Foreign Office is more than a little interested in Chu San Fu. As to why his men are to be secreted away, your brother did not choose to explain."

"I wish someone would," I blurted out.

"The Elizabethan policy, my dear Watson. Delay, play for time until things clarify. There is an adage of diplomacy which applies here. Make haste slowly."

"Well," said MacDonald, "my men have been informed that tonight's events are best forgotten. The prisoners have been turned over to associates of Mr. Orloff. I don't know where they are, nor do I want to."

"The safe-house technique has always been effective in situations like this," said Orloff.

Noting my expression of bafflement, Holmes came to my rescue. "A private residence which is not quite what it seems to be. Since, officially, it has no associations with government or police, it makes a nice hideaway or temporary prison."

"You've given me enough clues," was my exasperated comment, "but a criminal band attempted to enter our quarters illegally. Why all the secretive treatment?"

"To confuse Chu San Fu. If six of his followers simply vanish, he will not make a move until he discovers what happened. Were they captured? Are they peaching to the police? Have they simply run away? His hands will be tied until the matter is resolved and during that time we shall attempt to clear up the muddle surrounding this matter and discover what makes the Golden Bird so valuable. The answer lies with the Chinaman. He knows."

"But is not Basil Selkirk also involved?" asked Orloff.

"Watson and I had a meeting with the financier. He stated that he was after the Bird simply because Chu San Fu was. I'm inclined to believe this. Chu San Fu has the key to the puzzle. Barker found out what it was. Among Barker's possessions was a book which Slim secured for us dealing with the career of Jonathan Wild. I think Wild, long ago, knew the secret of the Bird."

"That's why his man, Harry Hawker, stole the statute from the shop on Rhodes," I said.

"The Rhodes robbery took place around 1850, Watson. Wild had been dead a full ten years by then. My theory is that what Wild knew died with him but a clue remained. Hawker discovered it, possibly in the same manner that the lamented Barker did. The answer may very well be in this book of Barker's, gentlemen, which I intend to study with much care."

Gilligan, MacDonald, and Orloff, after more musings, speculation, and libations, took their leave and this time the lights did go out at 221B Baker Street.

17

More Light in Dark Places

The events had been tiring indeed and when I awoke the following morning, I was somewhat shocked at the late hour. Mrs. Hudson and Billy had returned by the time I found myself in the sitting room. Holmes had breakfasted and the smell of his strong shag was heavy in the room. The volume dealing with Jonathan Wild was on the desk and Holmes sat by the fireplace, his fingers steepled and his aquiline nose pressed against them. I tiptoed out of the room to acquaint our housekeeper of my presence and needs. When I returned, Holmes had not moved a muscle, but he suddenly looked up as though startled by my presence.

"Ah, Watson, you are the late-abed today."

He sprang to his feet, crossing to the silver coffee urn.

"This should still be warm," he said, "and a cup will serve you well. Both of us in fact."

Holmes seldom deigned to perform domestic duties but on this day he bustled around, pouring coffee, urging me to be seated and talking all the while.

"You have ordered breakfast, no doubt?"

I indicated that this was so.

"Splendid!"

I had not lived with Sherlock Holmes so long not to recognize the signs. He had come upon something and

181

was quite delighted with himself and anxious to share his thoughts with his only confidant, me.

"Of course, I have been through the book. Badly written, but one section shows a spark of originality. The author, one Pierce by name, devotes a full chapter to the plans of Wild that never bore fruit. The schemes that the criminal did not or could not take action on. It is in this portion of the book that the only markings appear."

Holmes was at the desk, leafing through the book taken from Barker's dwelling. "Let me read this to you. 'Jonathan Wild was instrumental in a large number of jewel robberies but diamonds were his only passion.' "

Holmes's eyes rose from the page. "This portion is bracketed. A more specific marking comes later." He resumed reading: " 'In 1828, Wild spent much time and a considerable amount of money planning a theft of the Sancy diamond, one of the crown jewels of France. The stone had come into the possession of Demindoff and Wild intended to possess it despite my protestations that the gem was too well-known to be sold and I knew that Wild would never consider cutting it.' "

As Holmes paused for a moment, I offered a comment.

"The author, Pierce, seems to have been quite an intimate of Jonathan Wild."

"Or attempts to picture himself as such. His facts seem accurate. I do know that the Sancy was sold by Demidoff in 1865 for twenty thousand pounds. Or, at least, that is the story. I wonder if Wild actually did steal the stone!"

"Doesn't Pierce make mention of it?"

"Simply that the robbery did not go off as planned and Wild abandoned the idea. Here's the main point of interest: 'The one diamond that Wild really conveted was the Pasha of Egypt though he was never able to get his hands on it.' "

Holmes looked at me, his eyes alight.

"Barker drew a line through 'Pasha of Egypt.' "

"And when he died, that was the word that Lindquist heard: 'Pasha.' "

"Exactly. You can see my interest was immediately sparked."

"But what has the Pasha of Egypt diamond to do with the Golden Bird?"

"What indeed? At one time I mentioned that the pursuit of the Bird would seem more reasonable if it were encrusted with precious gems. Suppose, Watson, instead of jewels on the outside, to give the object a far greater value, there was one jewel, a world-famous diamond, on the inside?"

Holmes's idea was certainly intriguing. "Then all these thefts over a long period of time—they were not really after the Golden Bird but a diamond—the Pasha of Egypt."

Holmes head was shaking slowly in a negative fashion.

"As I have stated on other occasions, it is a capital mistake to theorize in advance of the facts. One begins to twist facts to fit theories, instead of fitting theories to facts. We need facts now, Watson, and shall have to seek them from experts. I have dispatched a note to Orloff asking him to arrange a meeting with Edwin Streeter."

"The name is unfamiliar to me."

"The royal jeweler, ol' chap. Streeter wrote a book in '83: *The Great Diamonds of the World.* I rather fancy he knows the diamond field inside and out and might provide the information that will crystallize this whole matter."

Holmes ran into a snag at this point since the royal jeweler was vacationing in the south of France at this time. However, Wakefield Orloff's intimate knowledge of comings and goings between England and the Continent came to the detective's aid. According to the security agent, Dr. Max Bauer of Germany was in England

183

at the time and Orloff was able to arrange a meeting between the famous gem expert and Holmes.*

Happily, the doctor was a follower of the exploits of my friend and was quite delighted to visit our chambers on Baker Street which gave me the opportunity of being present at a most fascinating exchange of information.

The professor had a round, jolly face topped with a profusion of unruly hair. He might have modeled for a character out of *Pickwick Papers* or perhaps a Bavarian toymaker. Orloff was not present, the doctor having come to our abode alone, for which Holmes thanked him warmly. Bauer stated that he was most happy to visit the world's greatest detective and to be able to meet the famous Doctor Watson. I decided that the doctor was a splendid chap indeed, and then Bauer and my friend got down to business.

"*Ach,* Mr. Holmes, you vill vant to talk about precious stones. Iss der any p'tickler vun vot intrigues you?"

"Diamonds, Doctor Bauer."

"A big field. You haf a p'tikiler von in mind, perhaps?"

"I'm interested in several. What could you tell me about the Sancy diamond?"

"*Ach,* von of ze most vamous. All crown jewels are. Like many great diamonds, it came from India. Before becoming part of ze crown jewels of Fronce, it vas in your country, you know. It vas sold to Queen Elizabet 'round sixteen hundred und vent to Fronce vid Henrietta Maria, de qveen of Charles, first. Den it vent to Cardinal Mazarin as a pledge. The Cardinal vas qvite a diamond fancier und left ze Sancy und seventeen other large diamonds to Louis Fourteenth. In 1791, der vas an inventory of ze French crown jewels und Sancy vas

---

* It is interesting to note that Dr. Bauer later, in 1896, published a book called *Precious Stones*. It was translated and published in England around 1903 and is considered one of the most comprehensive studies of gems ever published.

valued at one million francs. During ze revolution it vas stolen along mitt ze Regent und vas not recovered. Den ze beauty showed up as ze property of ze Spanish crown und came into ze possession of Demidoff."

"It was not stolen from him by any chance?" asked Holmes.

"*Nein,* ze Sancy hass returned to ze land of its birth. It is now ze broberty of ze Maharajah of Patiala. I saw ze stone ven it vas disblayed at ze Paris Exhibition."

"I see," said Holmes and I could see that he was writing off the Sancy diamond in his mind.

"Could you," continued Holmes, "acquaint me with some diamonds that are less famous?"

"All ze great diamonds are vamous but I see vat you are zearching for. Ze Nassak iss not so vell-known, dough it is better dan eighty-nine carats. It came from ze temple of Siva in India und vas acqvired in 1818 by der East India Company."

Holmes appeared interested. "Where is this stone now?"

"Right here in England, Mr. Holmes. Ze Nassak vas bought for seventy-two hundred pounds by der London jeweler, Emmanuek, und vas den sold to ze Duke of Vesminster und it has been in his family ever since. The Nassak iss large but you know it's not just der carats vat iss important. Ze Star of Este is a little less dan twenty-six carats but absolutely flawless."

"Is its present whereabouts known?"

"Indeed. It iss ze broberty of ze ruling house of Austrian-Este. Den der iss ze Pasha of Egypt."

"Ah, have I heard of that stone?"

"Pozzibly. Forty carats. Octagonal. It vas bought by Ibraham, Viceroy of Egypt, for twenty-eight thousand pounds."

"And it is still in Egypt?" Holmes looked disappointed.

"If it vas not, I dink I vould haf heard."

"Doctor Bauer, can you think of any of the great diamonds that have vanished?"

"Ze truly famous stones don't get lost. Und dey cannot be dublicated. Paintings—dot iss somesing else. Paintings iss manmade. For years, der iss vispers about famous paintings. Are dey original or a copy? But diamonds iss made by nature. Von look und de expert knows if dey iss genuine."

"I see," said Holmes, despondently. "Well, Doctor, I am most grateful for your assistance in this matter."

"Somesing vispers to me dot I vass not so big a help. You know, Mr. Holmes, everybody likes to blay in ze ozzer man's back yard. It vass ze Pasha of Egypt dat you vas really interested in, *nicht var?*"

Holmes had the good grace to smile. "Doctor Bauer, you should have been a detective."

"Dot I vill leave in your cabable hands. Und I shall make inquiries about ze Pasha diamond for you, Mr. Holmes."

The famous gem expert took his leave at this point, allowing Holmes to regard me with a wry expression.

"You see, ol' chap, the danger of becoming intrigued with a theory."

"But Barker did say *Pasha* before he died. Jonathan Wild was deeply interested in that one particular stone. Possibly, Doctor Bauer will uncover some additional information concerning it."

Holmes brightened up a bit at my thought and so the matter rested for a time. As he later confessed, he became convinced that he was following a will-o'-the-wisp with his diamond idea and he forced himself to concentrate on the irritating sifting of information in search of a pattern that would provide illumination regarding the matter of the Golden Bird. That he had the haunts of Chu San Fu watched, I am sure. Wakefield Orloff was a frequent visitor, a sure sign that Mycroft Holmes's finger was still in the pie. Nothing was heard concerning the shadowy international financier, Basil Selkirk. The entire machinery of plot and counterplot seemed to grind to an unwieldy halt. Holmes was in and out of 221B Baker Street at all hours and it was obvious that

186

he was annoyed with the lack of progress. As was his custom at times like this, he became secretive and did not communicate his latest theories, if he had any.

It was an afternoon, later in the week, that my friend returned to our lodging, his thin face more drawn than usual. I worried about his highly nervous state and not for the first time, having seen him drive himself unceasingly to the verge of absolute collapse and then, upon the solving of a case, stage a physical recovery that bordered on the medically impossible.

Without a word, he disappeared into his bedchamber, returning after a short period clad in his dressing gown and slippers. Seated in his favorite chair, he brooded in silence. I advanced no greeting, nor posed any questions, feeling that should he wish the comfort of communication it would be best to let him instigate it.

After another ten minutes, a long sigh escaped him and he rose in search of his pipe.

"Forgive me, Watson, but I have been much preoccupied of late."

"Small wonder," I stated, and secretly congratulated myself on having said nothing.

Holmes fished in the toe of the Persian slipper for his shag and soon there were clouds of acrid smoke.

"This matter of the statue has provided nothing but a series of dead ends," he said, bitterly.

"I thought you were on to something with that idea of the Pasha of Egypt diamond."

"As did I. The devilish thing about it is that I keep returning to that theory. Common sense finally led me to some digging into Oriental life. Did you know, old friend, that in the Chinese calendar this is the year of the diamond?"

"I say," I exclaimed, laying aside my paper, "that must provide some germ of a motive though I cannot think what."

"I can," said Holmes, and then, in keeping with a most frustrating habit of his, let the matter drop. Before

187

I could pose a question to explore this more thoroughly, he was off on another tangent.

"There is a line of inquiry which I have pursued that may pay off. I have a message that Orloff will be with us shortly and I trust that the news he brings will be of benefit."

Again the sleuth lapsed into silence and I consoled myself that the security agent would soon break it.

On the stroke of six, Wakerfield Orloff tapped on our door. Orloff was one of the very few allowed immediate access to Holmes at any time. While it was most frequently my chore to answer the door, this time Holmes sprang to his feet and opened our portal anxiously to usher the agent within.

Orloff's slightly moon-shaped face was completely impassive as he removed his lethal bowler hat with its steel-lined brim and placed it on an end table within easy reach.

"Well, man?" questioned Holmes, impatiently.

My friend's high-strung manner did not phase Orloff in the least, but then what would?

"We were able to secure the best man on metals available. His tests were time-consuming, but necessarily so. As to his findings, they will intrigue you. The Golden Bird is not in its original state."

"Ah," said Holmes, with gratification. He threw me a sharp glance. "No matter what happens now, Watson, we were right." His hawklike visage returned eagerly to Orloff.

"Our man," continued the security agent, "established that a portion of the base of the statue is of a gold of a different quality and age than that of the rest of the statue."

"Conclusion?" There was a tight smile on Holmes's lips.

"A large part of the base had been hollowed out as a depository for something. No indication as to what the object was but our man is certain that it was removed recently. The filler gold used to solidify the statue's base was poured not long ago."

"Selkirk," stated Holmes with conviction.

"Why him?" Orloff and I asked together.

"It all fits. Finally, we are dredging some sense from this morass. It is the diamond theory, of course. I'm obsessed with it but there does not seem to be any other logical explanation. Here are the facts." Holmes centered on Orloff for a moment. "In the Chinese calendar, this is the year of the diamond. Now, Chu San Fu's daughter is to be wed to Maurice Rothfils of the famous banking family. In the normal order of things, she will be presented at court."

I realized my head was nodding as I recalled the meeting with MacDonald some time back and his mention of this coming social event.

Holmes continued, savoring the words. I could see that his mind, at last, had a clue as to how to fit the pieces together. "The Chinese are renowned for their pride."

"They are not alone in that," I blurted, without thinking.

"But they make a fetish of it . . . a religion. Face is everything. What would a modern-day bandit like Chu San Fu desire above all things?" Holmes chose to answer his own question. "His daughter, presented to Her Majesty, wearing a gem that need not take second place to the crown jewels of England. That is why he's risked his men recklessly in an attempt to secure the Golden Bird. Somehow he knew that there was a famous diamond inside it."

"But why a diamond?" questioned Orloff. "I will agree that whatever was concealed within the statue figures to be a gem. Size alone narrows the choice to that. But why not a ruby? An emerald?"

"Because there are so few famous rubies or emeralds or pearls for that matter. Were this long-concealed treasure one of those stones we could probably name it now. But there are many famous diamonds and we seek a particular one. The daughter of Chu San Fu must be able to wear it openly. Therefore, it cannot be a stolen one. The solution to this entire matter is but a hair's breadth away. Somewhere there is recorded history of a unique diamond that will fit our requirements. Now I must find out its name."

"Would you wish to speak to Doctor Bauer again?" asked Orloff.

"Let me do some preliminary research first. As the eminent expert remarked in this very room: 'Diamonds are a big field.' I must narrow down the possibilities or I will but waste his time."

Orloff was not satisfied. "But what about Chu San Fu?"

"The Oriental has ceased to be a problem. Now we know what he is after or soon will. Basil Selkirk is the stumbling block."

Events proved Holmes wrong on both counts.

18

The Taking and the Rescue

The following morning, I had some medical calls to make. Again, Holmes had risen in advance of me or possibly he had never gone to bed. His manner never indicated whether he had slept or not. But somebody, and I suspected Billy, had been busy. Holmes was seated in his chair adjacent to the fireplace deep in a book and the desk had a number of unfamiliar volumes scattered on it, several open.

"What have we here?" I said, indicating the books.

"Research, Watson." Holmes's irritated and frustrated manner had disappeared. He was hot on the scent again and the fact delighted him. "Works by such experts on diamonds as Jean Baptiste Tavernier and our own Edwin Streeter. Benvenuto Cellini wrote some interesting comments on diamonds. Some scholarly work on social life by Capefigue and Brantome are also revealing."

"Good heavens!" I said with a rueful smile. "We are most often knee-deep in your criminal files and now we are inundated by books on diamonds."

"A momentary inconvenience, Watson."

"Have you discovered anything?"

"As yet, no. But I will. Once one knows what one looks for, the job becomes easier. Of course, we do have a last resort." I gazed at Holmes blankly, so he continued. "A cablegram from Berlin informs me that our client, Vasil D'Anglas, will be in London in two

191

days. Surely you realize, ol' fellow, that he knows the secret that was concealed in the Golden Bird."

"Why not just ask him, Holmes?"

"Will he give a truthful answer?" The sleuth laid his book aside. "Besides, he is a client. *We* must inform *him,* not the reverse."

Before I could think of a suitable retort to this, Holmes shifted subjects again.

"You know, this whole matter does present a most inventive idea. A diamond of great value is concealed. Not in some object which might be mislaid or lost. No indeed, but in an object of considerable worth itself. The greater treasure is secreted within the lesser. I cannot recall of a similar situation. Fascinating!"

Following my breakfast, I left Holmes pouring over aged books and descended to Baker Street to hail a hansom. There was one conveniently available and I stepped within it and was about to give the driver a Mayfair address. That is the last thing I remembered for a considerable period of time. . . .

When I awoke, I was lying on a pallet and someone was shaking my shoulders, forcing me back to consciousness. When my eyes became accustomed to the dim light, I was surprised at the gentleness of the hands that drew me erect and to my feet and half-supported me as a wave of nausea caused me to sag. The man was mountainous, with arms like the hawsers on a sea-going liner. His head was shaven and looked lost on a bull neck that tapered into the shoulders of a gorilla. His hamlike hands steadied me and he stood patiently till my brain stopped spinning. After a moment, he said, in a soft voice: "You come."

I had little choice in the matter.

There was the smell of earth and a musty odor that suggested the presence of the river, though the air was good and not damp. I was guided out of the small cubicle where I had evidently slept off some kind of narcotic that had rendered me instantly unconscious and helpless. There was a smarting in my eyes, but the nausea disappeared. I could not fathom what kind of drug had been used upon me.

We were in a narrow corridor with a dirt floor that slanted downward. There were doors on both sides at regular intervals marked with Chinese characters in a garish red paint. We came to a corner and a massive hand on my shoulder guided me to the left. I noted that I could have turned to the right as well. Wherever I was, and I suspected Limehouse, it was a labyrinth for the passageway split again before we came to a flight of rickety stairs. At the top, we passed through a curtain and into a sizeable room fitted with wooden benches and lit with gas jets. My guide extinguished the candle he had been carrying and unlocked a door on the far side of the room, gesturing for me to pass through it. The smell of incense assaulted my nostrils and I almost gagged, but the moment passed.

I was in a small room, its walls covered by tapestries. There were numerous candles and I noted the illuminating flame of each was motionless, like those in a church. It had a hypnotic effect and I jerked my head to dispell the sleepy passivity induced. My guide crossed the room and drew aside a tapestry exposing a heavily inlaid wood paneling. He scratched against it and the door behind us swung shut. I could hear its lock click. The huge Chinaman slid the wood panel to one side and indicated that I was to enter, so I did.

I was in another room of unknown size. Tapestries hung from ceiling to floor everywhere. Whether there were walls behind them or not was impossible to say. I heard the panel close behind me. I stood ten feet from a sizeable table that was elaborately carved. It could have been rosewood and it was oiled and polished to a subdued sheen. Behind it in a high-backed chair sat a Chinaman. His Oriental robe fit tightly around his neck and tended to slenderize his body. His face was a round yellow mask dominated by shrewd, slanting eyes. His head was domed and festooned with a few wisps of hair and from his chin hung two thin strands of white hair quite separated in the manner of some Chinese I had seen. While his white hair gave him a rather benevolent look, he did not seem of great age, though I would have been hard-pressed to guess his years. His fingers were long and the nails were of unusual length. One hand was gently stroking a small-headed animal with a pointed muzzle, short legs, and a long, nervous tail. It was regarding me with bright, inquisitive eyes. I looked at the small beast with familiarity. ___

"A very nice specimen. Herpestes, of course. His coat is in excellent condition."

The Chinaman was surprised. "You recognize a mongoose? But then, you were in service in India."

"I had that honor."

"Please be seated, Doctor Watson," he said, indicating a chair, placed lower than his and so arranged that the light in the room was centered on it. When one is associated for so long with a detective, one becomes conscious of these things. Also India, while not the Orient, makes one aware of the difference between East and West."

"I prefer to stand, a request which I am sure Chu San Fu would not deny a guest in his establishment."

The Chinaman was forced to look upward at me, a fact that nettled him though his impassive face gave no indication.

"I am sorry that you have been inconvenienced, Doctor Watson."

He was prepared to continue in the same vein but one cannot let that sort of thing go by. It is not the way the Empire survived.

"You are not sorry, at all. In fact you're not the least interested in me. My abduction by your hirelings was for the sole purpose of supplying a tool to be used against Mr. Sherlock Holmes. You may find a sticky wicket there."

My interruption and, indeed, entire manner was vexing to the man and he bit his lips in annoyance, regretting the act immediately. I shifted my position a bit to

194

one side, forcing him to look in a new direction and, since I had moved nearer to his desk, he had to look upward even more. Chu San Fu continued to stroke his mongoose, but I noted that his other hand was near a small gong on his desk. A quick flick of his really absurd fingernails would sound an alert to the giant on the other side of the wooden panel or other henchmen lurking behind the tapestries. I shook my head slightly.

"Really, sir, I am considerably disappointed."

His eyes widened, indicating that I still had him off balance. "You are disappointed in being here, of course, but . . ."

"Piffle!" I said, quickly. "I might just as well have been coshed by a ruffian or bagged, which is an expedience of the American underworld. In any case, here I stand and no doubt you have an emissary even now contacting Holmes with dire threats regarding my safety. 'Tis kidnaping, no more than that, a device of the criminally minded."

The Chinaman could not tolerate the position he was in and rose, with an attempt at dignity, so that his face was on the same level as my own.

"Doctor Watson, as you have anticipated, you are being used as barter in a trade which I will propose to Mr. Holmes. Your stay in my—ah—establishment—may be for some time. Holmes is not without resources and he may delay the exchange by use of subterfuge. There is not reason that your sojourn should not be pleasant."

Suddenly, he clapped his hands and a portion of one of the hangings was raised. Two exquisite Chinese girls stepped into the room. They could not have been more than sixteen with smooth oval faces and docile almond eyes. Their robes were of a tighter fit than is common, enhancing slim, nubile forms.

"Good food and spirits and companionship can help while away the hours, Doctor."

This charlatan had the effrontery to almost leer at me, as though we two men of the world understood such things. I drew myself up with an expression of haughty disdain.

"Sir, it is plain that we are wasting time. You would, no doubt, like to hear my views as to what Mr. Holmes has discovered and what his next steps might be. After my return, that is. If I return," I added, before he could make that obvious comment.

"Now, really," I continued, before he could regain the initiative, "what would I, who am no more than a biographer, know of the workings of the greatest mind in England. If I did, do you honestly believe that I would reveal anything to you?" I tried to infuse that last statement with sufficient scorn. "This is England, sir. Here, we are made of sterner stuff."

Chu San Fu angrily clapped his hands and the two girls disappeared from view. How many other followers were lurking within earshot I shall never know but the Oriental looked as though he wished no one had been present during our interchange. He turned his back on me for a moment and I could see he was breathing deeply. Then he flicked a finger at the small gong on his desk and there was a treble-sounding chime. Immediately, the panel through which I had entered slid open. My giant escort stood in the entrance with his bulging arms folded over his massive chest. Chu San Fu turned back toward me.

"You shall return to your place of confinement and we will see what Mr. Holmes's next move will be."

"Whatever it is," I replied, with considerable bravado, "it will entail the element of surprise."

As I began to retrace my steps, I noted a naked expression of worry in the Chinaman's eyes. Holmes had been right. Chu San Fu was a planner and a departure from the norm had thrown him off guard. I positively swaggered from the room.

My huge guardian escorted me back through the maze of underground passageways. It seemed that we followed the same route we had traversed before and I was struck again by the idea that this headquarters of

the Oriental criminal was nothing more than a miniature underground city. Other humans were present. I
could sense it, but we saw no one as we trod the dirt
flooring back to the cubicle in which I had awakened.
All the tunnels must have required the labor of large
numbers of people and I wondered how the excavated
dirt was disposed of. The thought that Chu San Fu
might have made use of an abandoned spur of the underground crossed my mind and I made note to mention it to Holmes as a possible clue to the whereabouts
of this hideaway.

My captor waited till I had seated myself in the cubicle and I sensed that he would assume guard duties outside my tiny prison with the stoic patience of an Oriental. Suddenly, I thought of the cellar at 221B Baker
Street and a huge Chinaman being disposed of by
Wakefield Orloff.

"You have a brother?" I asked, as my jailer prepared
to leave.

Unwinking amber eyes regarded me and his shaved
bullet head moved in a slight nod.

"He is quite all right. In good hands."

It may have been my imagination but it seemed the
amber eyes softened. Again, the giant turned to leave.
Before closing the door to my room, he glanced inside
again. "You all light?"

I nodded that I was. The door closed. A small candle
illuminated my limited quarters. Outside the door, I
heard the lock being engaged. Slim Gilligan could have
opened that lock in less than a minute. The door
seemed sufficiently flimsy that even I could have executed an escape. However, I could certainly not get free
of my massive guard so I abandoned any plans of
freeing myself.

Had I been privy to certain beliefs of India, I might
have passed the time contemplating my navel. Instead, I
thought back on the strange trail of the Golden Bird.
Obviously, Chu San Fu expected to barter me for the
Bird. Actually, I was not overconcerned about the situ-

ation, knowing that Holmes could surrender the statue without any great loss. The treasure it had conceleaed was no longer there. Comforted by the thought that I had not placed my friend in too difficult a position, I fell off to sleep. . . .

The sound of the door being opened roused me after a period. With the complete lack of windows and nothing but artificial light, I had no idea of the time. My amber-eyed jailer stood within the door as I rose to my feet, rubbing sleep from my eyes. Also present was a scrawny little yellow man with a close-fitting black cap set directly on the middle of his head. He had a blue coat buttoned from neck to belt-line and loose-fitting pants. He shuffled into the room in slippers, a black silk sash in his hands.

For a moment, I envisioned a professional strangler, but he revealed a toothless grin and indicated for me to turn around. As he slipped the sash over my eyes, I suppressed an indication of relief with difficulty. My wrists were secured in front of me with a thin cord that felt no larger than string. However, it held me firmly and I could detect the odor of hemp. I was then led from the room.

Bound and blindfolded, my journey can only be recounted via sound and conjecture. I was led down corridors, up and down stairs and around corners, certainly no attempt to confuse me since I did not know where I was to start with. Another of many doors opened and I knew that I was in open air again. Now there was the smell and the sounds of the river, reaffirming my idea that Chu San Fu's lair was in Limehouse, though we could have been anywhere in the Thames estuary. Hands held me on either side. Something about the texture of the sleeve fabric led me to believe that my other attendants had been replaced. Certainly, my giant friend was no longer with me. Neither of the hands on my arms could approach his in size. Then I was maneuvered into a conveyance that had to be a hansom. As it assumed motion, I tried to keep alert to any impressions

I might get, but could make little of our trip. I judged that we progressed for at least a half-hour with no more than one or two stops.

The sound of companion traffic seemed to increase. At one point, I was sure we crossed a bridge. Then the hansom came to a halt. There was the clatter of a dray, the sound of voices and close by I heard an internal combustion engine of some kind come to life. I opened my mouth to make a comment and a thin palm instantly covered it. A voice, not Oriental, cautioned me to remain quiet, and the manner was authoritative enough to encourage me to comply. Suddenly, the horse of our cab was gigged into action and we were in motion again. Our speed increased and, suddenly, the others who shared the hansom with me changed position. I was pushed to one side so that I was adjacent to the window of the cab. The blindfold was removed from my eyes.

The first sight was of another hansom progressing alongside and there was Holmes looking right at me with, I'm happy to say, an expression of intense relief. His eyes shifted to my captors, two in number I noted, and my friend nodded, seemingly a signal of agreement. I spied the coachman of Holmes's hansom, recognizing the form of Wakefield Orloff. Suddenly, I pictured the security agent jumping from cab to cab and disposing of those around me in jig time, something he was completely capable of doing. However, an agreement must have been reached and it seemed the terms were being mutually honored.

Orloff swung the hansom he was guiding closer to the one I was in and Holmes reached out with his long and wiry arm and passed an object to the outstretched hand of one of my captors—a small, dark man with a Balkan face. This Occidental—his companion was Western as well—took the object within our cab and removed the cloth bag that enveloped it, revealing the Golden Bird. He nodded to his companion who rapped on the roof of the hansom, which drew to a stop as did the one containing Holmes. I was urged from the hansom, which immediately took off to vanish in the traffic of the Strand. I scrambled into the adjacent hansom and leaned back in the seat with a sigh.

"My good Watson, you are all right, I trust?"

"Quite," I replied. "Actually, they treated me with considerable care."

Holmes's grunt had a tinge of menace. "I made it clear that if any harm befell you I would haunt their footsteps through eternity, if necessary."

He had a long-bladed knife in his hands with which he severed the cord binding my wrists and I was glad to massage circulation back into them.

"I cost you the statue," I began, in an apologetic manner.

"Purely a gesture, though Chu San Fu does not know this as yet. The Golden Bird will be returned to us shortly. I have plans regarding that. The important thing is that you are back, sound of mind and limb. What actually happened, ol' friend?"

As Orloff guided the vehicle back to Baker Street, I related my experiences and I have seldom heard my friend laugh so heartily as when I described my encounter with the Oriental criminal.

"Capital! Capital! I shall recommend a study of criminal psychology for Scotland Yard with you as dean, good Watson. No doubt, the Chinaman expected you to be frightened, or awed. That was his first surprise. Then he chose to appeal to your weaknesses to learn of my plans and to glean what knowledge he could of his burglar squad that has disappeared. Faced with an indignant and scornful doctor and threatened with a loss of face, he had to pause and regroup. The moment his emissary approached me, I pressed for a rapid exchange to get you out of the bounder's clutches. The statue was what he was after and since I agreed to the exchange plan on the spot, he jumped at the chance. When Chu San Fu discovers that the Golden Bird will not hatch a diamond for him, he will regret allowing himself to be pressed into rapid action. In his own heart, he will really lose face, a situation which we can exploit to the fullest."

19

The Revelations of the Royal Jeweler

It was late afternoon and I was most pleasantly ensonced in our Baker Street sitting room. Mrs. Hudson had clucked over my return insisting that a good meal was an absolute necessity. Since there were a number of guests, the dear woman ended up providing quite a spread, but she magically produced half a baked ham, a goodly portion of cold roast beef, cold cuts and even some *paté-de-foie-gras*-pie. Having taken a welcome bath, I made inroads on the provendor with some gusto, washing it down with good and heady stout.

Alec MacDonald accepted some of our best Irish whiskey for medicinal purposes. Both Holmes and Wakefield Orloff fancied an excellent vintage burgundy that I had chanced upon the year previous while Slim Gilligan was satisfied with a flagon of ale. The way the cracksman applied himself to the *paté-de-foie-gras*-pie made Holmes wince. I noted that my friend secured a goodly wedge for himself while he was still able to.

With so much criminological talent present, there had to be a council of war. However, the speculative and questioning nature of previous meetings was singularly absent. Action was the order of the day and firm convictions had supplanted tentative attitudes.

Possibly I have misrepresented the situation. Those allies of Holmes present were very definite in their thoughts. It was Holmes, the hero of so many *tour de force* solutions, who sounded the only questioning note.

"Gentlemen, I am much in your debt for recent assistance." Standing by the mantle, his noble head turned toward Inspector MacDonald. "The presence of any constables during the hansom exchange might well have panicked the forces of evil and our good Watson might not be with us now." His eyes swiveled to Gilligan and Orloff. "While there was reason to suspect the recovery of Watson would go smoothly, I felt more in command of the situation with you, Orloff, disguised as the cabbie and Slim curled up in the luggage compartment."

I coughed over a mouthful of stout, this being my first intimation that Slim Gilligan had been a concealed ace up Holmes's sleeve. My friend's delivery became more measured, as though his words were unpalatable.

"I have been committed to this affair from the start since I made a pledge to a now-departed friend. With the taking of Watson, another motive has insinuated itself as regards my involvement. Chu San Fu cannot be allowed to get away with such actions, as fruitless as they will prove. I intend to break him by one means or another and fulfill my promise to Nils Lindquist as well. However, to date there has been an expenditure of time and effort on the part of the authorities as well as a certain organization with which Mr. Orloff is associated. I cannot continue to impose on the facilities of others relative to what has become a personal vendetta."

Holmes might have elaborated on this, but he did not get the chance. MacDonald cut in. "I'll speak for the Yard, Mr. Holmes, to set the matter straight. I anticipated a bit of resistance from the Commissioner about this matter. There's not much on the books and it has been hangin' fire for some time even though we've been after Chu San Fu for years. However, there's a new scent in the air. Somehow, knowledge of the kidnaping of Doctor Watson's got round. How I dinna ken for I've not bruited it about. But there's a lot of angry men at New Scotland Yard and the Commissioner's one of 'em. Count us in, Mr. Holmes—all the way."

"Allow me to endorse those words," said Wakefield Orloff. "In addition, certain august personages are much concerned with the pending marriage of the Chinese princess and Maurice Rothfils. We cannot yet prove that she is the daughter of Chu San Fu even though our men in Hong Kong and Singapore are convinced. If they are right, this marriage will extend the cloak of respectability to areas not fancied by my superiors. This matter warrants a *carte blanche* on whatever assistance my organization can supply." His next words shook me. "Besides, I also have a personal axe to grind."

He had to be referring to me and I could not believe my ears. Save for infrequent flashes of warmth in his manner toward Sherlock Holmes, the security agent had always been as devoid of sentiment or emotion as a king cobra. I realized that were I down to my last farthing, I could still consider myself a man of means. Wealth cannot be counted in worldly goods alone. In addition, I was provided with the intense pleasure of seeing the super sleuth of Baker Street actually appear embarrassed. During our long association I could count the number of times that had happened on one hand and have two fingers left over. All in all, it had been quite a day.

Perhaps Holmes's eyes were slightly misty, I cannot be sure. In any case, he cleared his throat, took a sip of his burgundy, and then a lifetime of training took over. The cold, logical analyst was present again as his sword of vengeance was unsheathed.

"As Watson knows, I have been searching the field of famous diamonds and have narrowed down my search. Is Doctor Max Bauer still in England?" Holmes addressed this question to Wakefield Orloff.

"He has returned to Germany but the royal jeweler, Edwin Streeter, is back in London."

"I had the pleasure of reading parts of his well-known book. An appointment with the gentleman would be of assistance."

Orloff indicated with a nod that the matter would be arranged.

"I need the name of the diamond, the identity of the gem that was concealed in the Golden Bird. That is the password to open closed gates. Basil Selkirk has the stone, I'm sure of it. But the old rogue is a bit of a romanticist and I might get it from him. I also need the statue, but Chu San Fu is going to provide that. I intend to write him a letter saying that if he wishes the gem, he will have to contact me to arrange for a fee to recover it. I will also demand a return of the Bird."

There was a rare twinkle in the deep-set eyes of Inspector MacDonald. "You intend to take on the Chink as a client?"

"I intend to recover the diamond," said Holmes, and let it drop at that. He continued looking at MacDonald. "I'll want to be sure that my letter reaches Chu San Fu, and promptly, before he puts further plans into action."

Slim Gilligan broke a long silence. "I'll take the *billet doux*, Guv. Sydney Sid runs the biggest gin hall and slap-bang shop in Limehouse. 'E'll see that Chu gets yer message."

Holmes seemed satisfied. "Three men know the story of the Golden Bird. Basil Selkirk, Chu San Fu, and my client, D'Anglas. If fortune smiles, I shall be able to deal with all three of them."

During the war council and, indeed, thereafter, I must confess that I felt something of the center of attraction. When one is associated with a great mind like Holmes, one becomes acutely conscious of limitations. I knew full well that mine was, and always had been, the role of associate, biographer, friend. In the amazing number of cases dealt with by Sherlock Holmes, I rarely played a major role. My friend had often stated that a thought or comment of mine had sparked his brilliant intellect to follow the correct road, but that generous admission on his part was certainly open to question.

On this particular day, and following ones, I was treated to the revelation that when one associates with greatness there are attendant rewards. Baker Street residents, if they were alert enough to take note, must have felt that the area anticipated a major outbreak of crime. Constables were everywhere. Our placid backwater in the great metropolis was blanketed with representatives of the law. Obviously, Alec MacDonald was taking no chances that I might again be spirited away by minions of the lawless, or Holmes either. In times past, the world's only consulting detective had chafed at the presence of sinews of the law, but he took these protective measures in good grace. My friend seemed to consider Chu San Fu and his extensive criminal organization as a snake whose fangs had been removed. Why he adopted this casual atitude I could not fathom.

It was the following morning that we were honored by a visit of the royal jeweler, Edwin Streeter. He was a tidy man of medium size with keen eyes and a business-like manner. Obviously, he had been informed by Wakefield Orloff that the great detective required his knowledge of famous gems to solve a case of importance. He did not impress me as a waster of time.

"Tell me, Mr. Holmes, in what area does your interest lie?" he asked, immediately, after introductions. "Mr. Orloff indicated that it is diamonds that have caught your fancy."

"A large field, as Doctor Bauer informed me. However . . ."

Our visitor bristled. "If you have consulted with Bauer, you have little need of me, sir. He is one of the foremost authorities in the world."

"As you are. I have read your *Precious Stones and Gems* with great interest. I consider any book that can intrigue and inform one who is not versed in the field has the quality of lasting greatness."

Streeter's brusque manner vanished. "You are most kind, Mr. Holmes. Though I would think that in your profession a knowledge of gems would be automatic."

"A surface knowledge," agreed Holmes. "I find the present problem far beyond my resources and am most grateful that the government has prevailed upon you to come to my assistance."

It crossed my mind that Holmes had put the gentleman in a bit of a bind. By linking Her Majesty's government and Streeter's expertise, and the need of same for an undisclosed reason, he had put the royal jeweler on the spot as far as cooperation was concerned. However, this was probably unnecessary. Speak to the expert of his field and he instantly opens his book of knowledge, if only to prove why he is an expert.

"I am much interested in a famous gem, one of undisputed quality, which has disappeared. Does this suggest something to you?"

Holmes's question undoubtedly intrigued the royal jeweler.

"Mr. Holmes, men have died for diamonds. Wars have been fought over diamonds. But very few of the great diamonds just disappear. There was a famous theft in 1792 of three of the crown jewels of France. One of them, the Regent, was recovered and later adorned the sword of Napoleon. It is in the Louvre. The second, the Sancy, was also recovered."

"Yes," commented Holmes. "I am familiar with that stone."

"The last of the trio was a rare blue diamond. It surfaced again, but it had been cut. The larger portion is now known as the Hope Diamond. It is in America. The smaller portion has been lost track of, but it would not be considered a major stone in any case."

Holmes mulled over the expert's words for a brief moment and then embarked on a different tack. "In my research in the field, I am confused on one point."

Streeter smiled. "Mr. Holmes, historic diamonds have been a favorite subject for writers for a century or more. So much has been written that what is truth and what is fiction is sometimes hard to determine."

"The Pasha of Egypt diamond came to my attention," said Holmes. "I note that it was sold to the Viceroy of Egypt."

Streeter was nodding. "Fetched a good price, too. A fine octagonal brilliant of forty carats."

"Yet I note a strange similarity relative to another gem, the Pigott Diamond." Holmes referred to a book open on the desk. "The Pigott Diamond was disposed of to Ali Pasha, the Viceroy of Egypt. All trace of this stone has since been lost and, according to reports, it has been destroyed."

Streeter almost bounced up and down in his chair. Obviously, Holmes had touched a nerve.

"That information is printed in several authoritative texts, but is incorrect. The confusion is due to names, Mr. Holmes. I might better say: titles. The Pasha of Egypt Diamond was, indeed, sold to Ibrahim, Viceroy of Egypt. He held the title of Ali Pasha. But the Pigott —that is another matter. Fortunately, sir, I happen to be the leading authority in the world on that stone."

"And many others as well," said Holmes, diplomatically. "But do tell us about the Pigott and the confusion in recognized texts on famous stones."

Streeter was delighted to comply. "The stone got its name from Lord George Pigot, twice Governor of Madras. Though his name has a single *t*, the diamond is known as the *Pigott* with a double *t*. But that is of scant interest. Lord Pigot received it as a gift from an Indian ruler in 1763. They did things rather in the grand manner in those days. The diamond has been described as anywhere from forty-five to eighty-five carats. In any case, Lord Pigot brought it to England and undoubtedly regretted it since he was plagued by ill fortune and died in prison. Later, his family put the diamond up as a prize in a lottery and it is sometimes referred to as the 'lottery diamond.' It was sold for a mere fraction of its worth—six thousand pounds—to Rundell and Bridge, the London Jewelers. They turned a nice profit by selling the diamond to Ali Pasha of Albania for one hundred and fifty thousand pounds."

"I see," said Holmes, "where the confusion lies. The title of Ali Pasha has thrown researchers off the track."

"Exactly," agreed Streeter. "The Albanian Ali Pasha was a ruler of some historical significance. Known as the tyrannical 'Lion of Janina,' he wielded such power that the Sultan of Turkey sent an emissary to bring him back to Constantinople to curb his excessive ambition. Ali Pasha resisted and there was an exchange and he was fatally wounded. The Lion of Janina requested permission to die in his own throne room, in his own fashion, and this wish was granted."

At this point in his narration, Streeter almost preened himself. "Now, Mr. Holmes, I can give you information that is not common knowledge at all. As the eighty-year-old Pasha lay dying, he summoned a trusted soldier of fortune, Captain D'Anglas . . ."

"D'Anglas?" I asked. Holmes looked at me with irritation and I subsided.

Streeter continued as though he had not heard me. "The Pasha ordered his aide to destroy his two most precious possessions: the Pigott Diamond and his wife, Vasilikee. Captain D'Anglas crushed the diamond before the Pasha's eyes and he died. According to legend, his wife was not killed by the French mercenary."

"You say 'according to legend,'" said Holmes, thoughtfully. "If the Pasha's wife survived, might not the diamond have as well?"

"This was in 1822, Mr. Holmes. Since that time there has been no trace of the Pigott."

At Streeter's mention of 1822, Holmes threw me a knowing glance. His eyes then returned to the crown jeweler.

"How is so much known about the stone?"

Streeter was amused by Holmes's question. "Man's obsession with great diamonds is nothing new, Mr. Holmes. The Pigott was well-known. Lord Pigot acquired it in 1763. He died in 1777 and his family disposed of it via the lottery in 1801. At one time it was owned by Madame Bonaparte, the mother of Napoleon. There is a model of the stone which was made here in

England and still exists. It was an oval-shaped gem of the finest quality."

As he had been recounting the history of this famous gem, Streeter had been observing Holmes's manner.

"Do I sense that this is the information you are searching for?" he asked.

"You have certainly opened up avenues of thought," replied the sleuth. "Let us pose a hypothetical situation. Let us say the Pigott still exists. Who would it belong to?"

"To whomever holds it in his hand, Mr. Holmes."

"But it would be recognized?"

"A stone of that quality could not be ignored. We are speaking of one of the great diamonds of the world. An expert would immediately identify it by its shape and size. But proving it is another thing. Why, sir, if you had it, you could wear it on your watch fob and no one could say you nay."

Holmes had secured the information he wished. Soon thereafter, the crown jeweler took his leave. Of course, I was bursting with ideas.

"I say, Holmes, you struck a rich vein there! And the name of the French mercenary in the employ of the Ali Pasha . . ."

"D'Anglas—the same name as our client." Holmes had the satisfied look of a cat who had consumed cream. "D'Anglas's grandfather served the Albanian but did not follow his dying orders. The Frenchman had the Pigott and the ruler's wife, Vasilikee, as well. They had to be in it together. Note our client's first name—Vasil, in memory of his grandmother. The conspirators secreted the diamond in the Golden Bird and gave out the word of its destruction. They planned to secure the statue later and retrieve the prize within, but the Bird eluded them. Somehow the story got out, for Jonathan Wild heard of it. Through him, Harry Hawker, as well. Since 1822, the Golden Bird has had a value far in excess of its original worth. It has been a loadstone, a magnet for all who knew its secret. Barker left us the clues, ol'

211

chap. First the year—1822. Then, recall that in the book on Jonathan Wild's career, Barker ran a line through the reference to the Pasha of Egypt diamond. I mistook it as underlining, but he meant that the mention of this famous gem was incorrect."

"How did Chu San Fu learn the secret of the diamond?"

"We may never know the answer to that. But observe that Basil Selkirk seized on the clue I gave him, the year of Ali Pasha's death and solved the mystery."

Holmes's recreation of events covering more than half a century was interrupted by Billy, who informed us that an Oriental gentleman requested a few moments of Mr. Holmes time.

My friend cocked an eye in my direction. "My letter to Chu San Fu has prompted a rapid response. Show the man up, Billy, by all means."

When the page boy ushered a squat Chinaman into our chambers, my manner was frigid indeed. Nor was my friend a model of hospitality.

"Ah, Mr. Holmes—my name is Loo Chang. I am a solicitor."

He passed the sleuth a business card, which Holmes dropped on the desk without looking at it. Chang bowed in my direction. He was quite short and somewhat overweight, which may have contributed to the perpetual sheen on his face. His mouth was drawn in a constant smile and I wondered, for no particular reason, if it was present when he slept.

"I am here, Mr. Holmes, representing a client."

"We can," said Holmes severely, "dispense with evasions. You have been instructed by Chu San Fu to contact me relative to a certain piece of property, which he is interested in."

The Oriental's hands were spread, palms up, as though to indicate that he carried no weapons. "I do not know the object involved but I am empowered to negotiate a fee for its recovery. My client is a most generous man and will pay one thousand pounds for its return."

Holmes sighed as though his patience was being sorely tried. "You client's generosity is imaginary. Ten percent is a standard fee for lesser talents than mine. The price is fifteen thousand pounds based on the last valuation of the object. The thousand pounds you mention is to be paid in advance to cover possible expenses."

Chang looked shocked. "My client did not anticipate . . ."

He was allowed to go no further. "I do not haggle in matters of this kind." Holmes's right hand indicated the door. "Begone!"

"But, Mr. Holmes."

"Out!"

The sheen on Chang's face was more evident. He fumbled in his coat pocket, extracting a bulky envelope. "I will leave this thousand pounds as a retainer, Mr. Holmes. If my client agrees to your terms, he will notify you."

Placing the envelope on the desk, Chang backed toward the door with short, rapid bows to Holmes and myself.

"I bid you good day, gentlemen."

"One moment," commanded Holmes, and Chang halted by the door. "When your client agrees in this arrangement, instruct him to return to me the statue. When he does so, six members of his organization will reappear."

"The statue will be in your hands within the hour," the lawyer said, with a defeated air and then departed in haste.

"Holmes," I said, as soon as the man was gone, "you don't intend to give the Pigott Diamond to Chu San Fu."

"I intend to break him," was Holmes's grim response.

He crossed to the window with rapid strides, peering through the drapes. What he saw seemed to give him satisfaction for he gave vent to a chuckle.

"Loo Chang is departing with Slippery Styles, the human shadow, on his trail. Sooner or later the solicitor will return to his office. 'Tis then that Silm Gilligan will enter the picture."

Noting my blank look, Holmes continued. "Both Alex MacDonald and Wakefield Orloff are very interested in the names, locations and income derived from Chu San Fu's various enterprises. The Chinaman is very businesslike and organized and there should be more revealing information in the files of his lawyer."

I did not question this matter, realizing that Holmes was taking full advantage of his unofficial status and following a line of investigation not open to the authorities.

Holmes reverted to the matter of the diamond.

"By now, Chu must realize that Basil Selkirk has the stone. Rather than have him attack Selkirk's residence or involve himself in some similar skullduggery, it is best to let him think I'll secure the diamond. Besides, with Vasil D'Anglas arriving tomorrow from Berlin, I need the statue. That was our original commission, if you recall."

"But D'Anglas will expect the diamond to be in the statue. He, of all people, knows the secret of the Golden Bird."

"We have a touchy point there, Watson. The last legal owner of the gem died sixty years ago. Who does own it?"

"Streeter was definite on that point. The possesser in this case, Selkirk, is the owner."

"But we know something that the crown jeweler did not. My theory is that D'Anglas's grandfather secreted the stone and married Vasilikee, Ali Pasha's wife. Theoretically, Vasilikee owned the stone upon the death of her husband, the Lion of Janina. Which makes our client, Vasil D'Anglas, the man with the best claim on the gem."

"We are stretching things a bit, are we not?"

"My blushes, Watson. The fact is that I was commis-

214

sioned to secure the Golden Bird at the time when the diamond was still concealed within it. Therefore, I intend to honor the interests of our first client, Vasil D'Anglas."

"But how do you hope to get the diamond from Basil Selkirk?"

"I really don't know," said Holmes, to my surprise. "That could well be a two-pipe problem, at least."

As it happened, I was never to learn what plans Holmes made to separate the eccentric millionaire from the Pigott Diamond, for the following morning we received startling news indeed.

20

The Deadman's Code

Holmes and I had just disposed of a fullsome breakfast when there was a light tap on our door.

"Come in, Billy," said Holmes. He had the uncanny ability to hear and identify any footfalls on the seventeen steps leading to our first-floor chambers.

The page boy entered with an envelope in his hand, which he gave to Holmes.

"This 'ere just arrived, sir, by special messenger. 'E's waitin' downstairs in case there is a response."

Holmes tore open the envelope eagerly. It contained a letter in longhand and an additional sheet of stationery, which I noted was machine-written. This was what Holmes glanced at first and his lips pursed in a soundless whistle. He passed the typed sheet to me and began to read the rest of the communiqué.

The typewritten message was terse and shocking.

Basil Selkirk died in his sleep last night. The enclosed is being rushed to you to comply with specific instructions given to me by the deceased. I am further instructed to cooperate with you to any extent you may require. Please advise if I can be of assistance.

Cedric Falmouth,
Personal Secretary to Mr. Selkirk

"The blond youngish man," I said, my mind going back to our visit to the castle of the eccentric millionaire.

Holmes grunted, his eyes devouring words. Then he leaned back for a moment in thought.

"Billy," he said, finally, "inform the messenger to stand by until I reach a decision."

"Right you are, Mr. 'Olmes." The page boy was gone.

"Let me read this to you, Watson. As you may have guessed, it was written by Basil Selkirk in a reasonably steady hand." He held the expensive stationery closer to his eyes to study the ink. "Quite recently, I would say. Surely within the week . . .

My dear Mr. Holmes:

Though it may not have been your intent, you did bring joy into the dull life of an aged man. Even more important, you gave me, in these last days, for the sands are running out, a moment of triumph. It was your reference to the year of 1822 that gave me the clue that unraveled the mystery of the Golden Bird. During this final period, I have been able to feast my eyes on the most unique gem in history—a famous diamond that, officially, does not exist, but we know better, do we not? By this time, you have arrived at the truth regarding the Pigott Diamond. Alas, the cold that lurks within my withered shell is increasing and I foresee a lengthy passage to a land where I cannot take my treasure with me. Or anything else, for that matter, save a reputation that bodes ill for my reception beyond the pale. Therefore, sir, I leave the Pigott to you, but it cannot be as easy as that. You must work a bit for it though my little riddle is not so baffling that it will provide puzzlement for long. When this reaches you, I shall not be able to bid you Godspeed in person. Allow me to do so now . . .

Basil Selkirk

I crossed to stand behind Holmes and gaze at the letter and the last message of that chilling, yet strangely ingratiating, man.

C

QMKTXYN T

H

QMQE

KSOTEET

"Why, it is but gibberish," I said instinctively, but my words had a hollow ring as I said them. Selkirk would not have indulged in anything meaningless. I viewed the three lines of letters with narrowed eyes and tried to apply some reason to the riddle.

"Holmes, do the *C* and *H* have any significance?"

"Obviously separated from the body of the message for some reason. Selkirk expected me to solve this cipher. Therefore, it is not keyed to a prearranged text."

I was completely at sea at this point but, fortunately, Holmes explained his reasoning.

"As an instance, *Q* being the seventeeth letter in the alphabet and the first letter of the cipher might refer to the seventeenth word on the first page of a well-known novel. Or not so well-known for that matter. *N* being the thirteenth letter could refer to the thirteenth word on the second page of the same book and so forth. But such a cipher is dependent on a text known by the sender and receiver, not the case in this instance. Here we have a substitution cipher, I'm sure."

His eyes devouring the message, Holmes continued as though as talking to himself. "As a simple example, a reversal of the alphabet. Instead of an *A*, one uses *Z* while *B* becomes *Y*, and so forth. Usually, these are interesting little problems which intrigue the mind but seldom fatigue it. Here I sense difficulties. In the three lines of Selkirk's message, there are twenty-one letters. The letter *E* is by far the most commonly used in the English alphabet. But note, we have *E* used three times in the message. T is the next most common to our alphabet and it is used four times. In solving a substitution cipher, the basic step is to select the letter used most often and assume that it is E. The next most often used becomes T, the third A, and the fourth, O, and so on. In this case, the two most common alphabetic letters are the most-used in the body of the message. See also that Q is used three times while M and K occur twice. The other letters appear but once."

"Could not the C and H, positioned as they are, offer some clue?" I asked.

"I would think so. Give me but a moment."

Leaving Holmes deep in thought, I withdrew to the couch. Though confused myself, I had no doubt my friend would come up with something and soon. After all, he had authored a monograph on secret writings in which he analyzed 160 separate ciphers.

Suddenly, Holmes rose to his feet. "It won't do, Watson."

There was a tinge of annoyance in his voice and he crossed to the door and summoned Billy, instructing the page boy to inform the waiting messenger that we were on our way to St. Aubrey as rapidly as possible.

"There is something missing," he said, reentering our chambers. "A vital clue must be secured."

A short time later, we were on our way to St. Pancreas station where we boarded the first train stopping at the quiet hamlet of St. Aubrey. During our short journey, Holmes, to my delight, felt prompted to discuss methods.

"When one is faced with a problem, as we are, it is advantageous to divine another's thoughts. Therefore, I place myself in the late Basil Selkirk's situation. He has acquired the collector's dream, a famous gem and the right of ownership. But he has no desire to flaunt his possesion for death is imminent. He decides to leave the stone to the one who was instrumental in his finding it. To me. But how can he be sure I will get it? Advanced years tend to produce a distrust of everyone. Possibly an eccentricity of age or perhaps the fruits of long experience. He decides to send the location of the diamond in a cipher, banking that I will be able to break it."

"A fine summation of Basil Selkirk's final thoughts," I said, "but what do they suggest?"

"An association. Something in his immediate surroundings that Selkirk seized on as the key to the cipher he sent me."

A carriage awaited our arrival at St. Aubrey and it whisked us out of town and to the castle of the financier. The blond secretary greeted us with a harrassed manner and turned us over to a solemn-faced butler with instructions to assist us in any way. There was an air of secrecy everywhere and I later learned that Selkirk's death was not being revealed immediately for fear of the effect of the news on the financial markets of the world.

Holmes expressed the desire to view the room where the death had occurred and the butler, Meers, led us to Selkirk's study where he had breathed his last.

The room had a "much-used" feeling. There were well-filled bookshelves, a large teak desk, and a fieldstone fireplace with an ornate mantle, also of teak. The walls were wood-paneled and the furniture was heavily carved, highly polished, early Victorian. On one wall were four canvases of moderate size. Holmes gazed at these oils casually and a puzzlement crept into his eyes. The butler was standing by the door, awaiting instructions and Holmes turned toward him.

"Meers?"

"Yes, Mr. Holmes, sir?"

"These four paintings, I don't seem to recognize them."

"Doubtful that you would, sir. The artist was not illustrious, but Mr. Selkirk fancied them."

The great sleuth crossed to the wall and looked at the oils closely. Attuned to his moods for so long, it seemed to me that Holmes's features sharpened and that predatory look was upon him of a sudden. Not for the first time I noted that, on occasion, my intimate friend resembled a bird of prey.

"That will be all, Meers."

"Very good, sir."

As the butler disappeared, Holmes looked at me with that twisted half-smile that I knew sprang from self-reproach.

"Oh, what a fool am I!" he said.

Holmes was never quite satisfied. When a solution was in his grasp, and from experience I knew that it was, he most frequently regretted not having arrived at it sooner. The life of a perfectionist is not an easy one.

"I had but to consider the career of Basil Selkirk," he continued. "He was infatuated with communications. His business success was based on information accurately and rapidly transmitted. How reasonable that he would fancy four paintings by Samuel Morse."

"I never heard of him."

"As an artist, I daresay you haven't. Morse was an art student in England and, later, Professor of Art at the University of the City of New York. He was an American, you see. After devoting the early part of his life to painting, he realized that fame would never be his in the world of art so he applied his energies to other things. In 1844, the first message was sent by wireless telegraphy, which he invented."

"Most interesting," I commented, "but the association with our missing diamond eludes me."

"Because I have not touched on the relevant matter. The former artist also invented a telegraphic code based on dots and dashes, which bears his name. An interesting feature of the Morse code is that eleven letters of the alphabet have opposites. As an instance, the distress signal given at sea."

"S.O.S." was my automatic response.

"In Morse, the letter *S* consists of three dots or short sounds. The letter *O* is its opposite, being three dashes or longer sounds. Let me make this perfectly clear,

Watson. What are the opening notes of Beethoven's Fifth Symphony?"

"Dot . . . dot . . . dot . . . daaaaah," I hummed quickly. I had not attended all those concerts at Albert Hall and elsewhere with my friend for nothing.

"You have just signaled the letter *V*, old fellow. Three dots followed by a dash. The opposite of *V* is *B*, by the way."

"Wait," I said, excitedly. "The Selkirk cipher uses opposites based on the Morse code."

"Exactly," replied Holmes, seating himself at the desk and extracting the financier's letter from his pocket. I fiddled in my coat for a pencil and found one, handing it to him.

"Now," continued the detective, "the first line reads: *Q-M-K-T-X-Y-N-C-T.*"

"With the *C* off line."

"The very thing that might have alerted me. In Morse, the letters *C, H, J,* and *Z* have no opposites. Therefore, in this first line, I assume *C* is legitimate as well as the *H* in the second line. Now the opposite of *Q* is *F*. *M* becomes *I*, *K* gives us *R*, and *T* indicates *E*. *X* is *P*, *Y* is *L*, *N* represents *A*, the *C* is natural with *T* again indicating *E*. Watson, the first word is fireplace."

As my eyes swiveled to the fieldstone fireplace in the very room we occupied, Holmes worked out the next two lines in jig time and then regarded me triumphantly.

"Fireplace—Fifth—Rosette."

Sure enough, the mantle was adorned by a row of rosettes and I crossed to it eagerly. Counting from the left, I fiddled with the fifth rosette, but to no avail.

"Try counting from the right," suggested Holmes.

I did, of course, and in but a moment experienced one of the greatest thrills in my long association with the master sleuth. The wooden ornament turned a full forty-five degrees. There was a click and a section of the wood paneling over the mantle swung noiselessly open. I reached inside the aperture and removed a small casket. It was a work of art in its own right, but I curbed my natural inclination and crossed to the desk and placed it before Holmes.

"After all, you found it," I stammered.

Holmes waved this thought aside. "After you, ol' chap."

There were simple release catches on both sides of the casket, which moved under my thumbs, and I was able to raise the lid. The interior was lined with black satin and on it lay the oval-shaped gem, cut by a master. The incredibly hard stone seemed to drink in the light of the room and return it in magnified form. It was dazzling to the eyes, emitting a pure, yet dancing, whiteness like the fires of Arcturus burning in the blackness of unlimited space. This miracle of crystallized carbon, glowing with a life of its own, secreted within its flawless form, needed no expertise to pronounce it as genuine—for what cunning artisan could ever recreate such a miracle of nature. It rendered me speechless but not for long.

"Holmes, 'tis said that men, Selkirk probably among them, are absolutely dotty over such gems. I'm dashed if I blame them. It is something, is it not?"

"Cold to the touch with a fire that will not burn but a dazzling brilliance that can sear the soul."

I did not know if Holmes was merely musing or quoting.

"Yes, Watson," he continued, "it is, indeed, something."

With a visible effort, Holmes broke the mood of the moment and his long, flexible fingers extracted the diamond from the casket. He handed it to me.

"Ol' chap, your pocket handkerchief will protect the beauty."

As I carefully swathed the gem in linen and placed it in my breast pocket, my friend scooped up the casket, which he replaced in the hiding place over the mantle. Closing the small hidden panel, he regarded me for a long moment, his eyes dreamy with thought.

"You know, I have espoused a pragmatic philosophy throughout our long association. But at this moment, it is hard for me to conceive that such a majestic and quite unique creation of nature is not guided by an inevitable destiny. Can it not be that this ageless and invulnerable thing, which has seen empires fall and generations vanish, is simply passing from hand to hand down a preordained path to its fate."

I had certainly never heard Holmes speak in such a manner. As we departed from the castle of Basil Selkirk and returned to Baker Street, ours was a silent journey with my friend and myself buried in our thoughts.

21

The Resolution

It was late in the afternoon that our expected visitor from Berlin arrived. On our return from St. Aubrey, Holmes did not divest himself of his suit clothes as was his habit, but instead had extracted the small salon piece, which he fancied as a weapon, from a drawer of the desk. Alerted by this precautionary move, I had secured my revolver as well. Questions pounded at my brain, but I quieted their siren call and applied myself to the answers that had already come my way during the events that had crossed the sky of our lives like scud clouds in a high wind. The silence in our chambers was unusual and complete. Finally, with my thoughts collected, I regarded Holmes. His tall and whipcord frame stood by a window gazing with unseeing eyes at the passing scene.

"I say, Holmes, am I interrupting a chain of thought?"

"Not really," he said, without turning. "I was likening the gem in your pocket to a creation of that Oscar Wilde fellow. If you recall, Dorian Gray remained ever young, unsullied by the passage of time. In similar fashion the Pigott Diamond has burned with an everlasting flame for years on end."

"Possibly fueled by its effect on so many lives," I said, almost without thought, and was surprised when Holmes turned toward me with a look of interest. "I was just thinking that our pursuit of the statue and the gem has been a tortuous one, with a variety of incidents, but it has resolved itself to where the unknown elements are few."

"My dear Watson, ofttimes you amaze me. Please don't let your thoughts dangle in thin air, but elucidate."

If there was a twinkle in his eye, I chose to ignore it.

"Once you divined that the Golden Bird was nesting on a crystal egg, the motives became clear. As a dedicated collector, Basil Selkirk was schooled in the history of diamonds and, given the clue of the year of Ali Pasha's death, figured out that the Pigott Diamond still existed. Naturally, he wanted it and was quite willing to give up the Golden Bird as a means of removing himself from the scene."

"Pray continue," said Holmes, with approval.

"Chu San Fu's motive is certainly clear. Where could he get a comparable stone to adorn his daughter? Both Doctor Bauer and Streeter referred to similar diamonds, but they would be hard come by being owned by ruling houses or titled men of wealth. How he learned that the Pigott existed is not clear."

"Nor to me," admitted my friend. "Relative to Chu San Fu, let me interject some heartening news. You will recall that when his lawyer, Loo Chang, left here, I had arranged for Slippery Styles to be on his trail. That investment of effort produced rich dividends. Styles stuck with the Oriental and located his secret office. On my orders, Slim Gilligan burglarized said premises securing the lawyers files on the illegal activities of his client. Even now the Limehouse Squad is gloating over a veritable blueprint of Chu San Fu's illicit operations. In short order all of his opium dens, houses of prostitution, and similar noisome ventures will be shut down. I said I'd smash Chu San Fu, Watson, and we have."

As was so often the case, I regarded Holmes with a slack jaw. He had crushed a kingpin of crime who had laughed at the law for years and now revealed the fact as a mere afterthought.

In Holmes's mind, the matter being a fait accompli, Chu San Fu now commanded little attention. This was evidenced by his next words.

"Back to the matter of the fabulous gem, Watson. How the Oriental crime tzar or Jonathan Wild, master criminal of the past century, became privy to its existence is a matter of speculation."

"Our client, Vasil D'Anglas, must know more about the stone and its hiding place than anyone else," I stammered.

"True," agreed Holmes," and it would seem that the very man you mention, who can resolve the entire matter, has just alighted from a hansom at our door."

But a short time later, I heard a heavy and labored tread on our stairs. The ascent was interrupted by frequent stops but, finally, Vasil D'Anglas, breathing heavily, made his way into our rooms.

When Holmes and I had visited D'Anglas in Berlin, the man had not presented an attractive picture. Now, though the passage of time had been short, his appearance had worsened. His forehead seemed more craggy and overhung dull and deep-set eyes. His skin was shocking. Coarse and wrinkled with a dry, scaly look, the man reminded me of an elephant. While a surface examination seldom proved accurate, I had diagnosed his trouble in Berlin as acromegaly, a rare condition produced by the malfunction of the pituitary. It was with difficulty that I suppressed a desire to question our visitor regarding his problem. He had to know that his condition was critical and worsening, and certainly had placed himself in the hands of Berlin doctors. I recalled, from a series of articles in "The Lancet," that the Germans had involved themselves in more research into the mysterious pituitary gland than had our medical people. Just as well for our client that Holmes secured the Golden Bird when he did, for D'Anglas's sands were certainly running low, I thought.

Then my mind flashed back to our interview with Lindquist who had died the next day. Selkirk had just fallen before the grim reaper. Had someone, at that moment, offered me the golden roc as a gift, I would have refused it with enthusiasm. My mind directed a similar distaste toward the great diamond still resting in my breast pocket and I vowed to remove the fatal object from my person as soon as possible. Of a sudden, I felt that it radiated decay and death and that I would be contaminated by exposure to the priceless Pigott. A stimulated imagination can prompt weird fantasies.

D'Anglas, having greeted us both, had lowered himself ponderously into the chair adjacent to our desk. I secured his top hat from the man, placing it on the end table, but he clung to the thick, oaken cane, which aided his stumbling steps. The head of the stick was a heavy piece of bronze in the shape of a hammer. It seemed of Arabic design and I felt would have been of interest to a curator of antiques.

"Mr. Holmes, your cable filled me with joy. The despondency, which had weighed my soul ever since the news from Constantinople that the Bird had been stolen from Hassim's shop, was lifted."

His face shifted briefly in my direction and then returned to Holmes. "There cannot be another disappointment. Tell me that you have the statue."

Holmes, his pipe in his mouth, gave a slight nod.

The man's sigh of relief was akin to ecstasy. "Possibly it is not too late." A keenness infiltrated his dull eyes. "Let me savor this moment," he said. "Tell me, sir, how came you by the Bird?"

"As a gift or a payment," said Holmes. "Either interpretation has merit."

"I would like to see it." For the first time, D'Anglas's face reflected anxiety.

"Shortly." Holmes's manner was reassuring. "There is some information I would like to secure."

D'Anglas shoulders lifted in a shrugging motion. It was like movement of a water buffalo. The man was glandularly deformed but he certainly seemed powerful,

230

an impression strengthened by his oversized, knobby hands.

"Mr. Holmes, I have told you of the search for the Bird by my family. I spoke the truth."

"I know that you did. It is just that the story interests me and there is a great deal you did not tell."

D'Anglas's oversized face hardened. "You have the Bird. May I see it?"

"Of course."

Holmes crossed to the desk. Opening the second drawer, he removed the statue and passed it across the desk to our visitor.

The roc was dwarfed in D'Anglas's hand and he peered at the masterpiece for a long time. Then his knobby fingers with swollen joints oscillated in a gentle movement like the scales in a gold-assayer's office. The creases in his overhanging forehead deepened.

"The weight is not what I expected."

Holmes seated himself behind the desk, his eyes never leaving D'Anglas.

"The diamond is no longer in the base."

D'Anglas's hand tightened and, for a moment, I thought that he would crush the statue in his grasp, but his movement was momentary. Ponderously, he reached toward the desk surface, depositing the Golden Bird there. His hand rejoined its mate in his lap and round the strange handle of his stout walking stick.

"You know."

"Almost everything," was the detective's response.

"What of the diamond?"

"I have that as well."

The goldsmith's body had been inclined forward toward Holmes and now he leaned back, the frame of the chair creaking. His expression mirrored relief but there was a tinge of surprise as well.

"Am I to have the Pigott or does the pursuit go on?"

"I discussed this with Doctor Watson. When you commissioned Nils Lindquist to recover the statue, the diamond was still concealed within it. Since I fell heir to

Lindquist's case, we consider that the return of the statue involves the passing of the gem into your hands as well."

Two emotions—gratitude and astonishment—were fighting for supremacy on D'Anglas's face.

"But," continued Holmes, "I cannot afford to have loose ends lend confusion to my case histories. Not when answers are readily available. I have enough unresolved matters in my files now."

My mind immediately flashed to the affair of "The Engineer's Thumb" as well as that bizarre adventure of "The Greek Interpreter." Of course, "The Case of Identity," which Holmes had never brought to even a successful conclusion, had bothered him for years.

Holmes's manner had convinced D'Anglas that there was no sly ploy involved and he hastened to fall in with the suggestion of the great sleuth.

"If, as a bonus, your only request is the complete story, my knowledge now belongs to you. The quest of the Bird and what was within it has been the driving purpose of the ill-fated D'Anglas line for three generations."

If there was anything Holmes enjoyed more than a good story, it was a strange tale that coincided with his conjecture. It was he who now sat back in his chair with an expression of anticipation.

"We can dispense with the history of the Bird prior to this century. Let us begin at the court of Ali Pasha of Albania when the Pigott Diamond and the statue became one."

The goldsmith complied.

"Jean D'Anglas was a professional soldier, who first followed the banner of *Le Grand Emperor*. Then he chose to hire his sword in foreign lands and in Albania achieved a position of trust under the Lion of Janina. French by birth, he began to yearn for the peace of family life and applied his not inconsiderable talents to the goldsmith trade. Ali Pasha was a despot and a wealthy one, but he was a great fancier of art objects and much could be learned in his court. Of course, the ruler's main passion was diamonds."

Holmes never liked to be completely left out of an explanation and made a comment to indicate his familiarity with the narrative. "Passion, indeed! Was it not in 1818 that Ali Pasha paid Rundell and Bridge, the London jewelry firm, one hundred and fifty thousand pounds for the Pigott?" His eyes shifted to me. "Truly, an amazing price for the time. Can you imagine the worth of the gem now?"

D'Anglas's pendulous lips exhibited a small smile that carried with it a touch of bitterness.

"Sometimes there is more at stake than worth," he said. "You know of the ruler's receiving a fatal wound and his summoning my grandfather to his side in his last moments. My forefather had been working on the Golden Bird, repairing the base, and had the statue in his hands when he hastened to Ali Pasha's throne room. The wife of the Albanian, Vasilikee, had also been summoned. The three were alone when Ali Pasha gave his final orders. My grandfather was to take the diamond, which the Albanian always kept in a pouch tucked in his sash, and smash it. Following this, he was to kill Vasilikee. With the destruction of his two most precious possessions, Ali Pasha felt that he would be able to die in peace. My grandfather was at a crossroads since he had established a clandestine relationship with Vasilikee. Fortunately, he did not have to face a decision for the Lion of Janina died."

Though privy to a part of this tale. I did indulge in a sign of relief, which the goldsmith acknowledged with his dull eyes.

"Those were cruel times, Doctor, but knowing that his master was gone, my grandfather acted instinctively. In his hand was the fabled gem and there was the Golden Bird, its base still warm from fresh-poured gold. He pressed the diamond into the bottom of the statue and was artisan enough to remove the surplus gold and smooth the base. When the gold cooled and hardened, the Pigott was safely concealed in a perfect hiding place. Jean had Vasilikee secure some small diamonds and he smashed them to represent the wreckage of the great stone. He announced the death of his ruler and the ruination of the diamond. The court of Albania was in a turmoil, with various pretenders striving for the throne and the specter of Constantinople everywhere on the scene. My grandfather and Vasilikee were able to steal away without causing comment."

"The king is dead! Long live the king!" said Holmes.

"Jean D'Anglas and Vasilikee had a Christian wedding soon after. They chose to bide their time as regards the statue, on the theory that it would not drop from sight. My grandfather was adept to the goldsmith trade and prospered. The Golden Bird returned to the Ottoman capital and he made plans to secure it. But then the unanticipated thrust its surprising head upon the scene. The Bird was stolen from the Ottoman court by an aide of the Sultan who had fallen from favor. Choosing to flee the wrath of the Turkish overlord, he undoubtedly seized the statue because it was at hand and gold is a commodity of value anywhere. Only two people knew that the Pigott diamond still existed. But when the Bird disappeared, my grandfather was in a frenzy. He made every effort to locate the object, to no avail. He was a man obsessed. Everything had been risked for the great gem encased in a tomb of gold and now it was gone. Finally, he enlisted the aid of the English master-criminal, Jonathan Wild, to find the statue."

Holmes had to be delighted to hear his theories confirmed and he was nodding with the story.

"You feel that Jean D'Anglas told Wild about the diamond?"

"It would seem he must have. Wild was old at this time. Though he sent out inquiries through his widespread organization, he was not successful. Shortly afterwards, Jonathan Wild died. My grandfather had contracted a strange and fatal malady and he died as well,

234

leaving the legacy of the Golden Bird to my father. He also was a talented goldsmith and was commissioned by a Chinese noble to create some golden masques in Peking. When he completed his assignment in China, word spread of a robbery on Rhodes. Harry Hawker, now old himself, was recognized and as soon as the object of his theft was described, it was known that the Golden Bird had resurfaced again."

"Along with Harry Hawker," added Holmes. "Formerly, part of the Wild organization. Hawker had learned the secret of the Bird from his employer and when he recognized the statue in an obscure shop on Rhodes, he could not resist trying for it."

"That was my father's reconstruction, Mr. Holmes. The Rhodes robbery was in 1850, three years before I was born."

I gave a start which I hoped passed unnoticed. The man could not be so young.

"My father," our client continued, "made haste to return from China bringing with him a metal-worker of that country who had assisted him. As my mother told the story, it was rumored that Hawker had fled to Budapest so investigations were made there. In 1853, the year of my birth, a man was knifed on the waterfront of Constantinople. Something about the matter intrigued my father and he dispatched his Chinese assistant to Turkey. The man returned with the news that the victim was Harry Hawker. The Bird had disappeared again. The following year, my father, who had contracted the same dread affliction as Jean D'Anglas, died."

My medical background would not permit me to stifle a question at this point. "Then your own physical problem is of a hereditary nature?"

The oversized head turned to me and there was something strange in his deep-set eyes. "That fact, Doctor Watson, we can certainly accept. I, like those before me, was not only infected by a deformity but also by the compulsion to recover the Bird. I have pursued every lead, followed every rumor, for my entire adult life."

"This Oriental metal-worker you mentioned," said Holmes, who had gotten his pipe going again, "did he return to his native land after the passing of your father?"

Our client was nodding. "Yes, Mr. Holmes, and I agree with the thought that has occurred to you. The Chinaman was very close to my father."

The obvious crystallized in my mind. "Of course. That is how Chu San Fu learned about the Golden Bird."

Since my statement was not denied, I felt more of a part of this unraveling.

"After the death of Hawker," said Holmes, "better than thirty years passed before the Bird appeared again. Those who knew its secret sprang into action."

"I certainly did," said our client factually. "As did Chu San Fu."

"And Basil Selkirk," I exclaimed, and then corrected myself. "No, he learned about the diamond later."

"But now, the tale is told and the loose ends resolved. Watson, would you be good enough to place the object in your breast pocket on the desk?"

I was delighted to do so. The tale of fatalities and frustrations had made me all the more anxious to rid myself of the awesome diamond. Removing it from my handkerchief, I placed it on the desk's oaken surface and stepped back, relieved to be separated from the fascinating object.

Vasil D'Anglas, making use of his walking stick, levered himself up from his chair and stood staring down at the burst of brilliance that gleamed at us like a giant crystal eye. His deep, throaty voice had a removed quality, like a somnambulist's mumbling, but his words were audible.

"I am the first D'Anglas to view it since that fateful day in '22, yet it always has been ours. A thing of deadly beauty and the cause of the curse."

Suddenly, there was the gleam of the fanatic in his eyes and a wild look about his mouth. I saw Holmes step back from the desk and his hand went to his jacket pocket.

"Let the order be carried out." D'Anglas almost screamed this and then, to my astonishment, he moved with a speed of which I could not believe he was capable. His walking stick, clutched by its end, swirled about his head and then came crashing down on the stone. The bronze handle found its mark with astonishing accuracy and in an instant the magnificent gem was completely shattered into fragments and shards of crystal, devoid of value.

I have seldom seen Holmes astonished, but he was now. I was thunderstruck.

Panting, the wildness in our client's face disappeared to be replaced by a look of exaltation.

"Good heavens, man, what have you done?" I cried. Even as I spoke the words, I saw a look of sudden understanding pass over Holmes's face.

"Removed the curse," replied D'Anglas. There was a sharpness to his eyes that had not been there before. I explained it away as due to the violent emotions of the moment. "As a medical man, sir, you have no doubt diagnosed my affliction as glandular. The finest doctors of Europe suggest this, but they cannot name the fatal deformity which claimed my grandfather, my father, and has me in its embrace. I know what the doctors do not. Jean D'Anglas was ordered to shatter the diamond and, because of greed, he disobeyed. Since that time, the curse of Ali Pasha has dogged my family."

Considering the events of the last minute, his voice was remarkably calm. He turned toward Holmes, whose lips were twitching, from self-castigation, no doubt.

"Mr. Holmes, I have committed no crime. Destruction of one's own property does not warrant that accusation. I have merely fulfilled my destiny. The debt has been paid. I leave you with the Golden Bird and my heartfelt thanks."

Before Holmes or I could think of a thing to say, he

237

was gone. It sounds ridiculous but I swear he departed in a far more agile manner than he had entered.

Alone in our chambers, Holmes and I stared at each other. The climax of this strange case had certainly been unanticipated. A wry smile played round the mouth of the great detective.

" 'Ol chap, after all our adventures, it is you and I who end up with the statue. You might well say that we have been given the Bird."

About the Author

Physician, medical researcher, and man of letters, John Hamish Watson was the most painstaking and diligent biographer to grace the printed page. Born of an English father and Scottish mother in 1852, he spent his boyhood in Australia, returning to England to take his degree of Doctor of Medicine in 1878. Following a tour of Army duty in India, he was invalided back to England. There, because of the famous chance meeting with young Stamford at the Criterion Bar, he came in contact with that man who was to become his intimate friend and companion. The rest is history.

BESTSELLING AUTHORS
FROM PINNACLE BOOKS

LAUGH ALONG WITH
Larry Wilde

"America's bestselling humorist."
— The New York Times